"Rescuing children victimized by traffickers. A fascinating and engrossing read!" – Susan 1, Amazon Top 1000 Reviewer

"Plausible, well-written, military and civilian interaction. Real life situations. – Robert W. Busby, United States Dept. of Defense

"James N. Miller does it again! Another great book in the Cody Musket series." – Carol from LA

"I could hardly put it down! I've enjoyed reading all the books in this series. I would like to see another one." – Sheryl Young

Books In This Series

As Seen On

LibraryBub 2020 Top Mystery/Thriller Series

No Pit So Deep

The Cody Musket Story
Book Two

James Nathaniel Miller II

MUSKET
BOOKS™

Cover by Delaney_Design.com

Printed and bound in the United States of America

INTRODUCTION

Four years have passed since the romantic late-night wedding of Cody and Brandi Musket. Cody is cast as a future Baseball Hall of Famer, and Brandi has become one of the most admired women on the planet.

Their world is suddenly shattered when Knoxi, age 7, is abducted by a South American cartel in retaliation for the Muskets' fight against child trafficking. But Knoxi remembers the lessons Cody has taught her, and may prove to be too much for the traffickers to handle.

Get ready to be surprised by familiar characters who show up at just the right times, and by miracles inspired by real events which leave hardened warriors shaking their heads. Finally, newcomer Cody Jr., age 9, steps up and brings about an ending which shocks the world.

After the conclusion, read about real events that inspired parts of this story.

~   ~   ~

Supports traditional family values, but deals
head-on with adult subjects such as domestic
violence and human trafficking.
Contains no sexually explicit content.

the innocent

the children

CHAPTER 1

THE DARK ANGEL OF MOCA PUNACHE

One month before the abduction of Knoxi Musket

W as it a hoax? A mass hallucination? Was there really a man in a dark mask who had shown up just in time to save this tiny province?

The Peninsula of Moca Punache, a once-thriving tropical gem in the South Caribbean, had been torn apart by warring factions and plundered by renegades. In its weakened state, a mere handful of powerful, shadowy figures had seized control. They ruled by shakedown and murder, and they freely trafficked in drugs and people—especially children.

So hard had the territory fallen that it had become known as *La Puerta del Infierno—Hell's Doorstep.*

The cruelty had gone unopposed for over a decade, until one night when something happened that changed everything. The incident was first reported by the *Caribbean Courier,* a back-door tabloid whose distribution had never exceeded four hundred. The *Courier* article broke onto the scene like a storybook fantasy, going viral within hours . . .

> *"Joy at last to the people of Moca Punache,*
> *whose homes had been ravaged, streets bloodied,*

their children enslaved, their cries for help unheeded. Paradise lay fallen until that night when the Dark Angel appeared, wielding a fiery sword, exacting swift justice, avenging the slain, and setting free the little ones. Let the love lights burn once more in Moca Punache!"

This story, complete with photos, was the toast of social media. Blurry images of a masked avenger racing through the streets fueled the imaginations of multitudes. The *Metro Times* finally commented, saying:

"Just another tale from a region historically famous for inventing swashbuckling freebooters and romanticized heroes. If C.S. Lewis had had Twitter, even Narnia could have been made to look believable."

But amidst the controversy and burgeoning folklore, the real story had been lost. Something remarkable indeed had occurred at Hell's Doorstep that stormy December night. An angelic visitation? A ghost? A superhero? No one knows for sure.

Well . . . almost no one. Here's what *really* happened.

~ ~ ~

Cody Musket and his team figured to catch the traffickers napping. The mission to rescue eighteen abducted children at Moca Punache had proceeded like clockwork until the unexpected happened. Now, their escape plan was in jeopardy and they might have to shoot their way out.

Four of the kids had panicked and fled from the building. Cody raced to the exit door and yelled down the dark street. *"Wait! Stop! We came to free you! Come back!"*

One of Cody's own men warned him, "Charley Mike, let 'em go! We gotta get the rest of these children to the boat *now!* We're outta time! Don't go after those kids! It's too late!"

Too late? Cody ignored his own mission directive and ran like *The Flash* to catch the fleeing kids, leaving his men behind to protect the other fourteen children.

The fall of provincial government had forced scores of children to the streets. Many had died in the squalor, and others had fallen prey to traffickers who lined their pockets by dealing in displaced kids. The UN and regional authorities, mired in jurisdictional disputes, had neither the stomach nor resources to fight the traffickers, especially since no one wanted the children anyway.

The leader of the cartel was Salvador Escundo, a strong-armed killer backed by international power thugs. He had publicly executed Father Carlos Torrieto, the lone voice of opposition who had dared to appeal to outside authorities, and who had attempted to provide sanctuary for the children. Escundo had hung the Padre's body from the belltower, then burned his church to the ground.

The brutal martyrdom of Father Torrieto had scarcely made the back page of the *Times,* but had caught the eagle-eye of a rare league of avengers with no political obligations or bureaucratic entanglements—a league which officially did not exist.

Cody and Brandi Musket had established their *Planned Childhood Foundation* to provide safe houses. But in addition, Cody had secretly crafted an off-the-books shadow division of Planned Childhood codenamed *Rosa's Cantina*—its purpose to search and rescue with no one suspecting.

Rumors of its existence had surfaced, but Cody's canny associates had made his splinter company invisible—no money trail, no agenda, no profile. Even Brandi, for her own protection, did not know about Cody's secret league. Tonight, Rosa's Cantina had made a house call at Moca Punache.

Cody chased the fleeing kids nearly a half mile. After falling face-down in the mud and racing through puddled streets, he finally cornered the terrified children inside an abandoned hut near a railroad crossing.

The dirt floor of the one-room shack was like mud soup thanks to a leaking roof. Rodents scrambled for cover behind the wet cardboard walls. The dark room allowed Cody just enough light to make out the four scruffy little faces staring back at him—four small bodies gasping for breath after the long run—bare feet, tattered clothing.

The tallest was a boy who appeared no older than ten, but with combat-ready eyes, a do-or-die expression, and a long rusty knife in his belt. Cody could see puncture marks on the boy's left knee where the tip of the long blade had jabbed him while on the run.

The other three kids were even younger, all girls, whimpering, coughing, and crying.

Still breathing heavily, Cody explained that he had come to help. But one thing was clear—after having lived on the merciless streets, these four did not trust adults.

The boy had been forced to become a man way too fast, and now stood ready to defend the three girls. Without warning, the desperate child pulled the knife and charged into Cody, who quickly removed the weapon from the young hero and pushed him backward into the wall.

Cody held up his hand. *"Stop!* I only want to help! Do you understand me?" He waited, but got no response. He softened his tone. "*Help?* Do you know what that word means?"

Cody tried a few words in Spanish, but became tongue-tangled. The terrorized children cowered in the corner. Perhaps it was his dark clothing, the black mask, the gloves he wore. Words seemed useless, but he was compelled to find the means to communicate.

He removed his gloves, black shirt and mask, then dropped to a knee and invited them to step forward and feel the scars on his bare shoulders and back. The smallest of the four, a tiny girl with huge brown eyes and a runny nose, stopped sobbing long enough to bravely reach out and touch Cody's right shoulder.

"See?" Cody said quietly. "I've been hurt too."

She gazed up at him, her little mouth wide open. A tiny flicker of life came upon her frail cheeks. Cody took a long look. How many wishes did he see in her eyes? How long since she had eaten, since she'd had a bath or decent drinking water? When was the last time she had heard music or someone say, "I love you?" She could have been Knoxi, save for the brown eyes and the feet so dirty they blended seamlessly against the raw earth floor.

Like an impassioned general who wanted to fight beside his troops, Cody had desired to accompany a rescue team on a mission just once. Rosa's Cantina had been his vision. He had gathered the fiercest fighters, keenest planners, financiers, and experts to make the operation work, but had always kept a safe distance. His teams typically risked their lives to save children just like these in places just like this, but Cody had felt disconnected.

This time, he had put his own boots on the ground to observe his operation first hand. Despite his wealth, popularity, and glorious accomplishments in baseball, Cody had never seen an event so glorious as the wistful smile of this tender child who had just discovered hope by surprise.

But before he could blink an eye, the situation deteriorated. A blood-chilling voice from the street brought his happy thoughts crashing to earth as quickly as his F/A-18 had fallen from the Afghan sky eight years earlier.

"Señor! You cannot have my children! I must insist you send them out to me. I am already grieving for them!"

The ghastly voice had been recycled from the vilest pit. He recognized it—the same voice which had tormented him in the Afghan torture cell, had battered Brandi at the Pittsburgh theater, and had sounded off before shooting innocent people at the AME Church in Herronburg, Pennsylvania. Different faces. Same voice.

Now, it was calling him out at Moca Punache, waiting for him on the other side of the door.

The frightened girls clutched at Cody's belt as he stood up. One hyperventilated. But the swarthy young man with the ever-ready face stood firm, looked Cody in the eye, and held out his palm. He wanted his knife back. He was up for doing his part.

Cody looked down. The old knife was edged like a dagger, but long, dull, rusty. "Do you mind if I borrow your knife, son? I need a man to stay with these little girls to hide 'em and keep them quiet 'til help arrives. Can you do that?"

The heady youngster pointed to what was left of a mattress which lay on the floor. It had been nearly destroyed by rats, soiled by urine and muddy water. Cody got the message. He lifted the water-logged mattress and leaned it against the wall. The take-charge boy then motioned the girls to crouch behind it and hide with him. The four kids hunkered down.

"Birdcage, this is Charlie Mike, what is your situation?" Cody was calling the team members who had stayed behind to guard the other rescued children.

"This is Birdcage. All baby birds safe with us. Did you apprehend the other four? We're waiting for you at echo-two. Verify your location."

"Estimated three hundred meters west," Cody responded. "A

mud hut next to the crossing. Bogies danger-close, little birds in peril, situation critical. Do you copy?"

"Copy that, sending Romeo and Bravo One. ETA ten minutes. Can you manage 'til then?"

"I'll let you know in five. I got no ammo left."

"Señor! I am getting impatient! You have twenty seconds to send my children back to me or we will set the house on fire!"

Cody could already smell burning kerosene—a familiar sensation like the jet fuel smell which had routinely suffused the air aboard the flight deck of the USS *Harry Truman*. Kerosene had ever since reminded him of danger, and when he imagined the possibility of the kids burning to death underneath the mattress, he fought hard against the panic in his soul. He was compelled to gather himself. The coolest head wins the battle.

He reacquired his black disguise, which he wore to hide his identity, then took four deliberate steps toward the door. He hesitated while many thoughts raced through his head. Wasn't this exactly where he had wanted to be? Now, with his gut twisting and his ears ringing, he wasn't so sure.

He dropped his head. "God, I suppose . . . I mean, there's killers in the street, so . . . like if You ever wanted to roast somebody with lightning, seems like the perfect time to me . . . or not. I'd settle for a delay to buy me time 'till help arrives. Please tell me I didn't corner these kids just to get 'em killed. Yeah . . . that 'bout covers it, Sir."

A long, deep breath cleared Cody's mind. As he adjusted his mask, thoughts of Brandi made him chuckle. More than once, she had laughed at the "ridiculous" rumors about a behind-the-scenes paramilitary enterprise.

"I'll be perfectly clear," she would tell the media. "Planned Childhood is about safe houses, not about some dangerous *cloak and dagger operation.*"

How poetic. Little did she know that tonight he stood alone in mortal *danger,* his identity *cloaked,* his only weapon a rusty *dagger.*

The lowly whimpering of the girls behind the mattress returned him to reality. He swallowed hard. *Maybe tonight I die, but go with God and never let 'em see you sweat.*

"I'm coming out." Cody pushed on the squeaky door, stepped outside, and let it swing shut behind him. "Hello Salvador. You on foot?"

Cody recognized Salvador Escundo from photos, and he was surprised to see the leader of the cartel standing in the open with two associates.

"We both know you don't wanna hurt the kids," Cody said. "So tell your two boys to ditch the torches."

Salvador pointed his weapon at Cody. "You have caused me a lot of trouble, señor! I will shoot you and then pull off your mask so I can watch your face when we burn you like the priest."

"You can't depend on that pistola, Salvador. This here's a dark street, and your hand is shakin' so hard you won't be able to hit anything. Maybe you need to come closer, amigo."

Salvador's gun hand began to shake noticeably. The men kept their distance about ten meters away. Cody had hoped to draw them close enough to disarm Salvador and perhaps defeat all three in close combat, but for now he would have to keep them talking. Help was still seven minutes away.

"The children aren't here," Cody said. "I hid 'em somewhere else. If you kill me, you'll never find them. If you want this mask, come get it."

"But there are three of us and you are all alone, amigo."

Cody's bone-grinder voice fell into low gear, resonating through the suddenly quiet street. His black mask and hood made him one with the night, and the lights from the torches ignited his cold blue eyes. "Do I sound like the man who's alone, Salvador? Your hand is shakin' cuz you know I have the advantage. See . . . I'm not afraid to die, but you are."

The three men slowly back-peddled, looking around side to side as though expecting trouble. In the flickering flames, Cody read fear on their faces. Then, for no apparent reason, they turned and fled, dropping their lighted torches on the street. Cody blinked his eyes. Was this all a dream?

"Romeo, this is Charlie Mike. Say your ETA." Cody waited for a response.

Romeo responded, panting, "We're double-time to your location, ETA three minutes. Sitrep?"

"Bogies no factor. Last seen headed north. I got four little birds with me. *Expedite!*"

Moments later, Cody's help arrived. "So, Charlie Mike, how could you be out of ammo? None of us ever fired a shot, including you."

Cody cleared his throat. "I . . . uh, I slipped and fell in the mud during the chase. The nine-millimeter must've dropped out of my holster. I didn't wanna report that earlier 'cause it sounded so stupid."

"Uh . . . so, you had no gun and those baby snatchers just walked away? How does that happen?"

"I got no idea," Cody answered. "That's a question I'ma ask God next time I see Him."

"Yeah?" Romeo snarked. "Well, that could be sooner than you think if you keep separating yourself from us where we can't protect you. And you lost your weapon in the mud? You should leave these missions to us who are trained. What I mean is—"

Bravo One jumped in, "What he means is, you don't get to die. You're too valuable."

"Yeah, but these kids are fighters. I mean—"

"We already got the other kids on the boat," Bravo One cut in.

"And the Punta Gracia Police responded to our tip and collected the bad guys—wrapped in a neat package like we agreed. We need to expedite outta here"

Romeo added, "Salvador's done—him and his two jacks. We ran into 'em a few seconds ago. They were runnin' so scared they ran outta their shoes, yellin' about some black phantom ghost. Some townspeople tackled them right in front of us."

Cody shrugged. "Tackled 'em? So, what happened to them?"

"It wasn't pretty."

Bravo One quick-glanced up and down the street, his senses on full alert. "You can't do this again, Charlie Mike. You're too famous. Some bad guy's gonna recognize you even with the mask, then your family'll be in danger."

"Maybe I shudda' dressed as a clown," Cody said. "The kids were afraid of the mask."

Bravo One chuckled. "Well, obviously, Salvador was even more afraid. By the way, does your ol' lady even know where you are right now?"

"You kidding? Brandi thinks I'm conductin' a baseball clinic in Caracas with Bagwell."

CHAPTER 2
EASTER COMES EARLY

One day before the abduction of Knoxi Musket

The Anita Crown Cassidy Show, Fox News, New York— "Welcome back to our final segment of the Anita Crown Cassidy Show, ladies and gentlemen. We have been talking to Brandi Musket, wife of baseball star Cody Musket."

Audience applause.

"Now, Brandi, in these last few minutes, I have some serious questions. Let me first say that your popularity has not changed you in the four years since you married your famous husband. But don't you find popularity to be burdensome sometimes?"

"Yes. It can be hard, especially on Cody. After he struck out in the ninth inning with the bases loaded in the World Series against the Mets, he was bombarded."

"I wasn't talking about baseball, Brandi. I'm referring to the tight security, the bodyguards that escort your seven-year-old daughter to school—protection for your home due to yours and Cody's war against human trafficking. Your Planned Childhood Foundation is what I'm referring to."

"Well, Anita, I think—"

"And how do you feel about being called Mama Brandi?" Anita cut her off. "I mean, all those kids now under your care who have been victimized by traffickers—many with parents who have been murdered in third-world countries."

"It humbles me, Anita. I have been a victim of violence more than once, and I have the scars to prove it. After the first incident, I determined that I would never again let anyone treat me that way, and yet, two years later, there I was, attacked by three men in a public theater."

"Yes, we all remember," Anita said. "That's the night Cody saved you. It was a *huge* story."

"Yes, Anita. It was the first time I had ever seen Cody's face. I didn't even know who he was—a relatively unknown rookie baseball player."

"That's right, but after the incident went viral, you and Cody were both famous. And let me remind our audience that the three men who attacked you are still in prison, and will be there for a long, long time."

Audience applause.

"But, Anita, I was deeply traumatized. If you've never been a victim, you can't know what it's like."

"Yes, I can imagine, and it must be doubly-tough being married to a man like Cody. He travels extensively, and beautiful women always want to be seen with him, like at the MVP dinner I hosted in San Diego last year. I mean, that has to worry you."

"Anita, Cody Musket is a guy who would never be able to look me or his daughter in the eye afterward if he had cheated. When he comes off the road, he *never* hesitates to stare directly into my eyes."

Anita flashed her big brown eyes at the camera. "And I bet that's not the only thing he never hesitates to do when he comes home, right?"

Audience applause, laughter.

"Forgive me, Brandi, if I'm getting too personal, but you and

Cody are public figures, and rumors persist that Planned Childhood conducts clandestine missions to rescue children from traffickers in third-world countries where American authorities have no jurisdiction. That is positively heroic!"

"Anita, I categorically deny—"

"Like the breaking story we're following this morning," Anita interrupted again, "about the rescue of twenty-two-year-old American Melissa Randolph and four British teenagers last night in Syria. Any truth to those rumors?"

Brandi answered with a chuckle. "Those rumors always amuse me. Planned Childhood is about taking care of kids *after* they have been freed and about the *prevention* of abductions. It's not about some *cloak* and *dagger* operation. The Syria rescue is wonderful news, but we have no idea who the individuals are who saved those girls."

"You use the word *individuals*, Brandi, not the word *men*. Does that mean that some of those rescuers were women?"

"Like I stated plainly," Brandi insisted, "we have no idea."

"No idea? Really? Okay, so I have another question that might interest the women in our audience. We all know that Cody was held by radicals in Afghanistan years ago. When did you first discover his scars, and how did it make you feel?"

"That is *way* too personal."

Audience applause.

"But you're insisting that your husband had nothing to do with the recovery of Melissa Randolph and the British girls last night?"

"Anita, if Cody and I were involved in anything like that, I would know it. My husband and I don't keep secrets."

~   ~   ~

Houston, moments later

Cody had watched from his den. After the broadcast, he switched to Newsmax, where an update from Syria was already in progress:

> *"Melissa, you were abducted four months ago, and you're saying that you were then forced into prostitution. So, in your own words, can you describe what happened last night when you were rescued?"*

> *"Yes. Three men were driving me to a place of execution because I had become pregnant, and I've had complications with my asthma and diabetes. I had become too much trouble for them. I hoped they would ask for ransom, but they were afraid of being traced, so the easiest solution was to kill me."*

> *"Unbelievable! They had no use for you being sick and pregnant. Now tell us about the dark van that you described earlier."*

> *"We were driving over this bumpy road about twenty miles-an-hour, and this dark-colored van forced us into a ditch. My three captors . . . I mean, they like totally freaked out! They. . . drew their guns, but four hooded fighters came to the windows and shot all three men right in front of me! Blood flew everywhere!"*

> *"Good heavens! So . . .what happened after that?*

> *"I was screaming. The shooters carried me to their van. The four British girls were already in the van.*

> *We were all so scared."*

"So at this point, you had no idea what was happening?"

"That's right, Bonnie. I thought these hooded figures were from a rival Islamic group wanting to claim me for themselves. They seemed even more dangerous than the men who had already held me for four months."

"Oh, how horrific! So, then what happened?"

"We sped away, swerving, burning rubber, no windows in the back of the van. Then we heard a loud explosion behind us. It was so close it lifted our back wheels off the road. After that, we turned onto a smooth road and things quieted down."

"So, these dangerous individuals in the van; did you get a look at their faces? Did they say anything to you?"

"They um . . . they untied my hands and feet and gave us all drinking water. They never pulled off their masks, never even uttered a word the whole time, not even among themselves. I couldn't even determine their nationality. I was wheezing, trying to catch my breath."

"So, you had no clue as to your own fate?"

"Well, I started to sense . . . I mean these people were different. They were professional. Like, they didn't waste ammunition shooting their guns off, shouting Islamic slogans and stuff. One of them pulled out a portable electronic device. It terrified me until I realized he only wanted to place it on my

abdomen to listen for vital signs from my baby. He signaled thumbs up afterward and handed me an inhaler. I knew he was a man because I saw his hand when he pulled off his glove to use the device.

"Wow. Very observant. So, when did you realize that these individuals of unknown origin were there to rescue you?"

"It was when . . . when one of them handed me a cell phone. My daddy was calling, saying . . . saying he was proud of me and he'd meet me in Rome. We hadn't spoken since I was ten. He said he loved me at least a hundred times. They left us with the Red Cross in Damascus and the van sped away."

"Thank you, Melissa. Ladies and gentlemen, Melissa Randolph, the humanitarian worker from Little Rock, is free after four months of captivity— a happy ending shrouded in mystery. Who saved her? Speculation is that Melissa's father, an Arkansas rancher, may have paid someone to free his daughter at gun point. The rescue team may have incidentally encountered the British women and freed them as well."

Cody turned off the TV, tossed the remote onto the sofa, and glanced at his watch. He climbed the circular staircase to his loft, his private office. Once there, he rolled a tall Victorian davenport away from the wall, exposing a hidden closet. After entering the closet, he pulled the davenport back into place behind him.

He turned on the overhead light, sat down at a computer desk, and stared down at an antique rotary-dial landline phone sitting in front of him.

It rang. He answered, "This is Marty."

A woman's gruff voice responded, "Hi, Marty, this is Rosa's Cantina."

"Christmas comes late," Cody said.

"Easter comes early," was the response.

"So," Cody asked, "how did the egg hunt go?"

"Your basket was delivered on time, and we picked up four additional eggs for you. They were ours for the taking—sort of a collateral bonus—no extra charge."

"That's excellent service. What about your fellow egg hunters?"

"All hunters healthy and happy."

"That's good news, Rosa. Your payment for the basket has been deposited." He hung up the receiver.

Cody expected Brandi to call from New York any minute now that her Fox interview was over. But when the smartphone in his pocket rang, the caller ID told him it wasn't Brandi.

"Hello, Anita. I was expecting Brandi to call. You got pushy with those questions about the clandestine activities. When will you drop that act?"

"Me? Drop the act? Like you ain't the Merry Phantom of the Southern Caribbean?" she laughed. "Now *that* was a *real* act!"

"You mean that tabloid piece? Those pics weren't real. Smart girl like you should've known that. And about the Syria news—"

"C'mon, Cody, are you gonna actually deny you were involved in that Syria operation last night? How much did Old Man Randolph pay you to get his girly back?"

"You got no respect, Anita. I was right here yesterday. I never went anywhere."

"You're real funny. How long are you gonna keep Brandi in the dark about your under-the-floor activities? This time your boys killed some people. Once that starts, where does it stop?"

"Anita, you and I have never seen eye to eye on anything. I'm okay with that, but I can't handle the way you badgered my wife on your show."

"Look, Mr. Musket, I ain't no Oprah. She's black, beautiful, successful, and could always charm people on her show by bein' nice. But if *this* dark chick wants to make it, I can't do it by copyin' somebody else. I want that story, and I'm gonna get it!"

"I don't think of you as a 'dark chick,' Anita. Never did. I see you as a brilliant woman who . . . What I mean is, whatever you think about yourself is the way other people are gonna think of you. Take it from me, eventually you gotta stop bein' the victim. You're better than that."

"I don't need no lessons from you, Cody. And whatever I think of myself is no concern of yours. We could've had a good life. Why can't you admit there was something between us once?"

"That was all in your mind, 'Nita. I told you that years ago."

"Well, when the bad guys find out you're behind all this rescue stuff, there's gonna be hell to pay. Your whole existence will jack-knife when foreign governments find out you been violating their sovereign territory. They'll bury your little white fanny and your whole family."

Cody chuckled. "You still have a way with words, 'Nita. If I *was* involved, you wouldn't be much help."

"Then maybe what you need is an ally. I just want the story, Cody. We can spin it any way you please."

"Gotta go, 'Nita. Brandi's calling. You should chase a story worth reporting. Give those rescuers credit, whoever they are. They did what the US Government wouldn't even attempt."

He ended the call and took the next one. "Nice job. Glad it's over?"

"*Ugh!* I hate myself for letting that woman talk to me like that. Imagine her asking me about discovering your scars! Asking how it made me feel. I should be used to the questions by now, but she disgusts me."

"Hey, you're a natural. You were cool as cake. And don't be too hard on Anita. Her head got turned around a few years ago."

"What? How long have you known her?" She waited. "Cody, I mean, whatever happened before we met isn't important now, but—"

"No, it's your business too. You need to know why she resents you. I'll tell you when you get home."

"Tell me right now. I'm in the limo on my way to LaGuardia. I have plenty of time."

He waited and visualized her sitting in the back of the limo crossing her arms.

"Okay. Her real name is Anita Brown. When I was in flight school, she was a rookie reporter. She was always on the prowl for that one big story, but the station only gave her small assignments like civic clubs, interviewing soldiers from the base, stuff like that. When she interviewed me, we couldn't agree on anything. We were opposite sides on everything."

"So, you weren't exactly her favorite person, right?"

"I wish it was that simple. She had a weakness for US Marines. As long as she had an interview with some soldier every weekend and a Marine to play house with every night she was fairly content."

The phone went silent. "Brandi? You still connected?" He waited.

"I take it you were *not* one of those Marines who liked to play house?"

"Of course not, and *that* was the problem. The guys she couldn't have were the ones she wanted most. The night before I left for Miramar, some jerk beat her up. She blamed me, because I wasn't there to protect her."

"Tragic. But she's makin' it worse by playing it both ways."

"Yeah, I get it," Cody said. "And she still reminds me every chance she gets. I saw her face on a TV broadcast five years later when I was playin' minor league ball at Corpus Christi. She had changed her name to Anita Crown Cassidy and gotten herself hired by Fox."

"Cody, was she right about Syria? About your being involved?" She listened. His silence stopped her heart. "Cody?"

He finally answered. "If I *was* involved in somethin' like that, would you really wanna know?"

Brandi became quiet again. Cody could hear her breathe into the phone.

She swallowed quietly. "My flight arrives in Houston at two. I need to pack my things since we're leaving tomorrow for Madrid. And don't forget about our New Year's Eve reservation with the Berkmans tonight at Katie's Korral."

Chapter 3

Camelot is Falling

One day later, New Year's Day

Cody and Brandi seated themselves at Castro's Grill, a popular restaurant and bar near Terminal E. Their flight had been delayed for a second time. They were bound for Madrid, where their Planned Childhood Foundation would open its first facility on the European Continent.

The personnel at Houston's Intercontinental Airport had grown to know the Muskets, who were regular travelers. Cody, after four years, was now an established American League All-Star third baseman—an international celebrity. Brandi wrote a weekly syndicated column, and was known for her compassionate work with displaced children.

Everyone at Castro's Grill knew that Cody and Brandi were friendly but wanted as much privacy as possible. The Muskets' seven-year-old daughter Knoxi, on the other hand, seemed to crave the limelight.

She was articulate, funny, and smart, but her supposed innocence was an act. Everyone loved being manipulated by Knoxi Musket, and she had become quite adept. She had once marched into the kitchen at Castro's on July 4th and announced it was her birthday. She ordered a cake so large they had to reserve an oversized table just for the cake. Never mind her birthday was November 29th, and that everyone already knew that. When the pink cake was delivered, her favorite slogan was bannered across the top: '*Ya' neva' know, sucka!*'

On this New Year's morning, Knoxi and her parents were headed in separate directions. Knoxi would stay with José and Mia Bustamante at their Uvalde, Texas ranch while Cody and Brandi were in Madrid. José had been Cody's teammate for four years. The Bustamantes were already on the road in their truck, headed to Uvalde with the creative seven-year-old aboard.

Castro's was the Muskets' favorite airport hangout. The restaurant management knew the drill and was ever eager to cooperate with the Musket security team headed by Baker and Elena Rafferty.

On this New Year's Morning, Brandi and Cody sat down and ordered coffee. Baker and Elena had been delayed, but were due to meet the Muskets at their table any minute.

~   ~   ~

Interstate Highway 10, near San Antonio

"Do you ting your daddy and mama took off yet?" José could see Knoxi in the rearview mirror. She sat in the back seat, looking at her smartwatch.

"Nope. Not for another two hours," the seven-year-old responded. "Their flight leaves at 11:15. We'll almost be at the ranch by then, right?"

José peeked at his watch. "Pretty close," he said.

Knoxi loved to go with José and Mia to their ranch when her parents left the country. José had played no baseball for the past year. He was still rehabbing from Tommy John surgery on his right arm, but was planning to be ready for the start of spring training in a few months.

"Do you like your new school? Mia asked. "I understand you

have a boyfriend."

"Boyfriend? Heavens no! The boys in my school are all weird, like Tommy Castle who tried to pull my pants down the first day."

Mia's mouth fell wide open. "He did what?"

"Don't worry, I knew what to do. My daddy taught me. Now the only boy who even comes near me is Frederick, and he eats paste. *Yuck!!"*

"But that is a very fine school, no?" Jose asked, glancing back. "I hear famous rapper's son, uh, what his name? Calamine Lotus? His son go there, eh?"

"Yes, sir, but he's weird too. His pants are so tight he can't bend his knees when he sits down."

"But you can learn a lot there, can't you?" Mia offered.

"Yes, ma'am, but I wish I could go to a normal school with normal kids whose parents aren't so rich. And I don't like having a security team with me every day. Don't get me wrong, I love Stan and Willie. Willie lets me practice my fast draw with his Glock."

"Aye, yi,yi! Debes estar bromeando!"

"Ha-ha! Of course I was kidding, Uncle José!" She loved yanking his chain, provoking him to respond in his first language.

The threesome had left Houston two hours earlier in the Bustamantes' hefty extended cab, followed closely by a white SUV which carried their two-man security team of Stan Knight and Willie Townsend.

Morning traffic on Interstate 10 was light because Texans had rung in a new year the night before by partying late. Early risers had stayed home, glued to TV parades and sports. José pulled off the interstate near Wrong Way, Texas, a small town forty miles east of San Antonio. "We'll stop here at Cal's like we always do," he said.

Knoxi enjoyed Cal's because they sold trinkets and specialty items such as purses, wristbands, and necklaces. "I need to do some shopping," she would always say.

The Bustamantes had no children, so they loved spending money on Knoxi. She once had talked them into buying her a leather bullwhip billed as, "Hand made by Native Texas Comanches." Never mind the official tag which read: "Manufactured in New Jersey."

Despite the Muskets' pleading with the Bustamantes not to spend money on Knoxi, José and Mia couldn't resist. Knoxi could always look for the best deals by checking the latest hand-painted signs in the windows. She read at an eighth-grade level, and had spent so much time with José and Mia that she spoke perfect Spanish. The rule was, English spoken until they reached the ranch, and then Spanish.

~ ~ ~

Meanwhile, back at the airport . . .

"You want any more airport brew?" Cody held up the coffee pot.

"Are you serious? I'm already floating," Brandi told him. "Knoxi and the Bustamantes will probably reach the ranch before we ever take off from here." She chuckled. "By the way, those sunglasses make you look like Spider-Man. You think that's gonna keep autograph seekers from recognizing you?"

"Nobody wants my autograph since I made the last out in the Series," he responded, leaning on his elbow.

"Speaking of disguises," she said, "have you heard the latest on that Dark Angel story from that island near Argentina? This morning, they are claiming it's the murdered priest who has come back to life. There was a new sighting just last night."

"I don't pay any mind to that stuff," Cody said. "I saw a story about it on Facebone. And it's a *peninsula*, not an island. It's called Moca Punache."

"Well," she grinned, "for a man who cannot distinguish between a *facebone* and *Facebook*, you seem to know a lot about that story."

Just then, they looked up to see a rather squatty figure of a man standing next to the table. The booze smell had preceded him. With a dagger-hook nose, a beer-barrel torso, and skinny toothpick legs, he could have doubled for the villain who stole the moon in *Despicable Me*. Indeed, with flip-flops, shorts, and skinny white legs underneath his Humpty-Dumpty upper body, he could have passed for a man riding a large chicken. He stood there for a moment staring at the Muskets.

"Can we help you?" Cody asked.

The skinny-legged man focused on Brandi. "Miss Musket. I'd like to talk to you." Then he looked at Cody. "Excuse me, boy, I have business with the little lady here."

"It's *Mrs*. Musket," Brandi said emphatically. "And what *business* are you referring to?"

At that moment, Baker and Elena Rafferty approached the table and sat down. They had adjusted well to life in Houston since they had become head of the Muskets' security team.

"Sorry we were late. Took me a while to get the photos," Baker said. "Uh, who's your new friend here?"

Cody turned to the stranger. "I didn't catch your name, sir."

"Didn't rightly say, but the name is Ben—Doctor Ben Dover. I'm lookin' for an endorsement from the lady here for my new aircraft I'm developing."

Elena and Brandi stared at each other, and then both politely covered their mouths and tried to contain themselves. "Did you say your name is Ben? Dover? Doctor Ben Dover?" Brandi smothered her snickering.

"That's right, little lady. And my invention is called the Dovercraft XL. I just need an endorsement to get me going."

Baker's handlebar mustache began to buzz. "I can think of other ways to get you going, Doc," he growled."

"Well," Brandi said. "My husband is the pilot in the family. Maybe you should ask him."

Cody jumped right in. "Is the power plant normally aspirated? What's the max gross? What're the V-speeds? How about wing loading? Does it have speed brakes? Fowler flaps?"

"I don't know much about all that. I just know this little lady here needs to come flying with me." He seized Brandi's arm.

Cody and Baker stood up. "Not if you want to keep the use of your legs," Baker asserted.

Suddenly the table was surrounded by five men wearing leisure attire, ear pieces and weapons. One of them crossed his arms and spoke up. "Any problem here, Mr. Rafferty?"

"I don't think so, Jones. Your men can return to their posts."

The good doctor eased his grip. "Well, maybe some other time then."

Baker started toward Humpty Dumpty with intent to shoo him away lest he have a great fall, but Elena held her husband back and stepped forward. "There won't be another time, Mr. Dover. My husband likes to have his men shoot on sight. We're compiling a list. Your name goes at the top of it."

"Go sleep it off, doctor." Cody displayed his scowl for the first time. "And don't be flying any Dovercraft again 'til you're sober. And if I were you, I'd remember what this *little lady* sitting across from me said to you—the little lady with the *big iron* on her hip."

Doctor Ben scrambled away, trying his best to walk a straight line.

Brandi rubbed her arm where he had gripped her. "Well, that was different." Then she and Elena laughed so hard it inspired the eavesdroppers sitting nearby to do the same. "Ben Dover?"

The four sat back down.

"Knoxi texted me and said they're stopping at Cal's for gas," Brandi mused, still trying to wipe the smile off her lips.

"Yep. Mia will prolly buy her a bunch o' stuff like always," Cody snickered. "She can't resist spoiling our daughter."

"*Seriously?*" Brandi's face became an exclamation point. "Where have you been the past four years, Captain America? *José* is the one who can't say 'no' to our daughter."

Cody put his elbows on the table. "Remember when she talked them into buying her that bullwhip on her last birthday?'

"Yeah, but you have to give her some credit," Brandi insisted. "At least she learned to crack it."

"Sure, after I told her to choke up about four feet. She still wrapped it around her neck a few times. Don't most girls play with dolls? Girl stuff? I mean—"

"Babe," Brandi butted in, "Knoxi is *not* most girls."

Cody grinned, then straightened up when Baker, the former Navy SEAL, began rolling the ends of his handlebar mustache with his fingers. Something was up.

Baker glanced somberly at Brandi, and then back to Cody. He opened an envelope and pulled out an enlarged photo.

"We need to have a chat," Baker said. "Planned Childhood is drawing too much attention—the wrong kind, if you catch my wave."

"Roger that, sailor. We talked about that already."

Cody's nervous smile did not go unnoticed by Brandi. "Well, that's a good thing isn't it?" she asked. "We have nearly three hundred kids in our shelters now, and another eighty-nine that we've placed in good homes. Carlos LaVega of the Cincinnati Reds is going to adopt two of our Taiwanese children, and the Bustamantes are considering the adoption of the Sanchez twins at our Monterrey facility."

"We know, Brandi," Elena said. "But the other side of it—the Planned Childhood no one talks about—that's our concern."

Brandi caught her breath, confusion written on her face.

Cody looked straight ahead, trying to avoid Brandi's inquiring eyes. "Assuming there *was* another side," Cody asked, "what's your point?"

"My point is, this is no time to get sloppy," Baker responded, "especially with that Fox reporter nosing around. She's trouble. The traffickers have left you alone for four years, but now, they're zeroing in, putting the pieces together."

Cody tightened his lip. He could feel Brandi's icy gaze.

Baker placed on the table a photo of a shadowed individual sitting in the driver's seat of an automobile. "Have you ever seen this man?"

Brandi gasped. "Cody, that's . . . that's a familiar face, isn't it?"

"Where did you take this picture?" Cody asked Baker.

"Two blocks from your house. That vehicle has been parked under a big oak tree before dawn for the past four days. I finally sneaked over and took some pics around 0500 this morning. Do you recognize the driver?"

Brandi looked again. Her face turned ghostly gray. "CoGo's! Pittsburgh, four years ago," she said. "I recognize him."

Cody took another look. "The guy who resembled Will Smith? The hair is different, but, yeah, he's the same guy who drove that black SUV in Pittsburgh. The *Men in Black* we called them."

Elena's face was tight and drawn. "Are you certain?"

"Absolutely," Cody affirmed. "He was careless, letting you get close enough to photograph him like this. He's a real amateur."

Baker agreed. "But . . . never underestimate an enemy. Now, look closely at the individual standing beside the car. He and that driver had an animated discussion."

"Who is that?" Brandi asked as she took a second look. "Wait! . . . Cody, that's—"

Cody crushed his Spider-Man shades on the table. "We met him at a fund raiser in November. That's Porter Sanders, State Trooper."

"Well," Baker informed him, "he showed up at sunrise. Yep, it's Porter Sanders, supposedly your ally. These two geniuses had a powwow this morning just forty meters from your gate."

"What does this mean?" Brandi's tone was elevated.

Baker touched the call button on his phone. "It means I'm calling Willie right now. Knoxi's in danger!"

~ ~ ~

José turned into Cal's truck stop and headed for the fuel station. Stan and Willie pulled in behind them in their white SUV. José stepped out and prepared to fill the tanks while Mia walked toward the ladies' room. Knoxi stayed in the truck out of sight, doors locked, until Stan and Willie could stand next to her door— standard procedure.

As Stan and Willie parked, a burgundy van screeched onto the lot and stopped alongside them. A second van, identical to the first, skidded to a halt nose-to-nose with Jose's pickup. Six armed, hooded men bolted from the two vehicles, brandishing their weapons.

Knoxi knew she was in trouble. Her daddy had coached her: *Notice every detail. Don't panic. Don't resist.*

When she heard gunshots, Knoxi took cover in the floor of the king cab and held her ears. Her locked door flew open. A man with strong hands grabbed the collar of her red and white dress and then pulled her through the door.

José had initially frozen, but then had bravely attempted to stop the attacker from dragging Knoxi from his truck. The individual turned and pistol-whipped José, leaving him helplessly lying on the ground.

Knoxi's vision failed her momentarily as red-hot blindness seemed to invade her eyes from every direction. A second later, she came to her senses and realized she had jabbed a pencil into the neck of the pistol-whipper while his back was turned.

Meanwhile, Stan and Willie had punched 911 and dropped their phones onto the floor of their car to alert police. Despite the odds—six against two—they had drawn their weapons and prepared to defend Knoxi with their lives. When they raced toward José's vehicle, the crew of van number one intercepted them.

A gun battle ensued. Both agents fell. One of the gunmen was also hit.

The perpetrator with the pencil wound had slumped to his knees and then recovered. He drew back his gun hand as if to strike the seven-year-old. She raised her hands to protect herself but was immediately seized by another hooded individual who deposited her into van number two.

Mia came running toward the fueling area. *"¡José! ¡José! ¿Dónde estás? ¿Dónde estás? ¿Dónde esta Knoxi? Que paso?"* Then, she spotted José on the ground, holding his bludgeoned head. "Help! Help! My husband is hurt! *José! ¿Dónde está Knoxi? ¿Dónde está Knoxi?"*

As the two vans sped away, Knoxi's angry but muffled voice could be heard above the squealing tires and confusion. "My daddy's gonna kick you in the—" The remainder of her protests were overshadowed by shouts of victory from the fleeing perpetrators.

José attempted to raise himself. "They. . . they take her in *los camiones rojos! The red trucks. They take her!* He fell forward against the hood of his truck, blood running down the side of his face, remorse stealing away his breath. *"Lo siento, Mia,"* he sobbed. *"Lo siento mucho."*

~ ~ ~

Baker tried repeatedly to call Willie. The line was busy so he tried the emergency override. "Come on, Will. Pick up your phone!" Seconds were turning into an eternity. No answer.

Elena broke the cold silence. "When was the last time you talked to Knoxi?"

"Just minutes ago." Brandi fidgeted. Her voice wavered. "She texted me and said they were stopping at Cal's. That's near—"

"Yes, we know," Elena said. "It not near anything."

"What are you saying?" Brandi's heart pounded.

Suddenly, Cody's cell rang. He fumbled for the right button and then jammed the phone against his ear. "Take it easy José. What are you trying to tell me? Slow down, amigo!" Cody slowly lowered the phone to the table. Everyone sat in disbelief. The Raffertys and Muskets could hear José's broken English and mournful sobbing as he explained that Knoxi had been whisked away by armed gunmen, and that Stan and Willie had been shot. Cody's grip buckled the screen.

Baker called in his men. Rapid-fire commands rolled off his tongue. "Jones, Rafael, Dickerson, escort the Muskets home! Nobody gets close to them! You hear me? Aspro and Hoffman, you're with me! We're going to Cal's."

He turned to Elena. "Call 911! Find out if they have received any calls. Circulate these pics to law enforcement agencies from Colombia to Canada, including homeland security."

Elena was already on it, her cold green eyes tense and focused. "I'm goin' with you!" Cody leaped to his feet.

"Babe, stay with your wife," Baker told him. "You gotta let me handle this. Your place is with her, and I need you here for now. You may have to recruit some more guys. Stay with her! Tell me you understand!"

Cody looked back at Brandi, now standing alone with strangers staring at her. She appeared smaller, lonelier, more forsaken than at any time he could remember. He surrounded her with his arms. She briefly lashed out, her fists pounding his chest with the last ounces of her strength. Finally, she collapsed onto him. He carried her out, escorted by airport security and Baker's men. An EMS crew met them on the way.

Two hours later, Baker reported back after visiting Cal's. The news was not good. Stan and Willie had been flown by air ambulance to Houston for surgery. José had a concussion with lacerations, and Mia would not stop crying.

The FBI had taken over the investigation and would not grant Baker access to the abandoned SUVs. The getaway vehicles were found near an abandoned airstrip. State Trooper Porter Sanders' body was found nearby in a grassy field—a bullet wound through the chest. No one could find any trace of the remaining perpetrators or their little victim.

Knoxi Musket was gone.

CHAPTER 4
BAKER'S THE MAN

By the next morning, Cody had replaced his broken phone. At 8:45 a.m., he called Baker. "Where are you?"

"I'm at Brownsville airport," Baker responded. "I was up all night. How's Brandi?"

"Yeah, we were up all night too. Julia and Silverbelle flew down last night in Dawg's plane. Brandi can't hold anything down. She's in bed. Why Brownsville?"

"We got a hit on the pic. Security camera at the Brownsville airport caught our favorite driver getting into a very old Lear 23 last night with Colombian registration, along with two other—"

"Did they have Knoxi?" Cody interrupted.

"I think so, Babe. They—"

"You *think* so? What do you mean?"

"Babe, just listen. They loaded two coffins into the aircraft. Knoxi was probably in one of those, sedated, alive. The FBI believes someone at Customs was paid off, but it'll take a while to investigate. I have faster ways of finding out. I may be able to learn where they've taken her. Gimme a few hours. I have a specialist on the way here."

"I want Sanders," Cody said. "He's gotta be the catalyst. If he wants me, let him come. But comin' after my little girl . . ." He paused, then exhaled into the phone. "Specialist? So, what do you mean by *specialist?*"

"She doesn't come cheap," Baker said. "She'll get the info we want. Cooperation from authorities might not come easy. You may have to build your own team."

"Yeah, I'm already workin' on that."

"And, as for Sanders, he took a fatal bullet," Baker told him. "So far, no one has claimed responsibility for the abduction. Have you been contacted by anyone with ransom demands?"

"No," Cody replied. "No demands. What do they expect to gain?"

"They want you to stop opposing them, Babe. Stop ruining their business. You're getting too close. They think they can break you down—make you back off. If only they knew. It's like when Saddam showed off his US POWs in those old videos—beaten and bloody. He figured Americans would just freak out and lose hope. He had no clue. You sow the wind, you reap the whirlwind."

"That's what we'll do," Cody said. "Create a whirlwind."

"Listen, Babe, one other thing; the plane disappeared from radar near Colombian airspace. More than likely, they descended below radar coverage and landed at an unknown location."

Cody reacted, "You said it was an old Lear? A Lear 23? That's an antique. How do you know they didn't crash?"

"Because it isn't reported missing," Baker assured. "Odds are someone was paid off at that end too. Elena is working that angle."

"Copy that. Keep digging."

"How's Ray?" Baker asked.

"He wanted to stop the chemo and help search for Knoxi, but Whitney wouldn't let him. Brandi's worried about him, too."

"Yeah," Baker said. "And you know Brandi will demand to go on any rescue mission. She's as bullheaded as Ray and twice as dangerous."

"Copy that," Cody said. "But I won't let her go. I don't wanna lose her too, and she'll just be in the way. She *ain't* going."

CHAPTER 5

WHAT MISSION?

It was a warm, bright January morning, the third day since the abduction. Cody had been busy. Trying to juggle rescue mission plans and dealing with Brandi's deep anguish was taking its toll, especially since he had barely slept one hour per day during that time. How long could he hold up?

He sat down on the walkway behind their home with his head between his knees. A mimicking resident Mockingbird, which claimed the Muskets' backyard as its territory, landed ten feet away on the gatepost beside the pool. The rude bird always stuck around in winter because fruit trees were aplenty and Knoxi liked to cast birdseed on the pathway for its benefit. The barn served as a windbreaker for the obnoxious chattering beast when blustery Texas "blue northers" came whistling through. Cody was fond of saying that on those cold days the only thing between his backyard and the north pole was the chain link fence at the back of the property.

But on this calm, sunny morning, life was good—if you were a bird.

Cody heard footsteps behind him. It was Whitney. He stood to his feet. "Mom? What are you doin' here? I thought you were with Ray at the hospital. Doesn't he start chemo today?"

"We just came from there, Cody. He wouldn't stay any longer. He just has to be with his daughter right now. And, be warned, he's got it in his head to go with you. He's gonna try to force you to take him along."

"Take him along? Take him where?" Cody hung his thumbs on the front pockets of his cargos—his familiar mannerism when he was either telling a lie or about to lose an argument.

"Don't try to pull that on this ol' woman, Cody Musket. I know exactly what's going on. Look, Cody, listen to me. You gotta make him stay here. He's sick and he's not a thirty-year-old marine anymore, but I cannot convince him. You're the only man alive he listens to. You hear me? Make him stay here. You need able-bodied people to go on this mission, and he's in no condition. I mean . . ." She placed her hand over her face.

Cody supported her and led her to a nearby garden chair. She had always been a strong tower, never faltering, always ready to take charge. It was difficult for Cody to see his mother-in-law carrying such sorrow.

He eased onto a chair next to hers. "Ray's all warrior," Cody told her. "He's all heart. Right now, his heart is —"

"Don't even say it Cody," she interrupted. "I know he's broken-hearted. So are we all. But Ray can't go. You understand me? And neither can Brandi. It wouldn't be right. This is a job for . . . what I mean is, it's no job for my sick husband or my untrained daughter."

"Mom, you're the wisest among us. You're the only one thinking with your head right now."

"Cody, I've watched you these years. Everyone in the league knows you're one of the kindest human beings alive—sheltering kids, doin' baseball clinics. But no man would dare to make you his enemy, and for good reason. That's the kinda man this job calls for, the kinda man who's gonna get our baby girl back. I know it's dangerous and I don't wanna lose you either cuz I love you as a son, but . . . what I mean to say is that you are carrying the glory of God on your life, and you're the man to lead this mission. When you get there, you'll see why."

"What mission?"

"Do I look like I was born yesterday? I'm going back inside. Don't want Papa to even know we talked."

After she left, Cody glanced toward the Mockingbird. It had been strangely quiet during his conversation with Whitney. Now, it mimicked the cat and flew toward the barn.

Cody dragged his weary feet into the house, forced himself up the stairs, and collapsed into his office chair. He had not seen Brandi all morning and had spent little time with her while focusing on getting a plan together for a difficult mission. It was nearly noon. Julia, Silverbelle, and Whitney were with Brandi in the bedroom across the hall, trying to coax her to sleep. Soon, he heard someone else coming up the stairs.

"I have to talk to you, Cody." Ray was hoarse and short of breath. "Your security person told me you were in the garden. I guess I missed you there."

Cody moved the davenport away from the wall and invited Ray into his hidden war room. The two sat down.

Ray began by asking, "What do your people know?"

"Baker's still working on it," Cody said. "As soon as I have details, I'll fill you in. We're prolly gonna sortie to a small country near Colombia. The fewer people who know the details, the better. I have another guy putting an assault team together. It'll take another day at least."

"You look like you didn't get any sleep last night either," Ray observed, his eyes red and swollen.

"You look like you need to get back to the hospital," Cody told him.

"You sound just like Whitney," Ray spouted. "She's the proverbial mother hen."

"But she's right, Captain. We both know it. Thank God for mother hens."

Ray was silent. He sat back and folded his arms. "Let me guess, she's already talked to you?" He tightened his big fists, and placed them on the table.

Ray's voice dropped into his chest. "I know . . . Of course I can't go." His voice broke. "I'm unable to help when my granddaughter needs me the most. Please promise me one thing, Cody. Do your best to make Brandi stay here. She won't be any help. Only one thing will get Knoxi back, and we both know what that is. Brandi will be a distraction."

"Ray, what we both know is that Brandi's going. I don't want her to go either, but can you honestly see her staying here?"

Ray paused for a chuckle. "Loud and clear," he sighed. "If you tell her she can't go, she'll just get there ahead of you. Has she learned about Rosa's Cantina?"

"Not yet," Cody said. "It's getting harder to keep her outta the loop. You'd think she would've figured it out by now."

"For her own protection, don't let her find out," Ray said.

"I'm not sure she wants to know," responded Cody. "That's probably why she doesn't."

"What about that phantom ghost frenzy from Moca Punache? It's been a month, but that story isn't going away."

Cody shook his head, but had nothing to add in response.

Ray nodded and folded his hands on the tabletop. "One more thing, son. Don't go off half-cocked, motivated by revenge. When hate drives you, you aren't a whole person. It's gonna take a whole person to get Knoxi back. This is not a street fight. This is for all we love and believe in. Remember your martial arts training—stay within yourself, be committed to excellence and virtue, and don't be ruled by animal instinct. Bring our girl home."

Cody reached across the table. The two men clasped hands, their eyes filling with tears.

CHAPTER 6

WHERE'S CODY?

"**M**ama! Help me! Mommy? Where am I?" Brandi's sleepless eyes flew wide open. "Knoxi! I can't see you!" She threw the covers off the bed and reached for the light on the night stand. It was evening. Where had the daylight gone?

Whitney supported her shoulders. "It's okay, baby. You were dreaming. Daddy and I are right here." She reached up and turned on the light which Brandi seemed unable to find.

"I saw her, Mama! I saw her!" Brandi tried to catch her breath as Whitney handed her a glass of water half-filled.

Brandi took two sips then handed it back, rubbing her eyes. "Daddy? What are you doing here? You're supposed to be in the hospital," she scolded. "Where's Cody? I haven't seen him all day. I haven't seen him since forever! Why has my husband deserted me?" She lunged backward, turned over, and buried her face in the pillow, sobbing.

Ray's deep voice reverberated. "Cody's doing what is necessary. He's putting a plan together."

Brandi sat up again. "Plan? Plan for what?" She waited, but Ray seemed at a loss.

"Daddy, I saw Knoxi a few minutes ago, I tell you. She must be in this room somewhere. We need to find her."

She jumped out of the bed and started toward the closet, but Ray intercepted her, wrapping her in his big arms. "Baby girl, Knoxi isn't here. I'm sorry, I'm so sorry."

Whitney could only watch as heavy sorrow melted father and daughter into one. She joined them in a three-way embrace. "Baby, Cody is busy putting something together. I don't know what it is, but I know that man. He's just like your father, and he won't be denied."

"Have they found Knoxi? Where is she? I mean what's Cody putting together?" She looked at them inquisitively, but Ray and Whitney just stared at each other. "Won't somebody tell me something?" Brandi's patience was paper-thin. "I can't remember how long she's been gone."

"Honey, this is the end of the third day," Whitney said. "It takes time to prepare . . . I mean, your father and I don't know any specifics, but Cody's all over this. He's had experience—That is, he knows people who—" She stared at Ray. "This 'ud be a good time for you to say something, Papa."

Ray spoke up, "What your mother means is that Cody needs some space for at least another day or two. He needs a clear head."

"Well!" she insisted. "He should be with me while he's clearing his head."

Cody stood in the hallway. He had overheard their entire conversation but couldn't bring himself to enter the bedroom. He turned and placed his hands on the banister which overlooked the parlor below. He could no longer hold back red-hot tears which fell all the way to the bottom floor.

How many times had Knoxi reached up and pulled on his hip pocket to get his attention while he had stared over this handrail? He felt that little tug again, but spun around to find no one there.

Just then, Whitney came through the bedroom door, having left Ray to spend a few more moments with his daughter before returning to the hospital. When she saw Cody's tears, she embraced him.

"You go right ahead and cry, son. This ain't the first time some handsome man done cried on my shoulder. Nothin' wrong with that."

"I can't go in there. She doesn't need to see me like this."

"She needs you, period, Cody."

"But how can I keep my head clear if . . ." He clenched his fist.

"You'll figure it out, Cody. You'll figure it out. Meanwhile, you just remember there is no pit so deep that God is not deeper still."

Ray walked into the hallway. "I think the medication is finally working. Brandi fell back to sleep."

"Well, Papa, before your ushered her off to never-never land, did you explain why she can't go on some rescue raid?"

Ray pocketed his hands. "I'll leave that to her husband."

"Oh, you always wuz a big ol' soft wuss when it cum to your daughter. No wonder she's so spoiled. Come on, I'm gettin' you back to that hospital 'fore they give your room to somebody who'll actually stay put."

Cody stood and watched Whitney support Ray as they moved slowly down the stairs. Ray had always been the wise one, immovable, strong. He was the captain. Cody had learned to never make a move without consulting his father-in-law. Now, it was no longer on Ray. It was on him.

He splashed his face in the sink at the hallway bath, then tiptoed into the bedroom where Brandi lay. He sat in his rocker watching her sleep, remembering the first time he had seen her at the Cinema 18 in Pittsburgh. That night, unable to take his eyes off her, wanting to introduce himself, he had lost his nerve and just followed behind her.

In the four years that had followed, her beauty and mystique had only grown. She was soft like a kitten, and as hardy as a lioness. She was a giant, and would prove to be so again. He was certain of it. A brief wave of euphoric tranquility rolled over him.

Just then, he heard someone whisper. *"Pssst! Cody!"*

He glanced up. A woman stood in the bedroom doorway. She was tall, wiry, beautiful, with a familiar face. When he recognized Silverbelle, he hastened to embrace her like a kid lost at the mall whose big sister had just shown up. They moved into the hallway and closed the door behind them.

"Cody, have you had any rest?"

"I got stuff to do, people I gotta contact. One of 'em is your husband."

"He's with the team. They're playing at Golden State tonight. Both teams plan to line up before the game and pray for Knoxi. He said tell you we have cleared the schedule for the Gulfstream in case you need to use it."

At that moment, Cody spotted Julia quietly coming up the stairs. As she embraced him, his emotions gave way again.

"Cody, Tanner won't be here until tomorrow," Julia said. "He's rejected the offer from the Yankees, so he's meeting with his agent right now. Have you had any rest?" Julia's voice refreshed like a cool breeze. "You need to get outta those shoes and cargos and get under the sheet with Brandi. Do you hear me?"

"Listen to her, Cody," Silverbelle admonished. "Brandi won't awaken, but she'll know you're there, and she needs that more than anything."

Cody would have none of it. "What she needs more than anything is a clear-minded husband to put together a plan to get Knoxi back. She doesn't need to see me like this. Look at me."

Julia was quick to respond, "We *are* looking, and what we see is a man sleepwalking through the most important mission of his life. Your emotions are running wild. You are exhausted, and that won't help you get Knoxi back."

Silver ganged up. "You must rest, Cody. I see a man trying to be strong for too many people on his own. We love you. You're like a brother to us. Julia and I will occupy the sofa and the rocking chair for the night."

"Yeah, Cody," Julia agreed. "We'll be right there in the room if either of you needs anything."

They each took an arm and ushered him into the room.

Julia spoke quietly, "I'm going to turn on the shower. Can you get outta those clothes on your own or do you need some help?"

Normally, that would have been funny, but Cody had just enough juice left in his battery to disappear into the hot shower, dry off, change into his new Astros jammies which Brandi had given him as a Christmas gift, then re-emerge and ease onto the bed. With two angels—one in the rocking chair and the other on the couch—to watch over their bed, Cody finally let his guard down and slept soundly for five hours next to Brandi.

CHAPTER 7

HE WHO SOWS THE WIND

January 5, two days later

Media correspondents wanted comments, something to print. They called out questions repeatedly to Brandi and Cody as the couple was ushered through the lobby of Lancelot Aviation at Hobby Airport in Houston.

A Gulfstream jet was waiting for them to board. Morning fog was lifting, but the sky was still overcast. The weary couple wore sunshades to hide swollen, bloodshot eyes. They had scarcely slept for five days.

The room quieted as Cody held up his arms. "I can't give you any information yet. Brandi and I have no idea where Knoxi is."

A late correspondent arrived, followed by her own camera crew. "Where are you headed today?" She seemed out of breath, addressing Cody.

"We're flying to Panama City, Anita. A good friend to the ball club, Juan Aviles, has been kind enough to arrange for us to have some privacy at his cattle ranch in Central America until we hear news about our daughter. We need to get away from here."

"Is that the same Juan Aviles whose son played for the Astros a few years ago?"

"That's right. Juan has considerable roots in Panama. As soon as there is news, we'll make public statements."

Several reporters called out well-wishes as the Muskets passed through the security door to the area where the aircraft was waiting for them.

Cody supported Brandi's arm while they climbed the steps to board the aircraft. Brandi's choice words made her feelings loud and clear. "Anita Crown Cassidy, or *Brown*, as you said, was the last person I wanted to see here. She must have flown all night to get here and harass us."

As they entered the spacious cabin, Brandi removed her sunshades. She recognized the interior. It was Jungle Dawg's Gulfstream V. The Muskets had been aboard other occasions. Today, the ambience was different. Two vacant seats directly aft of the cockpit awaited their arrival, but the remaining fourteen seats were occupied by individuals wearing battle scars and hard faces. She knew the look—eyes that had seen the dark side, like Cody's the night they had met four years ago.

What were these people capable of? Was this the team Cody had assembled? She had not expected to be accompanied by such a ghastly breed—a more odious version of *The Dirty Dozen,* plus two.

The aircraft taxied to the runway as instructed, and then awaited departure clearance.

> *"Gulfstream Seven Juliet Delta, cleared for takeoff, runway three-zero-right, after departure turn left heading two-two-zero, maintain five thousand."*

A somber crew and passengers lifted off the runway at 8 a.m. The official flight plan specified a direct route to Panama City. But special arrangements had been made with Panamanian air traffic controllers for the plane to make a southern deviation over the Pacific Ocean for "sightseeing," descend below radar coverage for one hour, and then turn back north toward Panama.

As the Gulfstream climbed out of Houston airspace, morning sunlight was not to be found. The cabin interior of red, white and navy blue (Detroit Pistons colors) was festive, but outside the cabin the morning was drab gray.

J.D. ("Dawg") and Silverbelle Blue, international power couple and close friends of the Muskets, had provided their aircraft and flight crew. Additionally, Dawg had successfully energized fellow NBA players and other celebs to create public awareness, and to demand that all law-enforcement agencies push it to the limits when dealing with child trafficking.

To the American people, the abduction of Knoxi Musket was egregious on a scale not seen since the kidnapping of the Lindberg baby in 1932. It had taken Cody five days to recruit and organize a team of commandos, and to plan the secret mission to save their little princess.

"Gulfstream Seven Juliet Delta, turn left, heading one-seven-zero. Climb to flight level three-one-zero."

After they had leveled off at thirty-one thousand feet, Cody released his seatbelt and made his way three rows back. He knelt down in the aisle next to Sabre Maxwell, former Naval aviator and aeronautical engineer who had come along for the dangerous rescue attempt.

"Anything yet?" Cody asked.

"Not yet, but I'm monitoring."

"Can we pick up the signal in flight?" Cody wanted to know.

"Anywhere within ten thousand miles," Sabre responded. "If she calls, we'll have her exact location. Are you sure she'll remember the number?"

"Positive. She has it memorized. We always knew this time might come." Cody nodded and then walked back to his seat.

Brandi's frustration finally unwound. "Am I your lowest priority? You've kept me out of the loop on everything. Did the press know these hired guns were aboard? Why did you tell them we're going to Panama? A vacation? Are you kidding? And, by the way, where *are* we going? All you've told me is, 'somewhere in South America.'"

He took a deep breath. "Okay. First of all, I didn't exactly say *vacation*, and no, the press doesn't know about the team on board."

"Haven't I earned your '*need to know*' status after four years?" She put her shades back on.

He reached over to hold her hands, but withdrew and looked the other direction.

"Cody." She pulled off her sunglasses again. "Why won't you even touch me? I mean, for the past five days you've hardly looked at me. Do Mama and Daddy know where we're going? Do you trust them?" She stuffed her shades into her purse.

"While we were still making preparations for this rescue," he said, "I tried every way to discourage you from coming. Right up to the last minute, I was hoping to convince you. I mean, you have no idea what we may be walking into. You're so *bullheaded*."

His lecturing did nothing to brighten her day. "Cody, don't shut me out. I'm your wife. I'm a big girl. I need you to trust me, and even Wonder Woman needs to be held."

"I didn't want to give you the details. It wouldn't have helped. Too many unknowns. But now . . ." He was reluctant to finish his thought.

Brandi covered her lips with shaky fingers. "Cody, what are they doing to her?" She writhed in her seat, her eyes begging him to assure that Knoxi would not be harmed.

He tightened up. Not a moment had passed in five days that he had not asked himself the same question. He knew his wife, every inch of her. There was not a place in her mind he had not been, but if he held her now, he would be wrecked, and Brandi didn't need that. She needed him in one piece.

He spoke with no emotion, no eye contact. "If you knew the details, I mean . . . I can't honestly give you any assurances. And besides that, this is gonna be dangerous, and you aren't trained. I didn't wanna lose you too. I didn't want to be distracted. It's gonna be hard enough without having to keep up with you."

She turned away and trained her weepy eyes on the empty grayness outside her window, searching for just one ray of sunshine. At least he was talking now. Such insensitivity should bother any woman, but Brandi had learned to give him some space. She remembered when he had made the final out in the World Series, striking out with the bases loaded. For the next three days, Knoxi was the only person who could engage him in conversation. A strikeout seemed larger than life at the time, but that was only baseball.

Since the abduction, he was all business. It was his way. Would the wall he'd built around himself this time ever come down? What if they never found Knoxi?

"So, what was it that finally convinced you to let me come along?" she begged to know.

Cody shrugged his shoulders but said nothing.

"I know you only wanted to protect me," she acceded. "But now that I'm here, tell me where we're going? Cody, please?"

He reached over and finally touched her hand, his own eyes filling with tears. "I thought I knew the meaning of pain before this, but now . . ."

She reached for his knee. "*Ohhh, Cody.* I know you're hurting as much as I am. Neither of us can get through this alone."

He gathered himself. "Small country on the west coast of South America," he told her. "It's about the size of Rhode Island. Librador is a sovereign nation, but it harbors one of the largest drug and child-trafficking operations in the world." He wiped his face with his sleeve. "It's near Colombia."

"Does our government know? Does *anyone* know we're going down there?"

"No one knows, not even our own government. Right now, we have the element of surprise, but if the regime in Librador finds out . . ."

"So, why do we believe Knoxi's in Librador?" she asked. "Why not the Middle East or Europe, or —"

"Cuz Baker and Elena figured it out. The driver who parked near our house was spotted later by a security cam at the Brownsville airport. As we suspected, he was connected to that trafficking cell in Pittsburgh that you exposed four years ago, and the Pittsburgh cell was connected to a South American cartel."

"Okay, so Brownsville's on the border, and the driver was seen there. So . . . so did he have Knoxi?"

"He and an associate loaded two coffins aboard an old Learjet bound for South America. We think Knoxi was in one of the coffins, alive and sedated. It's how they smuggle things which—"

"What!" Brandi's stomach caught fire. "You think they put my baby in a coffin!?"

"We . . . we believe for certain." He swallowed hard. "But, I mean, coffins are built for comfort nowadays, aren't they?"

Brandi's mouth flew open. *"Comfort?* Sure, if you're already dead!" She began pounding his shoulder with her fists, then realized all eyes were watching. "Just so I'm clear," she snapped off, "we're having a conversation six miles above the South Pacific Ocean about whether or not our daughter is comfortable in a coffin while flying to South America in an obsolete plane used by smugglers?" The long sentence depleted her breath. She pulled out her shades and jammed them onto her face again.

Cody repositioned himself in the seat. "Uh, we're not precisely over the South Pacific yet, but—"

"Cody!"

"Okay, okay. The aircraft in question was tracked by radar as far as Colombia 'til it dropped below coverage. The Raffertys brought in someone who was able to obtain the destination. It's confirmed. Knoxi was taken to Librador."

"Confirmed? How did they obtain the destination? Bribes? Something else? Government channels?"

Cody looked straight ahead, grinding out his words. "The only channels here are the ones we make. Some very lawless people have our daughter. The US has no jurisdiction, no diplomatic ties with Librador. We're on our own. Those traffickers took a big chance coming all the way to Houston to snatch Knoxi. These "hired guns," as you call 'em, are gonna get her back."

"So why did they want Knoxi so desperately?" she demanded. "It must have taken months of planning, right?" She waited for him to answer. "Cody? So . . . so when were you going to tell me the other part?"

"The other part?"

Brandi yanked off her sunglasses and dropped them to the floor.

He turned away from her stormy eyes, grumbling, "You don't need to know anything else. Believe me, the less you know, the better."

"There you go again. Baker and Elena know about it and I don't? Who else knows? How long has it been going on? I can't believe you managed to keep it from me."

He stiffened. "Sometimes we see what we want to see. We know what we wanna know. I thought that if you really wanted to know, you would've figured it out by now."

"Cody Musket!" She pressed her fists against her own temples. "You don't get to say that to me! I wanna know everything that Anita knows!"

She waited, then sighed and stared into nothingness. "Okay,

so maybe I didn't always *want* to know, but we are way past that stage now. Cody? Can you at least look at me?"

Cody softened his countenance and folded his arms. "All right, but keep it down. No one else aboard knows what I'm about to say."

She waited with eyes focused.

"Traffickers like to hold abductees in no-man's land where laws aren't enforced," he told her. "We can't just nicely ask them to hand the kids over. Sometimes we have to get persuasive."

"Persuasive? You mean like with money?" She paused. "Or guns?"

"How do you think we bring so many kids into our facilities? How do you think we free 'em?" His face was like flint once more. "We do it any way we can."

"Well!" she whispered back emphatically. "If you go running in with guns blazing, how do you protect the children?"

"We've never . . . I mean the closest we ever came to losing some kids was a month ago when . . ." He stopped short and shook his head.

"Cody, where were you last month? A baseball clinic in Caracas like you said? With Jeff Bagwell?"

He bit his lip.

"So this is why they came after our daughter? Because you like to play Zorro when you're supposed to be teaching baseball to kids?" Brandi looked away. "You're right," she threw her hands up, "I didn't *want* to know." She crossed her arms. "But I wish you had told me."

"I only participated once, and I wore a mask so nobody would recognize me."

"Like a dark angel?" she simmered. "Well, Don Diego, sometimes *I* don't recognize you."

"I'm . . . I'm s—"

"Don't say you're sorry, Cody. I'm sure the kids you helped aren't sorry." She covered her face again and composed herself.

"So, are we going to attack these people? Like . . . like a raid or something? With weapons? How will you protect Knoxi?" She waited, hoping he would reassure her, but his stonewall face persisted.

"Cody, please answer me. What happens if we go charging in?"

He wrangled in a deep breath, then served up the naked truth, "What happens if we don't?"

"Ohhh," she groaned wearily. "Why does this happen? Why, why, Cody?" She clutched his arm and buried her face against his shoulder, her body writhing every inch.

"This is why I didn't want you to know everything." Cody wrestled again with his own feelings.

She sat up and looked through the window, her eyes focused a thousand miles away. "Librador may be a small country, but it's still a big place. Do you know where she is?"

"Not yet . . . but we're working on it."

"Not yet?" She raised her volume. "What do you mean by *not yet? You're working on it?"* She put her hand over her face. "Never mind. I don't wanna know any more." Brandi turned toward the window again, her shoulders quaking with the agony in her soul.

Others could hear Brandi's exhausted, hoarse voice squeaking like a dry hinge. Cody placed a pillow behind her head, reclined her seat, and softly floated his hand downward over her eyes to coax them shut.

After a quiet moment, he unfastened his safety belt, slipped out of his leather chair, and sat at her feet. He removed her shoes, and attempted to message the tenderness and warmth back into her rigid toes, but her pallid face showed no sign of relief.

She opened her swollen eyelids. "Cody, don't!" She pulled her feet away. "This is not the time. People are watching, and there's nothing you can do or say that'll make me feel better."

Pensively, he leaned back against the bulkhead and watched her for a moment. Earlier she had wanted him to touch her. But now?

"It was your dad," he told her quietly. "He convinced me."

"My dad? What are you talking about?" Her inquisitive expression was an improvement. She mellowed enough to move her feet closer until her toes found his warm hands again. "Cody? What about Daddy?"

"A couple of minutes ago, you asked what finally convinced me to bring you along. It was the captain. He practically *ordered* me to bring you."

She snickered. "You expect me to believe that?"

"Of course," Cody nodded, forcing out a grin. They both knew the real reason he had brought her along. Brandi would have simply found a way to come on her own had he refused. But this wasn't the time to tell her something she already knew. Right now, she needed to hear a good lie.

"So, you're *that* afraid of my dad?" She managed her first smile in five days. Moments later, she fought back tears again.

"I can't help myself, Cody. This is all *so* wrong. What are they doing to my little girl?"

Cody wrapped her feet in a blanket, then stood to obtain a washcloth from the galley. He returned to his seat beside her and delicately bathed her drawn and tearful face. She clutched his right elbow to her chest and rested her head on his shoulder. At last, she dozed.

CHAPTER 8

PEDRO ISLAND

Brandi blinked her eyes. Her sleep had been hard and restless. Sunlight shone through the window. Was she awake? Dreaming? The interior of the jet was familiar, but the loud voices were not. She was startled to see ocean waves streaming past the aircraft at high speed just below her window. Were they ditching in the sea? Cody seemed unconcerned, and everyone else had come to life—chattering, expressing relief that the flight was nearly over.

Something bumped the aircraft. She looked outside again and saw a concrete runway rolling underneath the plane. The landing gear had touched down.

"Cody, where are we?"

"Pedro Island," he told her. "A small bump of real estate in the Pacific west of Colombia, an abandoned naval training base. We'll stay here tonight, then head to Librador in the morning."

The team disembarked. An armed ground crew shielded the group as they made their way on foot to a gymnasium a quarter mile away. A man and woman who slightly resembled Cody and Brandi boarded the plane.

"Cody, that couple getting on the plane; who are they?"

"They're doubling for us," he said. "They were brought here yesterday so they could fly to Panama City and be seen from a distance getting off this aircraft. We gotta make everybody think we're holed up there."

Moments later, the Gulfstream taxied back to the runway and

prepared to lift off.

Juan Aviles, whose son Jesse had played ball with the Astros, was to meet the flight in Panama City and carry the Musket doubles to a secret location. If all went according to plan, the media would believe the Muskets were sequestered at the sprawling Aviles cattle ranch in Central America.

"Who put this elaborate plan together?" Brandi asked. "I mean, do you really believe that woman looks like me? She won't fool anybody."

"Don't worry," he said. "People will see what they want to see. No one will be close enough to know the difference. If the kidnappers find out where we really are, we lose the element of surprise."

"Cody, what if Anita goes to Panama and discovers that we aren't there? She'll find us. I just know it. She already thinks I'm a fool. I told her we didn't keep secrets from each other."

The entire company watched the Gulfstream whine back into the sky, make a shallow left turn, then pick up its heading for Panama City. The jet rumble grew quieter and quieter like the sound of distant thunder before finally fading out of earshot.

They glanced around as they walked toward the gymnasium that was to be their headquarters. The island airfield was deserted—no voices, no other aircraft sounds, just an eerie quietness except for the soft crunching and shuffling of their boots against the hot pavement.

A rusty water tower with faded red and white checkerboard paint stood next to an old military aircraft hangar missing most of its roof. Grass grew through cracks in the concrete road. Remnants of old communication lines dangled from the original poles and sliced through overgrown weeds as the sea breezes whipped them back and forth.

An alligator lived on the island. It was rarely seen, according to intel. No one knew how it had survived so long, but for one clue: *No other wildlife was present.* They kept their eyes open—*humans might be next.*

A faded *Naval Warfare Special Development Group* logo was hand-painted in red, blue, and gold just inside the entry door of the gym. On the right side of a lengthy hallway, old offices had been converted into sleeping quarters with mattresses on the floor. On the left side of the hall was the open gymnasium—no backboards, no athletic equipment.

Some of the window frames contained no glass. Fortunately, it was January which brought moderate evening temperatures—mid-60s Fahrenheit. Their plan was to be there only one night.

Cody had appointed Elias Chavez as his tactical commander. A decorated former Navy SEAL, he had been with Cody in Afghanistan. In all, ten men and four women comprised the armed team which would execute a rescue plan. Chavez had handpicked most of them. None of them had been involved in Planned Childhood rescue missions. For reasons of secrecy, Rosa's Cantina was a completely separate operation.

"Good to see you again, Mr. Chavez." Cody said. "Good job getting your people on board this morning. No one suspected."

"Roger that, Babe. Did you receive a profile for each team member?"

"Every single one," Cody answered.

Three of the female participants had trained for GI Jane duty in the British military but had never been allowed to participate in combat. Most of the others had special ops field experience, and each had superior ability in at least one military craft.

Sabre Maxwell, the former naval aviator, had recruited a retired army ranger named Domingo, a loner, a man of few words with an acquired reputation for settling things with his fists. His face was scarred and weather-beaten. When he spoke, he turned the air green with expletives, and he smelled like the southern end of a northbound donkey. He glared like the angel of death, and no one looked him in the eye. The others had already nicknamed him "T-Rex."

Following an early-afternoon meal, Cody held a briefing.

"You've been chosen for your specialty skills and character. You've all signed a confidentiality agreement, swearing secrecy about this mission for a period of seven years. We have landed on what is known as Pedro Island. US Navy SEALs have used it from time to time as a training base. It's off the beaten path. As you can see, all your gear and weapons are waiting for you at the far end of the room."

Cody then asked Chavez to lay out the mission schedule.

"At 0400 tomorrow," Chavez began, "a Sikorsky CH-53 Sea Stallion will carry us across the water into Librador. We'll arrive before dawn. Cell phones will be useless most places. Our satellite phone may be our only link with the outside world, but in certain areas it will be useless too. Something in Librador is jamming the signal. We donno what it is." He then opened a pouch and pulled out several large photos.

"We have satellite images of three compounds where they might be holding "Little Hummingbird." Here is her picture." Chavez held up Knoxi's photo. "We may need to do our own recon to determine exactly where she is. I don't have to tell you the risk to life and limb if our presence is discovered. This is a sovereign nation we are entering. I know you've heard this before, but no one's gonna help us if we get caught."

"Mr. Musket, how certain are you that your girl is even in Librador? The memo we received states that Juan Capistrano, the minister in charge of acquisitions and finance, is behind the abduction. Why would this Capistrano single your daughter out? Does this grabby bloke have some history with you?"

Her name was Priscilla Hayes, one of the three British women. She was weathered with gray-blond hair and a plain face. Wearing a black muscle shirt, ripped arms and abs, and a scar above her right eye, she could easily have passed for a middle-thirties roller derby queen.

"Also," she asked, "suppose something happens to you. How do we get paid?"

"Miss, uh, Hayes, I—"

"You can just call me Priscilla, Mr. Musket. I apologize for asking. This is just business for me and the other girls. But we're good. *Blinding good.* We came because you have a reputation, and everyone knows you are well-minted. We just don't fancy going home empty-handed, sir, that's all."

"Priscilla," Cody answered, "I've arranged for one-half million US to be wired to the accounts of each participant after this mission as agreed, even if I don't make it back. Your beneficiary which you listed will receive your portion if you do not survive."

Chavez lifted up pictures of Juan Capistrano and his three generals.

"Capistrano is the grandson of Juanita Capistrano, who established the largest trafficking cartel in South America in the early nineties," Chavez said. "Cody's father was the American DEA agent who led a raid on her organization several years ago. She was killed in the raid, and the group was crippled until the grandson took over."

Cody spoke again, "So the answer to your question, Priscilla, is *yes*. There is history between the Capistranos and the Muskets. We suspect this is *personal* as much as *business* for these thugs."

Brandi's lower jaw fell—her sudden realization that Knoxi's abduction was partly generational revenge.

Cody continued, "The dictator of Librador is Marcus Rizal. He has strong support from cartels and underworld figures throughout Central and South America. Capistrano is his enforcer and is given free rein as long as he brings in enough revenue for the Rizal Regime. This rogue government took power five years ago. It supports itself primarily by drugs and human trafficking."

"Capistrano brings in young women and children from all over the continent," Chavez added. "They round up orphans off the streets like stray animals. They snatch some from their homes, and others they buy for pennies. They use children for sex slaves, and they hold auctions in Librador." Chavez glanced at Cody, hoping he had not been insensitive.

A sobering silence gripped everyone. An ever-so-soft breeze whispered lowly through a cracked window pane. Cody swallowed hard and spoke again. "This bunch rarely ventures into North America, but eventually, if somebody doesn't stop them . . ." He clenched his right fist and pounded it into his left palm.

Another voice sounded off from near the back wall. It belonged to R.J. "Lefty" Seaman, a former Army sniper. "So, are we here to take out these brave and honorable gentlemen who like to snatch little children?"

Chavez jumped back in. "Absolutely not, Seaman. We would be outnumbered with no reinforcements and no heavy artillery. We have limited explosives and restricted communications. We aren't prepared to declare war on a whole country. We're here to get Knoxi Musket back. That's all."

The room was as quiet as death. Everyone could hear Chavez shuffling through the photos again. "One other thing, ladies and gentlemen." He lifted up a single photograph of a tall individual with dark eyes, black beard, and amber dreadlocks that resembled serpents dangling upon his shoulders. "This guy's name is Kola Mendoza—Capistrano's chief deputy. Be on the lookout. He's a very large man and extremely dangerous. He loves to burn things, especially living things. They say he's addicted to the screaming."

Chavez stopped when he turned and beheld Brandi's contorted face.

"Excuse me, sir." A stocky man with a pale complexion and suave hairstyle took the floor. He walked briskly to Cody and saluted. "I'm Jacob Greenberg from Syracuse. I don't know you Cody, but I owe you my life. I was an army reserve engineer when the Chinook I was in went down in Afghanistan in 2010. I was captured, and did not believe I would ever see home again."

Greenberg then turned to face the group. "I agreed to come on this mission as soon as I was contacted. I manage a successful firm on Wall Street. I still struggle with war-related stress, but I have a life because . . . Let me just say that I know something about the value of a dollar. Dollars couldn't buy what this man paid for me. Good to see you looking so well, sir. We're *danged-sure* gonna get your girl back."

Priscilla tightened her lip. A deep unity of souls welled up, so quiet that each could hear the thoughts of the others—*Musket may be a rich celebrity athlete, but this man is a brother, and this is a righteous mission.*

Chavez took center stage again. "The Taliban tried to kill Cody in Afghanistan and it cost them three hundred men. Traffickers tried to gun him down in Pittsburgh and they lost three hitmen. I guess Capistrano figured he would have a softer target with Cody's seven-year-old girl. But don't be surprised if that little Musket turns out to be *not so soft.* " A buzz went through the room.

"How do we know she's still alive?" Priscilla's chilling inquiry silenced the room again.

Brandi's eyelids closed. She could hear Cody draw in a deep breath through his clenched teeth.

"We may be able to pinpoint Knoxi's exact location," Cody said. "But, of course, she may have already been sold. In that case, she could be . . . anywhere."

Brandi shut her eyes again. The impulse to scream overwhelmed her, but she held on in the presence of such hardened warriors with whom she felt no commonality.

"There's another possibility," Cody wavered. "They may hold our little girl and demand other children as ransom." He stared through the floor. "If that happens . . ."

The others dropped their eyes. A brave fighter was in agony.

"Everyone, get some rest," Chavez said. "Tomorrow, we go hunting."

During the exchange, Domingo, the man they called T-Rex, had stood motionless near the entrance, staring at the floor. He was a statue—stocky, balding, leather-faced. His left forearm was solid ink-tats with the words *'Only the Strong Survive'* displayed prominently, and surrounded by choice metaphors from his unhallowed vocabulary.

Cody approached him. "Welcome aboard, Domingo. Where are you from?"

"Nowhere in particular, sir." His voice was cold, raspy and quiet. He showed no emotion as he turned and walked out the door.

~   ~   ~

From a distance Brandi watched through blood-shot eyes as Domingo left the building, then she slowly ambled toward her husband. She took his arm and leaned her head on his shoulder as they walked down the hallway in the opposite direction to find a moment of privacy.

"So, these fighters are not the same ones who perform secret missions for Planned Childhood?" Brandi asked.

"*Rosa's Cantina*—that's the codename," he said. "And, no, these people are not involved. They know nothing about Rosa's

Cantina. The fewer people who know, the less chance of leaks. These specialists have been picked partly because they're good improvisers. The intel out of Librador isn't reliable, and we might hafta' make things up as we go."

Brandi struggled to hold back her tears until she could be truly alone. "I don't understand why they took Knoxi. Isn't this just bringing more public outcry against them? I thought that was what they feared."

"They fear us more," Cody said. "They've changed their tactics because they're losing too many assets. Up 'til now, we've been untouchable. They're hoping that we've become peace-lovers, enjoying the good life. They think this'll break us, take the fight out of us. We have to be peacemakers, *not peace lovers.*"

"Peacemaker? Peace lover? What's the difference?"

"A peacemaker will fight to bring freedom," Cody answered. "A peace *lover* will sacrifice freedoms to avoid a fight."

She wasn't interested in hearing any of his wise-acre sound bites. "Cody, I don't care about peacemaking. I just want her back." She watched the floor move beneath her feet as they walked. "So, what will we do if they demand other children as ransom?" She broke, unable to contain her emotion any longer.

"That hasn't happened yet," he said. "They don't know we're coming. That gives us the advantage. Our plan is to maintain total secrecy, complete silence. You can see why I didn't tell you everything. The more you know, the worse it gets, and I didn't want to dump anything else on you."

"*Ohhh,* Cody. Why? Why did God let this happen? I'm . . . I'm looking for answers, but all I get is . . ." She wrangled with her emotions again.

He bit down hard. "I asked the same question when my leg was blown to pieces and I was dying at Kandahar. But if that hadn't happened, I wouldn't have met Nikki Corbett who showed me what faith is, I wouldn't have played baseball, and I would never have met you. I would still be in the Marines, none the wiser, thinking I owned the world."

"But if you hadn't met me—I mean, after all this pain, aren't you sorry?"

"Sorry I met you? And Knoxi? Don't even think that."

"But this has broken your heart." They stopped. She glanced up at him wearing deep remorse on her face. If only she could take it back. The last thing Cody needed right now was to be reminded that his heart was broken. Her shoulders ached from wanting to hold him.

He took a long, clearing breath—his usual first mechanism when things looked impossible. "You know . . . I heard somewhere that the most difficult trails on earth can lead us to the most beautiful destinations," he said. "I believe that's where this road will lead us in the end."

Cody left her for another briefing with his commanders. She smiled softly and watched him as he walked away. Did he really mean it? Beautiful destinations? *Oh God, please let him be right. And please keep Anita from figuring out where we are.*

CHAPTER 9

LITTLE MUSKET

Unknown location, North Central Librador

Knoxi had no idea where she was. They had made her swallow some red liquid after they had put her in the van. When she woke up, she was with other children. Most of them were crying, tired, hungry and dirty. Mean men were screaming at them in Spanish. She understood every word, and she had to fight to keep from crying. For once, she wished that she had not learned Spanish.

The children were locked inside a chain-link fenced-in area with a gate large enough for a truck, and a small walk-through gate for people. They received only one meal per day which consisted of a flour tortilla and one cup of water.

The kids found shelter from the frequent rains underneath three temporary structures that resembled carports. Most of the compound was muddy. They slept whenever they could find a dry mattress. A bed shortage meant they had to double and triple-up.

She stood in the middle of the containment area and scanned everything, starting directly behind her and moving clockwise in a complete circle. She memorized every detail, quadrant by quadrant, just like her daddy had taught her. "Scan 360," he would always say.

Selena was a five-year-old girl from Mexico City. She could not stop coughing. Two big men came in and took her away. She did not come back. Knoxi met a boy from Venezuela whose name was Ruben. He had lived on the streets in the city of Valencia. He had no family.

She soon learned that many of the children had no home and no parents. Now she understood the meaning of the word *homeless.*

During the first three days, soldiers were everywhere. They were rowdy and loud at night. The children barely slept. At the end of day two, five soldiers came into the pen and carried away four older girls. They were never returned, but Knoxi could hear them crying in a stone building nearby. When she stood on the table, she strained to see the building, but could not see the girls. It had bars on the windows.

On the fifth day, most of the soldiers had disappeared, and she no longer heard the four girls crying behind the barred windows. She could now count only four soldiers standing guard during the day, and only one at night. This was the first day it had not rained. When evening came, she looked up at the sky and saw a million stars.

Wistful memories came alive her thoughts. Were these the same stars she could see from her seat at Minute Maid Park when the roof was open?

She remembered what her mother had told her: "No matter where you go in life, listen every day for God to speak to you."

"God, if You hear me all the way from this place, I need to know what to do," she whispered into the endless starry sky. "Help me to get all these children away from these mean men. And God, why don't these children have homes? Why don't they have mammas and daddies?" She tried not to cry, but couldn't help sobbing again.

Most of the children were exhausted and had already occupied a bed for the night, but Ruben walked over to her and held her hand when he saw her standing alone crying. He didn't understand much

English, but he knew she was saying a prayer, so he held her hand firmly and bowed his head.

Knoxi smiled at him and continued in English. "Jesus, please help me get in touch with my daddy. These mean men are in so much trouble when my daddy finds out what they're doing. I miss my daddy and mama, and Grandpa Ray and Grandma Whitney, and I need to know what to do!"

She wanted to cry again, but took hold of herself and cleared her head with a long breath—a practice she had learned from her father. She wiped her eyes and stood quietly with her new friend.

At that moment, she remembered a game she had once played with her daddy at the Bustamante ranch in Uvalde—*the camouflage game.* He had taught her to hide in plain sight by camouflaging herself with something from the natural surroundings. The sweet memory made her miss home even more and she fought back tears again.

Just then, the night guard walked by outside the fence. He carried a cigarette in one hand and a half-empty bottle in the other as he had done each night. As she watched him stumble along, an idea filled her head. She glanced at the deep puddles left over from the rain, then looked up at the floodlight, which created a bright spot on the ground about twenty feet inside the gate.

Ruben's curiosity grew as he watched her. *"¿Huh? Qué —?"*

Knoxi responded. *"¿Rubén, puede usted guardar un secreto?"* She wanted to know if he could keep a secret.

She told him she was going to escape later that night, and that she would need his help. After the escape, he was to spread the word secretly that she and her daddy would come back and save them all.

Ruben's eyes got big. *"!Tu papá debe ser gigante, eh?"*

"¡Sí!" she answered. *"He's the biggest man you'll ever meet! Es el hombre más grande del mundo!"*

"Bigger than Hulk?"

"Yes! Even bigger than the Hulk!" She answered. Then she continued in Spanish, assuring him that her father was a friend of Jesus, and that he and Jesus loved all the children in the world.

"You papa friend of Jesus? I never meet a friend of Jesus before!"

She explained her escape plan and the part he would need to play. He agreed.

But when darkness deepened, Knoxi began to waver. What if she got caught? Would they carry her away never to bring her back like some of the other girls? What would they do to her?

Fighting off terror, she recalled being with her daddy when he had spoken these words to the Naval Academy graduating class:

"When your pain is greater than your fear of
doing something about it, you must act."

She had never understood it before, but now she knew the meaning. The idea of never being free again was more painful than her fear of the present danger. She must get word to her daddy.

Trembling like the last rose of summer, she stood near one of the small gates and watched for the guard to come by again. Each night he had carried a bottle and sipped from it with every other step. Tonight, she was counting on it.

When she saw him coming, she took off the red dress she had worn since the abduction. She dropped it to the ground where the spotlight was focused. After that, she ran into the dark area beside the gate and covered herself head to toe with the black mud from a residual rain puddle. Then she lay down in the mud. In the darkness, she was *camouflaged.*

Ruben, as planned, shouted frantically for the guard to come inside. He pointed to the dress and held it up for the guard to see. The drunken soldier unlocked the gate and staggered in to investigate. While the guard's back was turned, Knoxi rose from the puddle, tiptoed through the unlocked gate as quietly as a snowflake, then galloped off into the darkness on tiny feet swifter than a little stealth pony.

She ran until she came to some buildings. She was out of breath, and now began to panic once more. She had hoped to find help, but the small village was like a ghost town. Every night she had heard music coming from this direction, but tonight there was none.

The mud on her skin had dried and was now cracking and falling off. She didn't know which way to go. Gazing down the deserted street, she could no longer manage her fear. Alone in the night, she began to sob again. The trees along the side of the road cast long shadows in the moonlight. It was creepy.

Who would help her? How far was she from her home? Would more bad men find her?

"Please, Jesus, what do I do now?"

She stepped cautiously down the middle of the street, still crying. Toward the far end of town, she finally saw a faint light. After walking a little farther, Knoxi glanced around. She saw no other signs of life in any direction.

She ran as fast as she could toward the distant light. It got bigger and bigger as she approached. At last, she stood in the street before an old frame building. Shutters covered the windows. The light shone through wooden swinging doors that resembled the ones in her favorite cartoon called "*Showdown at Dry Gulch Saloon.*"

She tiptoed cautiously onto the porch, knelt down, and peered underneath the saloon-style doors into the building. She stood up and parted the doors slightly, looking with one eye through the crack. A man wearing a white apron was cleaning tables. He looked very distraught with tears on his face. He was older than her daddy. A picture of Jesus hung on the wall. After weighing all options, she decided to place her bets on the sad man in the white apron who loved Jesus.

"Por favor, señor, necesito ayuda."

When he turned and saw her standing in the doorway with muddy tears streaking her face, he immediately held out his arms.

"Rapido! Rapido! Entre pequeño. Come in here, Come in quickly!"

Knoxi stepped inside and stared up at him.

He pulled a towel from the rack and wrapped it around her, intending to put her in the bathtub immediately, but Knoxi insisted she needed to use a phone. He explained to her that Capistrano had confiscated every cell phone in town, but that he had managed to hide an older satellite phone.

He paused for a moment. What was he doing? A tiny girl wearing a thin coat of mud shows up in the middle of the night and asks for a phone? Was he dreaming? He connected the sat phone and handed it to her.

Knoxi dialed the number and waited to hear the five beeps that her daddy had told her to listen for. Afterward, she turned the phone off and handed it back to her kind host. Her smile cracked most of the muddy shell off her face. A dirt trail followed them as he carried her to the bath.

He left her to soak and then returned with clothing just her size —jeans, a shirt, hat, and little hiking boots. Knoxi wanted to know whose clothes and boots she would wear. The answer made her cry again.

CHAPTER 10

TOMMY JOHN

D arkness had fallen over Pedro Island. The team would retire early. They planned to be airborne by 0400.

Brandi lay down on a double mattress in a room designated for the Muskets. Cody had not arrived yet.

The sleeping quarters were dimly-lit by moonlight shining through windows with no glass. She placed her head on a pillow and picked up her cell phone. A very weak signal was indicated. Several text messages popped up which had apparently been sent to her during the flight that morning. One message caught her eye—one she had never expected.

"Brandi. I'm so, so sorry. This text is too little, too late, but I had to say it: I feel responsible. I pushed the story too hard. I said too much. Now they've targeted your family. I issued a statement on Fox this morning retracting my accusations. I am in Panama City, and I have released my eye-witness report verifying your presence here. And wherever you and Cody are tonight, please be careful. Bring her back, and know that I will not sleep or stop sending prayers to God until I know Knoxi is safe. — Anita Brown."

Thirty minutes later, Cody, Sabre and Chavez entered the room. Cody would share the mattress with his wife, while the other two men each had a bed in an adjoining room. Outside, a rusty clamp on the flagpole clanged repeatedly against the mast in the breezy air. It would be a long night.

Cody lay with eyes wide open. Their world could collapse in the next few days, and he would be powerless to stop it. What would he do if Knoxi were lost forever? Could he and Brandi survive another heart wreck? He could hear her breathing next to him, but they were miles apart. They had suffered separately by his choice.

He had denied his heart. A good commander is not allowed to have feelings. A leader must remain in one piece, focused. His heart would have wanted Brandi to come with him to Librador, but duty and discipline reasoned that she would be an additional burden. In the end, nevertheless, he had no choice but to bring her.

Lying on his back, staring up at the flaky paint which had left bare spots on the ceiling, he remembered something Brandi had once told him: *"The only heart that cannot be broken is one that has no love in it."*

Before meeting Brandi, he had no love in his life. He had not granted his heart permission to break, but with Brandi's trembling body touching him, he could deny the truth no longer—he was broken into a million parts. Time froze as he drifted away from mission plans, soldiers of fortune, and what tomorrow might bring.

Memories of the good life now flooded his thoughts. Knoxi's first words, "You never know," pounded on his heart's door. On her fifth birthday he had taught her a camouflage game at the Bustamante ranch—hiding under a pile of leaves in the field, moving through the Purple Sage bushes while carrying leafy branches as a cover-up—the delight on her face when she thought he couldn't see her.

She once sneaked into the barn and painted herself yellow with a special body paint designed for a pre-school play. She then hid from him in plain sight, standing next to the yellow wall near the horse stalls. He passed by several times, calling her name, ignoring her muffled giggling. Finally, she tiptoed up from behind and tackled him. He pretended to be surprised, rolling on the ground with her while they laughed their heads off.

The musty mattress squeaked as Cody rolled onto his side facing away from Brandi. He could feel her trying to snuggle from behind, trembling, sobbing. Her pillow was wet, but he had pretended to not notice.

She needed him, but tomorrow was too important. Cody couldn't afford to lose it now. He summoned his strength, but his self-control deserted him. He helplessly turned and threw his arms tightly around her.

Suddenly, they were electrified by a loud buzzer. Brandi screamed, clutching and sinking her fingernails into Cody's shoulders. Fire alarm? Were they under attack? Was it all a nightmare?

Sabre jumped up and stuck his head in the doorway. "Do you hear that?" Everyone was now standing, bewildered by the obtrusive sound. Chavez entered the room with a flashlight.

Sabre opened the black case he had been carrying. "Okay, here goes."

"What is it?" Brandi's huge eyes focused on the device.

"Wait." Sabre paused.

"Well?" Cody was impatient.

"Wait . . . Hang on. That's it! We got her! Here's the lat-long readout!"

"What's that device?" Brandi was hands-on-hips while the others closed in.

"It's what we've been hoping for!" Sabre shouted, his voice booming like a combat pilot after a dogfight. "Something I've been working on ever since I retired from the Navy. Needs no network support, no triangulation in the traditional sense—just a portable device that can be used in the field."

Cody screamed back, "Did it give you—?"

"Affirmative, Babe." Sabre's vocal tone slid into an easy cruise. "It gave us her exact coordinates. We only need to check the lat-long on the satellite photos to see what's there."

"Yes!" Cody shouted. *"Yes!"* It was the round of high fives he had been waiting for. "We know exactly where she is—latitude and longitude."

Brandi jerked Cody's arm hard enough to turn him around. "You wanna tell me what's going on?"

By now the rest of the team had arrived. Sabre had the floor.

"I've been working for the Department of Defense for the past eleven years, developing this device that can instantly pinpoint the location of a phone signal. It's at least one thousand times faster than any other call tracing device in the world. It has a range of ten thousand miles."

"Sabre is more than just an airplane pilot," Cody said. "He's an electronics genius. That's why the Defense Department enticed him away from the glorious life of piloting a tanker jet in the Navy. They sent him to school again, and then employed him to finish developing his invention."

"I've been able to do what I love while being at home," Sabre said. "And this device allows a call to be traced anywhere within a ten-thousand-mile radius in one second or less. Someone just needs to dial the number. Still not fully tested, but it definitely worked tonight."

"What's the name of this invention?" Brandi wanted to know.

Cody rolled his eyes. "Now that's a typical woman's perspective. Everything's gotta have a name."

Brandi slapped him on the shoulder. "Well, I think we should name it. I mean, even *Tommy John* got a surgery named after him."

"Tommy John?" Cody smirked. "How'd you come up with that?"

"Hey, I like it!" Sabre interrupted, "Tommy John it is."

"Are you straight up serious?" Cody vented. "You're gonna name this thing you invented Tommy John?"

"Sure, Babe. Tommy John has a ring to it."

"So!" Brandi shouted. "Let's go get my daughter! *Our* daughter!"

"I second that!" Cody reached for his boots.

"Wait a minute," Chavez grumbled. "Now that we know where she is, we'll use the lat-long data to construct a plan that'll work. We want to insure Knoxi's safety, so we can't just fly in there like a bunch of happy-butt plebes. It'll take us a few hours to figure out a strategy."

Cody ground his teeth, paced back and forth beside the makeshift bed, then plopped down on the mattress mumbling to himself. It was awkward. Sabre stepped up, "Ladies and gentlemen, can you give us the room?"

Everyone filed out, leaving Sabre alone with Cody and Brandi.

Sabre sat down. "Listen, Babe, we should get one thing straight. We all respect the fact that you learned wisdom when you earned your stripes—the kind that never go away. And your presentation at the Academy last year was amazing, but—"

"Just get to the point," Cody grimaced.

Sabre paused and refocused. "Okay, fair enough." He started again. "Look, these people are prepared to follow you to Hell if necessary, with or without the money, but leave the tactical aspects to these professionals who have done this before if you wanna get your daughter back in one piece."

Brandi backhanded Cody's knee to get his attention, then rubbed his shoulder. His head cleared. "Okay, okay, I get the message." He blew off some steam. "Tell Chevy to carry on. Brandi and I will try to get some shuteye 'till everything's a go."

Brandi laughed. "Shuteye? *Ha!* After this? Not even hardly! But I'll take whatever time I can get with my hubby!"

~ ~ ~

Note: Tommy John was a left-handed New York Yankees pitcher who suffered an injury to the ulnar collateral ligament (UCL) in his pitching arm. This common injury had ended careers for many pitchers until Dr. Frank Jobe performed an experimental surgery on Tommy John in which the torn UCL in his left elbow was replaced with a tendon from his right forearm. The operation extended John's career and became an accepted medical procedure known as Tommy John Surgery.

~ ~ ~

At 3 a.m. Chavez alerted Cody and Brandi. "The coordinates place Knoxi at a building in this satellite photo." He displayed the picture. "It's not one of the compounds we looked at earlier. This building looks like a store, hotel, or maybe a bar.

"Why would they be holding her there?" Brandi asked.

"Ma'am, if you want my opinion, she may have escaped from one of the compounds. Otherwise, how could she have gotten access to a phone?"

Cody pounded his fist. "That's my girl. Let's go!"

They heard their ride flying in from the east. The helicopter set down on the road in front of the gymnasium.

As the rest of the team walked out to board, Cody held Brandi back. "You're not going on this trip. You're staying here. We should be able to snatch her out of there and head straight back here. We'll be back before you know it."

"Cody, you can't force me to stay. I'm going." She began to cry and then clenched her fists and stomped her foot. "She's my little girl, and I can't stay here wondering if both of you will come back. You brought me all the way here, and now you tell me you won't let me go?"

"Look. I wasn't crazy about bringing you in the first place. I'm tellin' you it isn't safe. We don't have any idea what we'll walk into. You haven't been trained for —"

"Neither have you, Cody! I'm going!" She was steamed, crossing her arms.

He knew that look. "Get your boots and helmet," he conceded. "Follow me." He shook his head and picked up both backpacks. "You're just like your dad—stubborn, bullheaded. *Ugggh!"*

"Thank you," she snapped.

She put on her boots, picked up the helmet and marched out with head held high. They walked to the giant Sikorsky without speaking, then climbed aboard.

"The helo ride is gonna be shorter than expected," Sabre said. He had waited for Cody and Brandi before boarding. He sat down next to Cody. Brandi looked up at the overhead cables and some visible wiring. She wouldn't look anyone—especially her husband—in the eye.

Without having heard a word, Priscilla, the former British spec-ops trainee, knew exactly what had just occurred between Brandi and Cody. She cast a jealous glance at Brandi, who returned a polite but sterile smile.

"What's our ETA?" Cody asked Saber.

"Bout forty-five minutes." Sabre glanced at his mission notes. "The building is in the lowlands, twenty-seven miles from the coast. We don't have to cross any mountains. Lots of jungle, but looks like a clearing just a half mile from where Knoxi called. We'll use spotlights to verify before attempting to land."

They flew at treetop level to avoid radar. When they reached the coordinates, their searchlights revealed that the satellite images were not accurate. A landing attempt would not be safe—day or night. They would have to rappel sixty feet to the ground in the darkness with ropes.

Cody turned to Brandi. "You'll have to go back to Pedro Island. I'll send someone with you to keep you safe 'til we return. Rappelling requires a lot of training. You'll break your neck. I haven't rappelled from a helo either, but I learned the basics at that mountain survival course in Colorado."

"What about a parachute or something?" she asked.

"Are you kidding?" Cody grinned. "A parachute or something?"

"I'll get you down there, luv," Priscilla offered, standing behind her. "It's called a spider jump when two go together. I can rig the rope and harnesses so we can both go."

Brandi turned around. "Are you serious?"

"How much do you weigh, ma'am?"

"Uh . . . 'bout a buck thirty-five."

Priscilla looked her over and shook her head.

"Okay. More like one-forty-five," Brandi admitted.

Cody objected. "Well, I dunno—"

"It's okay, Babe," Chavez spoke up. "Priscilla's the best one here. She murdered out. If anybody can get Brandi to the ground in one piece, Prissy can."

"Murdered out?" Brandi asked.

"It means she convinced the brass she was good enough to instruct in the rappelling school," Cody spouted off.

"I'll get you down, ma'am, I promise . . . With your husband's permission, of course."

Brandi, arms crossed, stared at Cody. Her eyes were easy to read: *'At least someone cares.'*

"Thank you, Priscilla, from *both* of us," Brandi said, her blue eyes still fixed on Cody's face.

"Go ahead, Prissy. Take her down," Chavez said. "We'll get your gear to the surface for you." He helped the two women get ready for their descent.

Brandi could not see the ground as they left the helicopter. Her trip down the rope in the early morning darkness was like falling into a deep, dark hole. Priscilla had instructed her to watch for the surface, stay loose, bend her knees, and let her legs take the shock to protect her back and ankles. Brandi was an athlete. She could handle it. Everyone made it down safely. The Sea Stallion left immediately in hopes of avoiding detection.

The huge rotor blades sent echoes like an army of horses galloping away through the jungle, becoming more distant each second. Soon, all was quiet. No one moved. They stayed low, eyes and ears on alert. Had the enemy detected their presence? Would they face armed resistance?

After a few moments, Chavez spoke quietly. "All right, we need to keep the noise down as we make our way to the building." Then he glanced toward Brandi. "Glad to see we all made it to the ground safe."

Brandi looked around and then lowered her eyes. Reality took hold. Standing on this jungle battlefield with fire-tested warriors, she was out of place—a rose among thorns. Cody moved next to her and placed his arm around her shoulders. He looked at Priscilla and nodded his thanks. Priscilla acknowledged, then looked upward toward the treetops. The fading moonlight exposed her plaintive, suddenly misty eyes.

Movements were slow and deliberate, cautiously approaching

their target. Brandi feared their presence might be compromised by the sound of their boots walking over the small crunchy rocks. Most of all, she feared they would not arrive in time to save Knoxi. Couldn't they go faster? She resisted the urge to bolt full speed ahead on her own.

The jungle itself was eerily quiet—not even a breeze to rustle the treetops, no insect or bird sounds. The silence was ominous, baffling.

Brandi nearly tripped when she walked into a scrubby fern bush. In the dim, pre-dawn light she could not determine the height of the tallest trees. When she had landed after rappelling earlier, something sharp had grazed the side of her right ankle. Good thing she had worn boots—no injuries, but the object had torn through the leather.

She was shivering. Deprived of sleep for a week, she had just rappelled from a helicopter into a dark, silent abyss. Never had life posed so many questions. Never had her soul known such fury in the midst of the quiet. A fire in her belly had driven her thoughts toward that building all night long.

Over and over she had tried to visualize what this moment would be like. But now, so close to the objective, her legs and feet became numb with a foreboding compulsion to turn back. Could she face what they would find in that building? Would her hope end in the next thirty minutes? *Will my baby be there? Alive?*

Cody was steady. She knew he was feeling the same fears, but his rock-hard arm firmly around her shoulders would suffice for both of them.

Finally, they spotted the tavern. Cody spoke to Brandi quietly, but with a stern voice. "That structure is our objective. You keep down. Let us handle this. I want you to stay here out of sight."

"I will, Cody. I promise." She trembled all over as she hid behind a large rock.

"You stay with her, Babe," Chavez said. "Leave this to us. It's what we do."

Cody whispered forcefully, "Chavez, are you really gonna tell me to stay here when my little girl's in that building?"

Sabre weighed in. "Babe, you don't wanna leave your wife alone out here." He gestured toward Brandi, hoping Cody would notice she was visibly shaking like a lamb lost in the wilderness.

"All right, you win." Cody grimaced and took one long glance toward the building. "We'll stay outta sight." Cody and Brandi hid behind a volcanic rock the size of a railroad car

CHAPTER 11
AIN'T GOIN' TO NO COAST

Their target building was now fully visible in the dim morning light. They stopped at the tree line about 150 feet from the dilapidated structure. Chavez sent four scouts led by Domingo, the one they called T-Rex, to recon the small Tavern up close.

Moments later, Domingo sent word to Chavez: "No sign of Little Hummingbird. Gotta open the door to shop for a birdcage."

The rest of the team moved into position on every side of the structure, leaving Cody and Brandi hidden in the trees.

Chavez prepared to lead an assault team through the front door, but just then, a window shutter near Domingo swung open. The soldiers trained their guns, but were shocked when a small girl with dark hair appeared in the opening and stretched her neck to see over the window divider.

"Hold your fire," Domingo whispered loudly to the others. "Somebody get Musket!"

"Is my daddy with you?" The little face in the window now had a voice. The wary rescuers focused eyes on the child.

Domingo's growly voice responded, "Is your daddy Cody Musket?"

The scrappy girl pulled herself onto the window ledge and jumped. Domingo caught her at arms' length, held her off like any normal man would fight off a bobcat, and then lit up the morning with a string of unholy utterances that brought Cody and Brandi rushing from their hiding place. By the time they had raced to the scene, Knoxi was choking Domingo with hugs and drowning him with kisses.

T-Rex carefully set his rifle on the ground, dropped to one knee, and stopped fighting with the little girl. No one, friend or foe, had ever before targeted Domingo for a hug.

Knoxi yelled when she saw her parents, "Daddy! Mama! I knew you were coming. I told the other children you would save them!"

Brandi and Cody fought each other to be first to hold her. "Other children?" Cody asked.

"Affirmative!" Knoxi answered. "Mr. Santiago is inside. He's very sad because bad men have his wife. They killed his little girl. He wanted me to be his little girl, but I told him I already have a daddy."

The raiders lowered their weapons, momentarily speechless. They had never before rescued a child, nor would they have believed that a seven-year-old girl would invoke such a verbal response from T-Rex, and then wrestle him to the ground.

Rapidly-approaching daylight forced them to scamper inside the building immediately. They couldn't afford to be spotted. The rickety old tavern featured an aging bar with several cracked mirrors hanging on the wall. Eleven tables sat on an uneven floor with wooden planks that squeaked when walked upon. The air was musty with the smells of burnt toast, beer, and weed.

Cody extended his hand to Knoxi's gallant host. *"Señor Santiago, gracias, gracias."*

"Un honor, Señor."

Then Knoxi spoke. *"Señor, digale a mi padre acerca de su esposa.* Tell my daddy about your wife."

He was Benito Santiago. His family had owned the tavern for two generations. He was forty-five years old. Benito's grief overtook him as he told about his wife and little girl—the story he had kept hidden from townspeople for fear of retribution.

His wife had been taken two months earlier. Benito would often venture near Capistrano's compound where he could sometimes observe her from a distance. She was a very desirable woman of twenty-seven, the mother of his murdered daughter. He had asked God each day to send someone to bring his wife home, but God was silent.

Chavez translated, and then took Benito into the kitchen to quiz him about Capistrano's facility and the strength of his forces. Together they drew a map of the entire compound.

The tiny girl told the rest of the group how she had escaped, and that Benito had hidden her at great risk. She described the living conditions inside the compound, and revealed the layout and number of guards on duty. She mentioned the four older girls who had been taken away, and said she had heard them crying in the nearby building.

Priscilla needed some air and stepped over to the swinging doors. She lit a cigarette and gazed toward the street. Wiry muscles on her arms tensed while she listened to Knoxi.

"How many children would you estimate, Fort Knox?" Cody pulled his daughter close.

"Fort Knox?" she asked.

"That's your codename from now on. How many children?"

She sat on Cody's lap. "I counted exactly forty while everyone was sleeping. Some from Mexico and some from other countries. Ruben is from Venezuela. He helped me escape. I remembered what you taught me about scanning three-sixty, one quadrant at a time. I memorized everything in sight."

Cody looked around the room—warriors all, hardboiled and battle-scarred faces, locked and loaded, weapons at the ready.

"This is my girl," he said.

"I told Ruben that Marines never leave anyone behind. I asked him to pass the word that I would bring my daddy to free everyone. I told him those bad men would be in so much trouble when my daddy found out what they were doing, because my daddy loves children and he's a friend of Jesus!"

Cody's pride brightened his stern cheeks. "Were you scared?"

Her lower lip puckered. Her smile no longer hung on. She threw her arms around Cody's neck and began to sob on his shoulder. The others breathed a collective sigh of relief—she had at last proven to be human. Priscilla could not resist turning around to witness the sight of the tiny hero surrounded by Cody's huge forearms.

Knoxi looked her father in the eye. "I listened for Jesus to talk to me," she said, sniffling, "and I remembered you told me that just because you're afraid, it doesn't mean you aren't brave."

Cody wiped Knoxi's tears, unable to conceal his own.

Domingo came front and center and took off his hat. "Honey, you are pure *baddass!"*

Domingo then inquired, in his own way, if she could confirm that more children like her were being held against their will. Knoxi seemed unfazed by his limited and profane vocabulary.

"Yes, sir," she responded. "And I made a promise to them. I can tell you're a sweet man, but you sure say a lot of bad words!"

Several of the men and women covered their mouths.

Brandi's facial muscles unwound like the loosening of a tight rubber band—the goodness of God, the sweet release from an excruciating six days. Her daughter was not only safe, but in complete command. She had not spoken a word until she was nearly four years old, but could now hold the saltiest men on earth in the palm of her hand in two languages.

"I'm not surprised about finding more children here," Cody said. "Librador means one who writes his own currency and sets the terms of commerce. It is also synonymous with the Spanish word *'gaveta,'* which means a hidden drawer in which to hide valuables. Capistrano kidnaps children then keeps 'em hidden until international buyers come in here. Capistrano writes his own ticket and makes the terms. The kids are sold to the highest bidders."

No one made a sound.

"How many of you are thinking the same thing I am?" Cody's face straightened. "I know y'all didn't sign on for more. All you gotta do is head out tonight toward the coast. You'll be picked up from there by the helo and will receive every penny I promised. You did your job. But—"

Saber stood to his feet. "Excuse the interruption, Babe. Take a look around you."

Every assault weapon in the room was now lifted overhead—a weapons salute, a signal of solidarity. No speeches necessary. Their collective thoughts ran loud and clear: A seven-year-old girl had left her dress on the ground, camouflaged herself with mud, had run through dark streets in an unknown region two thousand miles from home, and had promised forty kids she would bring help. *We ain't goin' to no coast!*

Chavez and Benito reappeared from the kitchen. Benito had provided valuable intel for a raid on the compound.

Chavez gave Cody the rundown. "Benito tells me that Capistrano and his army are not even here. They headed south to the mountains where a group of farmers is trying to escape the country. Farmers here can't survive because they're required to dedicate half their fields to marijuana and give it to the regime."

"That makes sense," Priscilla said. "If he loses the farmers, he has nobody to provide his yearly supply of bobo bush."

"He left only a handful of soldiers to guard the kids," Chavez continued. "He wasn't expecting us. That's why the town's almost deserted, and why there were no soldiers in this tavern last night."

"So, the resistance is light," Cody concluded. "Capistrano will have to come all the way from the southern mountains to catch us. Our timing couldn't be better, but it'll still be a race. We can't get helicopters into this jungle, so we gotta head outta here on foot."

"Right," Sabre joined in. "It'll take Capistrano only a day to get back after he learns we ripped off his latest harvest of little people. He's heavily armed and equipped with personnel carriers."

"I'll scrounge around town and see how much food I can round up," Brandi suggested.

"No, you won't!" Cody bristled. "It still isn't safe out there."

"Wait! I got this, Babe." Chavez stepped in and asserted his position as tactical commander. "I'll assign someone to go with you, ma'am. Can't take anything for granted. Not everyone in this town is on our side."

Brandi nodded her appreciation. Cody gritted his teeth.

Chavez spoke to the entire group again. "Tonight, we go to the compound and wire explosives to create a diversion. Before dawn tomorrow, we set off the fireworks, snatch the wife and the children, and haul our fannies outta here. There are no vehicles available in this village, but maybe we can find some on the way."

After they had disbursed, Chavez approached Cody alone. "Babe, I know she's your wife, but maybe you could consider—"

"Consider what? What are you saying, Chavez? Do you think she should have come along?" Cody had not cooled down after Chavez had stepped between him and his wife.

"I know you think I was out of line, Cody. But she's here, like it or not, and we have a lot of kids to take care of."

"What would you do if it was your wife?"

"I've had two, Babe. Neither of 'em stuck around. I'm not the best person to ask."

"I'm gonna call Dawg," Cody said. "He can charter a ship out of Colombia to meet us at the coast. Where's the satellite phone?"

CHAPTER 12

KNOXI'S BRIGADE

C ody stayed at the tavern with Brandi and Knoxi while the team invaded the compound. The raiders left at midnight to prepare the surprise attack.

Cody slept restlessly. Brandi slept soundly for the first time in a week. Just before dawn, the building shook. Loud explosions could be heard coming from the compound a half mile away. Flashes of light reflected through the windows and off the inner walls of the tavern. It was happening.

All three jumped out of bed. Benito could not be found. The Muskets assumed he had followed the team to the compound—not part of the plan.

"Mama, what's all that noise? Is it a storm?"

"We need to get ready, Knoxi." They had spent the previous afternoon gathering items for their exodus—food, medical supplies, clothing. The soldiers had discovered blankets in a deserted building near the tavern—enough for all the kids to sleep on. No one could explain why so many blankets lay in an abandoned warehouse.

Some merchants had been afraid to help, fearing retribution from Capistrano. As a result, they were unable to gather enough food and drinking water to last more than one day.

The twenty-seven-mile journey to the coast with so many little ones would take at least a week. How would they find food? Shelter? And what about Capistrano and his army? Sleep had refreshed Brandi, but now reality overwhelmed her. *Fleeing with forty kids? What were we thinking?*

Just as the first rays of sunlight peeped through the windows of the tavern, they heard voices screaming, crying, shouting. Bursts of gunfire in the distance were an ominous sound that Cody had not heard since Pittsburgh four years earlier.

When Knoxi saw her father cover his ears, it frightened her. "What's happening to the children, Daddy? Why are they screaming? Why are you scared?"

Brandi knelt down and embraced her daughter as the sound of boots pounded upon the wooden porch. The front door swung open.

Chavez appeared in the doorway with a grim countenance. "Take a look," he said, pointing to the street.

In front of the tavern stood a sea of children—poorly-clothed, dirty, terrified.

"We lost two of the kids," Chavez reported. "But we counted thirty-eight survivors, all unharmed. They're scared. One kid saw his brother take a bullet in the head. He sat down next to his dead brother and wouldn't move. We had to carry him. He wouldn't speak. They call him Paco. We think he's about six years old."

"What about resistance?" Cody asked.

"Either dead or fled. One got away. No tellin' if he was able to get word to his boss. But either way, Capistrano will know by the end of this day."

"And Benito?" Cody inquired.

Chavez shook his head.

"Benito's wife?" Brandi asked.

Chavez stared at the porch underneath his bloody boots. "Sorry, ma'am."

Cody hesitated to ask one more question. "So, what about—"

"I know what you wanna ask me, Cody. The answer is no. We didn't find the four older girls Knoxi told us about." Chavez closed his eyes and caught a fresh breath.

"But," he added, "we found items confiscated from children. Mostly footwear. So . . . at least the kids won't be barefoot in the jungle."

"Any other casualties?"

"Priscilla has a flesh wound on her arm. That's it. We did everything we could."

"Nice job, Chevy. Much better than any of us could have hoped."

"Cody's Marauders are ready to move out, sir. It's your ball game now."

"Cody's Marauders?"

"We wear the name with pride, Babe. We've all decided."

Brandi held Cody's arm. "Are you okay, Babe? I mean—"

"Fine. I'm fine," Cody replied with urgency in his voice. "We need to move on. No time to mourn the dead. The clock's ticking."

Chavez looked out at the mortified child brigade. "We need to settle these kids down. We aren't gonna control 'em if we can't get their attention. They're screwed in the head right now. Too much shooting. Too much blood. And then, there's little Paco, the kid who saw his brother shot."

"I got an idea." Cody picked Knoxi up and lifted her to his shoulders.

In a few seconds, the sounds of distress softened. Little heads turned and the street became quiet.

Knoxi raised her hands. *"¡Hola, a todos! ¡Vamos a casa!"*

The children cheered—raising hands, bouncing, clapping. Cody set Knoxi down. Her legs were in motion before her boots touched the porch. When she ran into the crowd of children, they greeted her like a sister—one who had kept her promise.

No time to grieve. Word would surely get to Capistrano. The adults handed out blankets, boots and clothing for those who needed them. Then, Fort Knox gave the order to move out. "*¡Muévanse!*"

"Okay, Sabre, you'll navigate," Cody said. "Lead us out of here!"

"Right, Babe. We follow this road out of town, then catch a trail that leads straight north. We'll see some farmhouses along the way with small roads. Maybe some of farmers'll help us. These satellite photos should get us there."

They began their march. Brandi and Knoxi stayed back with the kids, while Cody, Chavez, and Sabre led the way. The marauders guarded the flanks and rear, keeping watch for spies while making certain all the children could keep up. They weren't in a mood to lose anyone else.

"It's just a matter of time 'till Capistrano finds out we blew up his compound," Cody said. "So, how do we keep his army from finding us?"

"Gonna be hard," Chavez admitted. "He has informants, spies everywhere. The secrets of jungle warfare survival are: Don't be smelled before you're heard, don't be heard before you're seen, and don't be seen."

"How do we pull that off with these kids?"

"Like I said, it's gonna be hard."

"We'll need help," Sabre joined in. "We have to pray that farmers and forest dwellers we run into can be trusted. We need to keep moving in a straight line and pay close attention to the satellite images. We'll pass through jungle, and then through a portion of the rainforest."

Brandi overheard. "What's the difference between jungle and rainforest?" She and Knoxi moved to the front.

"Most people can't tell the difference," Chavez answered. "The rainforest doesn't always have thick underbrush, but has taller trees that can form a solid canopy over the top. Sunlight barely gets through, so it's easy get disoriented. People get lost and never found. And there's other dangers."

"What other dangers?" Brandi wanted to know. She and Knoxi moved forward to join the three men.

Chavez glanced at the tight-lipped Cody and shook his head. "Not now," he stated flatly. "Too many little ears listening."

A morbid chill rocketed from Brandi's chest all the way to her toes. Her legs scooted her forward, positioning her between Chavez and Cody.

"I wanna know," she insisted, barely above a whisper. "How can I help if I'm not informed?"

Chavez wasn't anxious to step over the line with Brandi again and incur the wrath of Cody whose burden of command had obviously given him a short fuse.

"Go ahead." Cody breathed out. "Tell us both."

"Okay," Chavez agreed. "I'll give you the short version. This is not gonna be a cake walk. Start with the wildlife, like jaguar, black caiman, cougar, anaconda, vampire bats. I could go on and mention huge hairy spiders that'll scare the crap outta these kids, and piranha that can—"

"All right, we get the picture," Cody interrupted. "Besides the critters and varmints, what about heavy undergrowth like trees, vines, and other stuff? And what's the chance we find some roads to follow?"

"Won't know 'til we get there. But I promise you we won't find any five-star hotels along the way. Could be headhunters. Could be mercenaries who would love to collect a king's ransom from Capistrano."

"What about fresh drinking water?" Brandi asked.

Sabre joined the conversation again. "No major rivers on our route, just a few small streams. This is the dry season, but that's relative. Isolated storms with flash floods come outta nowhere."

Cody tossed in another chilling tidbit. "Our sat phone's inop ever since I called Dawg to arrange the boat. It's definitely on the fritz, not to mention some sort of jamming interference of unknown origen."

"Daddy, what are critters?" Knoxi had slipped up beside him undetected.

"You weren't s'posed to hear that" he told her.

"You said *critters* and *varmints*," Knoxi insisted. "What are those?"

"Baby, your daddy was just saying . . ." Then Brandi turned to Cody. "Come to think of it, Captain America, what's the difference between a critter and a varmint?"

He glanced at her with that '*are you serious?*' facial expression. "Critters crawl," he muttered. "Varmints walk. People can be the worst varmints of all. Question answered?"

Brandi got the message. "Come on, baby, let's go back and walk with the children where we belong."

"Copy that, Mama! Let's get away from these varmints."

CHAPTER 13

PACO

T he long walk was underway. When Brandi looked back and could no longer see Benito's tavern in the distance, the realities were overwhelming. No phones, no internet, no transportation—complete separation from civilization—gigantic palms, volcanic rock, crunchy soil as far as her eyes could see. Oh, how much larger it all seemed when traveling on foot!

Brandi thought of the ancient Hebrews who had fled from slavery in Egypt. They, too, had faced impossible odds. Was her apprehension even a taste of what they must have felt? Following this guy named Moses whose leadership mettle had not yet been forged, they found themselves backed up against the Red Sea with the Egyptian chariots approaching. What wonder must have filled their heads when suddenly the water parted so they could walk over on dry land.

Oh, God, when we find our backs against the wall, will you part the water for these children?

Terrain in this area was strewn with rocky ground that limited the underbrush. Trees, however, particularly palms, were aplenty.

Domingo found a dirt bike in the woods with a full tank of gas. Apparently, the rider had met with ill fate, but no sign of a body was found. He suggested to Cody that he could use the bike and lag behind to scout for Capistrano. He could report back quickly several times per day.

"Good thinking, 'Mingo. Do it. Remember, your PNR has limited range, so you will need to get within one kilometer of us to communicate."

After Domingo sputtered away, a disturbance arose at the rear. Children were calling out. *"¡Paco! ¡Paco! ¡Vuelve! Come back!"*

Paco had run off. The kids had tried to call him back, and several had run after him. Chavez held up the march and scrambled to the rear. Paco, the traumatized child whose brother had been shot earlier, had stripped off most of his clothes and had taken off like a gazelle into the jungle.

"¿Por cuál camino se fue?" Chavez asked. They all pointed into the jungle in the direction he had fled. The few who had run after him had returned panting, declaring that Paco was way too fast to catch.

Brandi and Knoxi stood together looking at the youngster's clothing lying on the ground. "Why did he run off, Mama? Where's he going without his clothes?"

"He witnessed his brother shot this morning," Brandi told her. "He's really sad, not thinking straight."

"What's your plan, Chevy?" Cody wanted to know.

"I vote we try catching him, but it's *your* call, Babe. I don't wanna lose any more kids, but we don't have any time to waste. Capistrano isn't going away."

"Why did he leave his clothes here?" Brandi was confused.

"My guess, ma'am? It's because he's traumatized. No telling what some of these kids have been through."

"We're goin' after him," Cody said. "Let's gather up his clothes. He's bound to be tired, and he can't go far with no shoes— not on this stuff." He pointed to the rocky ground.

"Okay." Chavez pulled together a search team. "Dakota! Hampton! Seaman! You're with me!"

Brandi handed Chavez Paco's things. "Here are his clothes, Mr. Chavez. Can you catch him?"

"In answer to *your* question, ma'am, Dakota is the best tracker here. Joe Hampton and Lefty Seaman are former rangers. We'll find Paco. Just hope he hasn't fallen into a hole or quicksand."

Knoxi reacted, "*Ohhhh*, roger that."

Chavez had parting words for Cody. "Babe, you and the rest stay here and guard the kids. Make sure they keep their heads down. If you don't hear from me in thirty minutes, start the kids moving again. We'll catch up."

"Copy that," Cody nodded. "Thirty minutes."

The marauders and kids hunkered down for a thirty-minute rest. The children were whiny and fatigued with growling stomachs and jittery nerves. They were naturally afraid around adults with guns, and Paco's running off naked through the jungle had done little to ease their apprehensive feelings.

~ ~ ~

Dakota's real name was Bobby Adahay, which means "Bobby who lives in the woods." He was a native Cherokee American, a Yale Graduate, and a decorated former Army Lieutenant. His square cheek bones, weathered face, and fifty-year-old rough-and-tumble body belied his smooth-as-velvet Groucho Marx voice. He was born in the Okefenokee Swamp in Southern Georgia, but his family had moved to South Dakota when he was young. Hence the nickname, *Dakota*.

Chavez, Seaman and Hampton followed Dakota while he tracked the small boy. The path was easy to find. They saw where he had fallen, and they kept tracking until they came to a mound that was home to several tall, slender palms. Suddenly, the trail disappeared.

They circled the area, but found no sign of Paco. Dakota stopped in his tracks and remained motionless for several seconds.

He detected the odor of human urine. One of the tall acai palms began to drip around the base. He looked upward.

Paco was frozen, clinging to the trunk approximately thirty feet up, hugging it with arms and legs that shook with fatigue.

"How did that tiny kid get up there?" Chavez stared.

"Beats me," Dakota said. "He can't hold on much longer."

"Yeah," Hampton agreed. "He won't be able to come down on his own, 'til he falls. Gimme a hand!"

"What chu got in mind?" Dakota asked.

"First, cut some bark off this other tree," Hampton said. "I gotta have a couple of ten-foot strips."

Dakota knew what Hampton was up to. He also knew the danger. They sliced the bark with a machete to get it started, then peeled off the long strips by hand. Hampton yanked off his footwear and began looping one of the strips back and forth around his ankles and between his heels to form a web.

"Okay," Hampton said. "You guys should stand underneath in case the kid falls. I might not be able to catch him since I'll be busy climbing and trying to hold on."

Hampton began shimmying up the tree using the webbing between his feet to push himself upward. He looped the second strip of bark around the tree as a safety belt.

"I've heard of people who climb like this," Dakota said, looking up at him. "Where'd you learn this?"

"Jungle training for a mission we never deployed on," Hampton told him. "Today's the first time I've done it in a real emergency."

Paco began to slip. Hampton was still seven feet shy of reaching the exhausted child. "He's gonna let go! Gonna fall!"

When Paco let go, Hampton made a valiant effort to catch him but the sweaty youngster was difficult to grasp, slipping right through Hampton's grip. Somehow, the child managed to latch on to Hampton's ankle. Hampton slid down the trunk with the child holding on, and the two came away with only minor scrapes.

The four men cleaned Paco up. His face and neck were still spattered with dried blood. His brother had been shot while running next to him during the escape that morning. His feet had a few cuts from running over the rough ground, but were heavily callused. This kid was used to running barefoot on hard surfaces.

They tried to get Paco to talk, but he did not respond to Spanish or English. They could only guess what country he was from and what language he spoke. Paco showed no emotion, displaying what soldiers call the *thousand-mile stare.*

"This kid's a climber," Hampton said. "Some tribes about two hundred miles from here survive by climbing trees for the fruit. They work naked. He may be from that region."

After they got him dressed, he refused to follow, so Dakota picked him up and carried him over his shoulder. The boy never made a sound.

"Babe, you read me?" Chavez called Cody on the comm. "We have recovered the sombrero, and we are returning. Do you copy?"

"Chevy! Get back here on the double," Cody whispered. "We have company. *Hostiles!*"

CHAPTER 14

THE WOUNDED

Chavez and the others expeditiously found their way back to the brigade. Cody, Brandi and the marauders were crouched inside an area of heavy growth, trying to keep the kids quiet and out of sight.

Chavez took cover next to Cody. "Hostiles? Where?"

"They crossed in front of us 'bout ten minutes ago, fifteen of 'em. They were loud, well-armed, and headed east. If we hadn't been delayed with Paco, we would've been out in the open and they would have opened up on us. That would've been ugly."

"I want to send Hampton up one of these trees," Chevy told him. "We need to know if the hostiles are still heading east. If they are, we'll be safe if we keep going north and stay quiet for a while."

"Why Hampton?"

"You kiddin' me? You should have seen that guy. He's an animal. Climbs like a crazy man."

"What if they spot him?" Cody asked.

"Hampy knows how to hide behind the trunk while he climbs, and I wanna know where those guys are going." Then he turned around. "Seaman, Dakota, cut a cuppla' strips of bark from this tree."

Everyone was amazed as Hampton capered like a monkey up the stem of a slender palm to about fifty feet above the ground. He began surveying with his field glasses.

Suddenly, a gunshot cracked the air and echoed through the forest. "Everybody down!" Cody warned with a growling whisper.

Three more shots rang out, followed by the cries of an animal. It sounded like a canine, possibly a wolf.

Next, a falling object, Hampy's field glasses, hit the ground at the base of the tree. Everyone stared upward to see Hampton rapidly sliding down the trunk, the bark strips smoking from the friction. He hit the ground hard, uninjured, but breathing heavily.

"Lost my grip on the glasses," he panted. "I saw the hostiles. They're 'bout a hundred meters east. They musta' shot some animal. Couldn't see what they were firing at, but they shot one of their own by accident—one idiot who stepped out in front and caught a bullet in the back." He paused to catch his breath. "Now, there's just *fourteen* of 'em remaining. Somehow, I don't think this bunch has all their faculties online." He unwrapped the bark from his feet and began acquiring his footwear again.

Chavez stepped it up. "Cody, Dakota, on me." The two men followed Chavez forward to examine the trail left by the disorderly squad.

"Look here." Dakota picked up what was left of a home-rolled joint, still smoking. "Reefers. They're everywhere."

"That doesn't make Smokey the Bear very happy—throwing these down in a forest," Cody said. "Of course, Smokey's an American. This isn't America."

"Right, Babe," Dakota said. "But it sure made those buttheads happy enough to take target practice at some canine and plug one of their own in the back."

"You think it could've been a wolf?" Cody asked him.

"Not certain, but I sense it was domesticated."

"How could you possibly know that?"

"Just a sense, that's all," Dakota answered.

Chavez called Priscilla on the comm. "Prissy, get 'em ready to move out. I want Kershaw and Hodges on our flanks at least forty meters out. I don't wanna run into another parade of smiling assassins."

They cut their way through dense brush, followed animal trails and dirt roads. Chavez sent Dakota ahead as a scout. The two marauders on the flanks were all ears and eyes.

They hoped for rain. Water in the canteens would not last long. By mid-afternoon, everyone was exhausted. Marauders took turns carrying Paco who was in his own world, wherever that was.

They had counted on wild game as a food source, but animals were scarce. Satellite photos showed streams ahead, but those water sources were another day's travel. The kids, having been captive, now became portraits of hopelessness again, facing fatigue, hunger, and fear of being recaptured. This was just the first day. What would it be like five days from now?

Night was fast approaching. Topographical images depicted a clearing within a few hundred meters, so they trekked northwest to find it. Dakota took point to check it out first.

Brandi's feet were heavy, as if carrying everyone's burden. The children were edgy, noisy, frightened. How could they possibly make a six-day journey without alerting every living thing within shouting distance?

And where would they find food for so many? Some palm species provided fruit, but harvesting it would have taken too much time. Marauders picked fruit along the way, but only what they could snatch on the move.

Dakota radioed back to Chavez. "I'm at the clearing. Hodges made it here too. It's safe for now. We could bed down for the night."

"Roger that. Any five-star hotels?" Chevy snapped.

"Yeah, but they don't take American Express. How 'bout a teepee?"

"A teepee? Reserve it. We'll be there in ten."

"Reserve it? You think I'm some rich Indian? Nobody off the

reservation even knows me."

Hodges cut in, trying to catch her breath after the long hike. "We should jus' all go home now, ladies and gentamen. Dis video game's over."

"Only one problem," Dakota said. "This game's like dancing with a grizzly—you can't quit just cuz *you* want to."

"That's a roger."

Cody spoke up, "I heard you spec-ops types have a motto; do all you can, and if things look impossible, joke around."

"Yep, somethin' like that," Chevy confirmed. "And we didn't learn that in special warfare school either."

"Does it help?" Cody asked.

"Of course not. But if you survive, it makes a heckuva story for later. And if you end up a casualty, at least you die happy."

When the main group finally reached the clearing, they had no choice. Time to stop. Exhaustion had overtaken them, and traveling by night in the jungle was not an option. Darkness would fall within the hour.

Domingo reported that he would ride into camp within five minutes. So far, he had seen no one trailing them, but it was only the first day.

Brandi wanted Cody's attention, but he was preoccupied setting up camp: Did everyone have a blanket? Was the perimeter safe? Did they have any remaining food? Water? How's Paco doing?

Knoxi approached him. "Daddy?" Cody didn't respond. "Daddy!"

Cody gave her a quick glance, but walked the other direction. Children were crying. Paco sat holding his ears, rocking back and forth.

Cody met with his leaders. "What little food we brought with us was consumed this morning, and the water's nearly gone."

Knoxi took matters into her hands.

"Mama! Put me on your shoulders."

"What?" Brandi asked her. "What do you have on your mind?"

"I need to talk to the children."

The kids had responded to her that morning when Cody had lifted her. Could it work again?

Brandi hoisted her up. Knoxi waved her arms and called out. One by one, the kids noticed. She began singing "Jesus Loves the Little Children" in Spanish, and then asked them to sing along.

Priscilla stood near the edge of the clearing and snuffed out her cigarette. She strolled toward the group when Knoxi became the choir director.

Gradually, most of the children joined the chorus, singing in thirty-eight different keys. Brandi set Knoxi down and took hold of Cody's arm.

"Listen to me, commander-in-chief. Someone must pray. We have no food, no water, no shelter. We can't do this. *I* can't do this."

Cody lowered his head to let off some steam. "Okay, what do you expect me to do?" he asked her.

"Cody, they won't listen to me. I'm just the dumb tenderfoot female. You gotta step up. Tell 'em your wife is gonna pray. They can either join me or look the other way."

Cody held up his hands for quiet. The children stopped singing. Everyone focused except Paco who still sat alone. Cody announced that Brandi was going to lead everyone in a prayer for food, water, and safety.

Some of the marauders scoffed. A few looked the other way.

Priscilla was especially vocal. "Leave me out of it, luv. Good to know we have a choir and someone to say prayers, *but we need food.* We haven't seen even a bloody squirrel all day. How do you plan to find enough food this late when it's nearly dark? I just hope I don't run out of smokes. We're toast in a couple of days anyway."

"Okay, Priscilla. We get it," Cody muttered. "But I just want everyone to know that God listens to my wife because she listens for Him. Priscilla's right. The odds aren't good. We gotta have food and water."

He put his arm around Brandi and told her she had the floor.

A few snickered, but they respected Cody, so they removed their head gear and waited for Brandi to petition God for help. Domingo, who had arrived by this time, was uncomfortable. He walked far enough away to miss the prayer.

Brandi called out to Heaven for provision and protection. Her voice was the only sound—no insect noises, no breeze. The scent of Homo sapiens had rarely impinged upon this tiny region of the earth. Perhaps the critters and varmints were silenced by the untoward presence of human encroachers.

After Brandi finished her prayer, two rifle shots rang out. Domingo, who had wandered about fifty meters away, lit up the wild with a voluminous trail of vocal impiety. The gunshots and his subsequent bellowing terrified the children.

"Everybody get down!" Chavez shouted. The children stood frozen, screaming and crying.

Domingo howled like a man who had just won the lottery. *"Wahooo!"*

Cody and Chavez, guns raised, moved toward the howling. When they reached Domingo, his right boot rested on the head of a large bear which had wandered into his sights. Two shots had brought down the fatted animal. And, even more amazing, the bear was clutching within his iron jaws a newly-killed marsh deer. This was the first time anyone had seen Domingo crack a smile.

Sabre came upon the scene belatedly and shook his head. *"Seriously?* This is a male Spectacled Bear, the only bear species on this continent, and it's on the endangered list."

Dakota walked forward and examined the nose and mouth area of the bear. "That's not all," he said as he pushed back the upper gums to examine the teeth. "These bears live in the Andes high country. They're never found in these lowlands, and they aren't quick enough to catch a deer like this." He ran his hand across the neck, admiring the magnificent animal. "I mean, these guys eat berries and nuts, and they'll sit for days on a tree branch waiting for fruit to open rather than stalk a fast animal like this."

Chavez lowered his weapon. "How do you figure it?"

"I have no clue," Cody answered. "But you better get the kids settled again, Chevy."

Chavez gave the good news to the children. Several of the men dragged the animals into camp. The youngsters stared at Domingo. Suddenly, the smelly T-Rex was their hero. Their big eyes followed him, but none ventured close.

Chavez glanced over at Paco—still alone, showing no reaction.

They prepared a fire and began to roast the meat. The sun had fallen out of sight, leaving only the fading glow of dusk.

Just then, they heard an animal whimpering. All eyes were drawn to a spot about thirty feet away, where stood a gray mixed-breed canine that would have put new meaning into the term *shaggy dog.*

His eyes were nearly hidden by matted gray hair, and his tail hung down ragged and motionless. The forlorn dog's right hindquarter had a bloody crease, and he favored his right front paw. His three good legs were wobbly and trembling.

Chavez walked slowly toward the animal. The dog growled and showed his teeth, but held his ground. Everyone watched while Chavez raised his rifle, stepped forward, then stopped. "This must be the canine running from the bravo bunch earlier," he said.

"Looks like a bullet grazed his right hindquarter, then took out his right paw. A dog makes a fine meal, Babe."

Brandi charged front and center. "You can't be serious, Mr. Chavez. Just look at him."

"Hmmm, not much meat on him anyway," Chavez responded. "Wonder how long it's been since Ol' Shaggy had a meal."

"The smell of fresh roasted meat must have drawn him out of the bushes," Seaman said.

Chavez lowered his gun and stepped forward slowly. When he stood about three feet away, the dog gnashed his teeth and growled, issuing a warning and signaling no retreat.

"He wants some of that meat," Dakota announced. "He's determined. He's dying but refuses to quit. That's what I call a soldier."

Brandi stepped cautiously toward the hurting animal, holding out her hand. The dog whined, then decided to bare his teeth once more.

Chavez warned her. "Move back, ma'am. This animal doesn't trust humans. I got a good look at his eyes. He's not gonna let me treat those wounds. He'll die out here."

"It's no wonder," Brandi said with feeling. "He looks like he doesn't have a friend in the world, and he's just been shot at. I tell you this dog was sent to us as a message. Count on it!"

"No disrespect, ma'am, but I should put him outta his misery. Besides, we don't have any food to spare."

"What do you mean we don't have food to spare? We just had a bear and a deer handed to us. We have plenty!"

Cody grabbed Brandi's hand and whispered. "You might want to think about backin' off a little."

Chavez waded back in. "If I had a tranquilizer, I could—" He stopped speaking, having suddenly caught movement with his right peripheral. He turned to look. It was Paco, confidently walking forward, stretching his right hand toward Old Shaggy. The boy was as good as dead if someone couldn't stop him. Chavez froze, unable to pull the trigger.

No one took a breath, but everyone was shocked when the dog whimpered, got on his belly, placed his chin on the ground, and gazed up at Paco. The wounded animal extended his left paw and inched himself closer. He swished his tail through the air and whined.

Paco knelt and stroked the dog's shaggy head, then spoke quietly to the desperate animal. *"Queremos ayudarte, chico."*

Brandi placed one hand over her heart and slowly dropped to her knees. "Cody, Paco speaks Spanish."

But the dog showed no reaction to Paco's Spanish, and appeared to be falling asleep.

Paco had another idea. "Wassa' matta, big boy? Why you no let this man fix you foot?"

Shaggy sat up. His tail came to life. He put his hurt paw on Paco's knee and began licking the boy's dirty face.

Brandi stood. "Cody! Paco speaks English!"

"Yeah, so does the dog."

The children frolicked and gathered around Paco and Ol' Shaggy.

"So, what do you think now, Mr. Chavez?" Brandi smiled.

Chavez put his weapon down. "Hey! What can I say? This creature loves kids and speaks English. What's not to like? I'm gonna bandage this wounded animal, and then let's eat—all of us."

They feasted on the roasted meat—plenty of tasty nutrition for a late-night meal and enough leftovers for another one. Paco never left the side of Old Shaggy, and fed the dog out of his hand. The children all wanted to touch the hurt animal.

Hodges came over and knelt next to Paco. *"Saweeet Jesus!* Now I've seen eva'thang. I might jis have to adopt me a boy and a dog." She placed her arm around Paco. The child warmed to her touch and smiled for the first time.

Afterward, a brief thunderstorm dumped enough water to fill low spots in the rocky ground—puddles large enough to allow all to drink, and to enable the grownups to refill all twenty-nine canteens they had managed to get their hands on.

The kids splashed and played in the puddles. The shaggy dog laid down in the water and drank while the children stroked and talked to him in their own languages.

After the storm, came a calm, warm night. Knoxi placed her blanket next to Paco and his dog.

"So what are you gonna name your dog? Do you like what Mr. Chavez calls him? Ol' Shaggy?"

"I no like that name. I tink I call him *Los Heridos*."

"That means *The Wounded*," Knoxi said.

"Si! I call him Los Heridos, The Wounded, because God bring him for all these wounded ones."

CHAPTER 15

HODGES

Everyone settled after the brief shower. The kids bedded down on dry blankets, and the demeanor of the adults was light, but guarded. No more joking. Cody figured it out—the humor and horseplay among these specialists was reserved for times when facing impossible odds. The immediate crisis had passed, but the mystifying events had raised deep questions. Hunger, fatigue, fear, crying—all had turned on a prayer, for now.

Cody noticed that several men and women who had scoffed earlier managed to make eye contact with Brandi after dinner, nodding or tipping their caps. Cody leaned back against a tree trunk with Brandi resting her head on his shoulder.

"Excuse me, ma'am, sir, I wanted to meet yawl, but seems like it hasn't been no good time to introduce m'self 'til now. I don't talk much 'cept when somethin' moves me, and this is wunna those times. I'm Justice Hodges. Most folk call me 'June.'"

Hodges extended her meaty hand. Cody and Brandi welcomed the decorated US war veteran and invited her to sit. The meal and the dog had calmed the spirits of the children. Darkness had fallen. Quietness prevailed.

"I 'specially wanna talk to you, Ms. Musket, cuz I saw your father's picture in *Achiever Magazine.* They published his fourteen leadership principles. Oh, honey, he's wunna the mos' handsome men I ever did see!"

Brandi grinned. "That's exactly what my mama thought when she first set her eyes on him."

"Oh, I know the story—about that monster who took advantage of her helpless estate when she was jus' sixteen. I read about it. Your mama is such a hero. But I will say, you have such pretty blue eyes."

"That's *all* he gave me—the blue eyes," Brandi said. "I never knew who her attacker was. He was never caught, and my mother couldn't identify him. Ray Barnes is my *real* daddy."

"Well, ma'am, I never had a daddy. An' my mama . . . well, she took me to the salon when I was thirteen and give the woman five dollars to cut my hair, and that's the last time I saw my mama. I remember her last words: 'I'll be right back, Junie, I'll be right back.' But, my mama . . . she never came back for me."

It was quiet for a long, awkward moment, then Brandi broke the silence.

"So, you've decided to adopt a boy and his dog," Brandi said. "I suppose congratulations are in order."

"Well, ma'am, I dunno if authorities would allow me . . . allow me to *legally* adopt. I mean, I ain't real good wit people no more since Kandahar. But this mission is different than I figured. I mean, like tonight, when the food jus' showed up like a gift all wrapped in ribbon and bows. Hallelujah! I do think Saint Peter missin' one bear and one deer, cuz Jesus done cut 'um outta His herd and sent them down to earth jus' for us."

"We're glad you're here, Ms. Hodges," Cody said. "Your profile says you received a Purple Heart and a Bronze Star for valor at Kandahar."

"That's right, sir, but we both know what that means—we jus' do what we gotta do."

"That's precisely why you're here, June. You do what you gotta do under fire," Cody affirmed. "And, please call us Cody and Brandi."

"So, why did you come on this mission, June?" Brandi wanted

to know. "Somehow, I sense it was more than just the money."

"I think . . . I think it was for the people. To be around honorable people, that's why I come. It gits lonely. Besides, when Cap'n Sabre Maxwell invite me, I can't refuse."

Cody responded, "Sabre saw something in you, Specialist Hodges. He was in-country on a fact-finding for the DOD when he heard about your incident with the Humvee."

"I know, Cody. They say I lost my memory 'cause of the head injury and the shrapnel, but I rememba' it like yestaday." She reached into her pack and pulled out a stogie. "You mind if I smoke?"

Cody looked around and snickered. "Hey, it's a free country, right?" All three stared at each other, then chuckled guardedly.

Hodges smiled. "I do believe I'ma like you folks. Yessir! You just as friendly as my hometown of Saint Jo."

Brandi noticed the scars on the side of June's neck and behind her ear. "So . . . your life has been lonely since you were discharged from the Army?"

"Yes, ma'am. I cain't be around people no more. My husband took all he could stand and finally said I wasn't the same woman. I told him good riddance. Now, I'd give anything to have him back."

She lit up the stogie and blew a cloud into the air. "My life done changed forever the day I . . . the day I rescued Major Duffy from that Humvee." She took another drag. "Turned out to be my downfall. And what's worse, the major died later anyway." She smothered the stogie against her bare left hand and showed no reaction.

Brandi glanced at Cody. He looked away.

"Cody and I know what it's like, June. I mean, once in a while, it helps just to—I mean to say, if you ever feel like talking . . ."

"Like I was sayin, I rememba' like it was yesterday. I mean, they was waitin' for us at grid tango-alpha eight-one—a bouncy road through a narrow canyon. I was ridin' the turret. Major Duffy was a famous sniper—over ninety kills. There wuz five of us. When the IED exploded—" She stopped, lit up the same smoke again, took three quick draws, then tossed it into one of the pools left over from the shower. "Do you want me to go on?"

"Up to you, June. We're good listeners." Brandi's empathetic smile and amiable face made her adept at getting difficult words out of people. She had received plenty of practice with her husband.

"Well, ma'am, afta' the explosion, things got messy *real* fast. My ears wuz ringin' and I kept hearin' that poppin' sound inside my head. Didn't know if I wuz alive or dead. Then all-a-sudden my mind cleared. Evabody screaming. Bullets buzzin' past my face. The vehicle was on its side. I was trapped. We wuz takin' serious fire. Susie Aguilar—'Aggie', we called her—she moved in the line of fire and pulled me free, then she took one in the gut."

Hodges paused, lit up another smoke, and blew another cloud into the air. "After that, Bobby Frazier dragged me to cover."

Brandi leaned backward against Cody, her right hand over her mouth to hide her emotions. Hodges glanced at her. "I'm sorry, Brandi. You don't need to hear no more of this."

"Oh, please, June. What happened? Cody and I . . ." Brandi recognized the look—the distant, empty stare, like once-upon-a-time in Cody's eyes.

"Help was on the way," June went on, "but it was still five miles out, and we wuz gonna be dead by then. Somethin' had to be done.

"There was this drop off beside the highway—good place for cover if we could just git down there. I could see the major crawlin' on the road, leavin' a blood trail, bullets bouncin' all around him. Aggie was screaming because of the gut wound. Then, I seen that

Bobby had been shot in the head after he pulled me to safety." She took three long drags again, flicked away the butt, then gazed into nowhere through steamy, sad eyes.

Brandi wanted to take her hand, but didn't know if she should. Cody had gone barefoot during the rain. Now, in nonchalant fashion and without speaking, he stretched forth his legs presumably to make himself more comfortable as he sat, but also revealing the gruesome scars he lived with every day. The former Army Specialist covered her mouth with her palm while huge tears rolled from her blinking brown eyes.

"After that, the only ones left wuz me, the wounded major, and Aggie who had took a bullet for me. Aggie was callin' me, over and over . . . I cain't never forget . . . like it was yestaday . . . 'I'll be right back, Aggie . . . I'll be right back. That's what I told her . . . like it was yestaday."

A soft mist began to fall from the overhead darkness.

"Oh, Justice," Brandi's voice wavered. "You couldn't have saved them both. No human should have to make a decision like that."

"They told me I dragged the major behind a rock an' got shot two more times. I don't remember that part. They gimme a medal. But I 'ventually figured it's like someone said—they don't give you no medal for what you done in the battle. They give you the medal cuz you have to live with what you done in the battle."

Brandi and Cody were quiet. Any response would have been shallow, inadequate.

A few rain drops fell at random, but Brandi folded her hands and looked up to see stars now peeking through. A full moon broke between clouds on the horizon. She could hear the dog whimpering softly as he rotated among the children.

"June," Brandi asked, "do you remember earlier when that dog showed up? I said he was sent to us as a message."

"Yes, ma'am." Hodges wiped her eyes with her fingers.

"Remember how lonely? Forsaken? Wounded? Growling at us when we only wanted to help? Take a look at the shaggy ol' dog now."

Hodges looked up. Los Heridos, Old Shaggy, was making his rounds, tail held high, ears on alert, limping from child to child, licking faces, making whining noises. A guard dog on duty.

"That dog was in pain too, June, until he adopted those kids. Now just look at him. Did you ever see a prouder animal? Just let some bad guy try to snatch one of those little ones. That dog will know about it way before you or I."

Hodges raised her eyes toward the horizon. A savory lunar glow from the rising moon reflected the misty rain droplets on her smooth facial skin. She shut her eyelids.

"You'll never chase off the shadows by isolating yourself, June." Brandi paused for a deep breath. "The pain of losing Aggie may never go away, but your sorrow will lose its grip on you when you lift up your hand to the helpless. So many hurting people need your compassion and your bravery."

June leaned forward and wiped her face with her fingers again. "I couldn't tell nobody, cuz mostly nobody understands."

Cody cleared his throat. "Brandi's father is the wisest man I know," he told her. "If you've read his books, you may remember his number-one leadership principle: '*The ability to bring healing to others is granted in deepest measure to those who carry scars.*'"

"Yes, I read that. It's just had to understand sometimes." Then she looked at Brandi. "I know you carry scars too, Ms. Brandi, and I can feel how you luv people who been hurt."

"That's right. My scars are not visible when I'm wearing my clothes, but we all three share a common bond, a fellowship of suffering."

"Y'all don't act like no famous people." Hodges lit up another smoke, took one draw, then snuffed it. "I should stop smokin' these. I wasn't completely honest wid you folks. I cum on this dangerous mission cuz . . . I figured if the tobacco didn't kill me soon enough, a bullet might find me here in this country, and the money would go to my ex, since I still love him. I mean, I didn't see no purpose for me no more."

CHAPTER 16

FANGS

When morning came, they handed out leftovers. Greenberg had led a detail to dig a latrine during the night. Chavez dressed the wound on Priscilla's arm again. Afterward, they broke camp and hit the trail.

With each passing hour, their escape route was more imposing. Brandi fought the constant sensation of being swallowed up by the sheer mystique of the jungle. Never had she felt so small, nor her surroundings seemed so large. Who or what might be hiding in the shadows?

The euphoria of the night before had worn off. The miraculous arrival of food and water, the dog which had changed Paco's world and brightened up the kids, and Justice Hodges taking a first step to healing by trusting someone else with her story—these events had been enough to lift spirits for one day. But what about today? Brandi knew it would take more miracles to get them home.

Enormous webs with giant spiders stretched across their path. Narrow trails and the sheer density of some areas made progress exhausting and slow.

By the time they entered a small section of rainforest, Brandi was clueless. Which direction was north? Towering Brazil Nut and Kapok trees rose nearly two hundred feet straight up. Kapok trunks housed poison dart frogs, birds in the nooks and grooves, and displayed foul-smelling white and pink flowers.

Bats hung from limbs. Brandi caught her breath when she spotted a green anaconda on the ground at the base of one of the trees. Cody glanced back to see if she had spotted the sizable reptile which had kept its distance about thirty feet away. Thankfully, the children had not seen the well-camouflaged snake. Brandi scanned the trees above for more such slithering creatures, having heard they sometimes lurk among the leafy branches.

The canopy formed by broad leaves in the crowded treetops made it impossible to know the location of the sun. An eerie, mid-day darkness made it even more difficult to spot wildlife. If only she could regain her sense of direction. Once, she was certain they had made a complete 180-degree reversal in direction.

Soon they came to a less dense area. The morning sun shone intermittently between moving low clouds. A refreshing mist fell. The tiny droplets illuminated by beams of sunlight filtered down between the leaves, creating the bizarre illusion of light rays piercing into the dense jungle floor.

Cody was aloof, and the wall he had built around himself grew. With each passing hour, the chance of detection by spies, snipers, or local informants increased. Brandi felt isolated despite the presence of so many children pressing against her.

By contrast, Knoxi seemed to thrive on the adventure. She mingled, conversed, and laughed from time to time. Speaking Spanish with other kids seemed to invigorate her. But as the morning wore on, fatigue dragged everyone down again.

Brandi's feet ached, as did most of her body. Her right ankle now burned each time she took a step. Something was wrong, but she would not complain and hold up the entire brigade just because of a little discomfort.

At noon, they stopped and finished off the food. They gave everyone a drink, but saved enough water for that night. Cody and the edgy marauders kept a gun in one hand while they ate with the other, taking smaller portions to allow more for the children.

Berries and palm fruits were barely enough to go around. They would need another source of food soon.

Brandi took the opportunity to check her right ankle to determine the source of the burning pain. She sat on a log and removed her boot, which had been pierced by a sharp object after rappelling from the Sea Stallion. The torn place had now collapsed inward, rubbing her ankle raw. She wanted to ask Chavez to examine it, but tensions were high, and the leaders were antsy. She pulled a towel from her pack and slipped it inside her sock as a cushion.

She removed her other boot while awaiting the order to move out. The fresh air felt good on her feet. She looked up through the trees to catch a glimpse of blue sky, and she relaxed momentarily in the gentle breeze. She shut her eyes.

Just then, she felt something crawling on her right foot. She was electrified when she looked down to see a large spider creeping upward across her sock and onto her ankle. It was hairy and brown with a red face and huge fangs.

She panicked, then regained her senses. Sudden movements might prove deadly. She did not know if this beast was venomous, but two things were certain—it was as large as a Texas Whataburger, and she couldn't take her eyes off it. Suddenly, it raised its front legs and began to extend its reddish fangs into the air, all the while looking Brandi straight in the eye. Then, as if taking a director's cue in a horror flick, it commenced swaying from side to side, swinging its front legs overhead like a sports fan doing the wave.

She wanted to scream, but contained herself. Her world began to fade as blood rushed from her head, but her vision returned when she heard a silky-smooth voice behind her.

"Don't move." Dakota's confident, whispery words cooled her urge to leap out of her skin. He floated noiselessly around her, then used his machete to brush the waving creature onto the ground. He sliced the hideous arachnid into two squirming curled-up balls of tremoring spider legs, each as large as a man's fist.

"Bad spider," he said.

Cody knelt and frantically pulled up her pants leg. "Did it bite you?"

Others had arrived with all eyes trained on her leg. No one breathed.

"Oh! I didn't know I was surrounded by such a great cloud of witnesses," she said as she placed her fingers on her temples. "No. It didn't bite. I'm fine." She pulled the leg of her fatigues back down, then shuddered. "Thank you, Dakota. Is that species venomous?"

Chavez cut in. "Deadliest spider in the world, ma'am. Enough venom to kill at least twenty men."

Knoxi and some of the children came running. They screamed when they saw the smashed remains still withering in the dirt.

"¡Uff!" Knoxi yelled to the children. "¡Es una gran critter!!"

"That swaying and showing those red fangs is a defensive move," Dakota informed Brandi. "You must have scared it." Then he smiled. "It's a Phoneutria Nigriventer, better known as *Brazilian Wandering Spider* because it doesn't live in a nest. It just wanders through the forest."

"But we're a long way from Brazil aren't we, Mr. Dakota?"

"Well, Knoxi, that's why they call it the *Wandering* Spider. There is also a spider here that walks on water. They call it the—"

"Wait," Cody interrupted, clearing his throat. "Enough information for now, Dakota. Thank you."

Cody sat next to Brandi on the log and dropped his head into his hands. "That was way too close."

Brandi put her boots back on, but not without thoroughly shaking them out first.

CHAPTER 17
THE ORBITING LIGHTBULB

They started walking again.

By mid-afternoon, the pain in Brandi's ankle and both feet became almost unbearable. Cody noticed that she limped.

She tried not to grimace with each step. She would not cause more stress for Cody, and she was not about to be carried by anyone. When he asked about it, she played it down.

They finally stopped before sundown at an ancient stone structure with strange markings and grotesque wooden sculptures which frightened the children. Some cried and said they would be too scared to sleep there.

"This place might be as old as twenty-five-hundred years," Sabre said. "Most likely some sort of temple. It may be hard to get the smaller kids to settle down because of the carvings, but shelter is hard to come by out here."

Brandi sat down on a stone walkway next to a broken retaining wall. She struggled to remove her backpack and helmet. The fatigue had finally gotten the best of her. She was light-headed, but her body felt the heavy weight of exhaustion. She leaned back against the wall, closed her eyes, and refused to move a muscle.

To settle the kids, Knoxi asked permission to tell them a story.

"This ought to be good," Cody said. "Let's hear it."

Priscilla came near and sat down.

The story was a repeat performance—this time in Spanish. Knoxi told about escaping from the compound after dark, running into town, saying a prayer, and finding Benito's tavern with the light on. When she told them she had jumped into Domingo's arms and kissed him, they sounded off loud and clear: *"Ooohhh!"* Their twisted facial expressions further displayed their repulsion. But Knoxi assured them Domingo was a *"hombre dulce"* (sweet man). By the time she had finished, the kids were limp and motionless.

Cody came and sat next to Brandi. Her eyes were partially open. He had seen her only briefly that day. Now, he noticed the jagged cut on her right boot.

"How did you rip this?" He scooted forward and lifted her foot.

"Easy! Take it easy with my foot." She labored to fill her lungs. "It happened after I jumped out of the Sea Stallion. It was dark. I couldn't see what I hit. A sharp rock most likely. Knowing how you felt about my rappelling, I decided to not mention it."

"I didn't know you got hurt. It's why I didn't want you rappelling with no training," he scolded. "How bad is this gonna be?" He carefully lifted up her foot again and eased the boot off.

"Cody, please," her voice hoarse. "I get the picture. You didn't want me coming here and jumping out of a helicopter." She paused a moment, then looked him in the eye and laughed so hard she couldn't stop.

Cody of the iron jaw wasn't looking for laughs. "What's so funny?"

"Umm," she tried to regain control. "Don't you think that's hilarious? Do you realize how that sounded? Me jumping from a helicopter?"

Cody's leathery expression never changed.

"Okay." She straightened her face. "The ripped place on my boot folded inward and started to rub my ankle, that's all."

Her sock was soaked through with perspiration and blood. When he removed it, she winced.

"Your foot's swollen. How could you walk like this? Brandi,

you should've told me. Lotta blisters. Bleeding. It's more than just a sore ankle."

She closed her eyes again, now fighting tears.

Cody lifted her other ankle. "How's this one?" He carefully uncovered her left foot. "Yep, swollen and blistered, just like I thought. I gotta call Chevy over. He's got some heavy-duty stuff that special forces use for blisters like these."

"I'm not used to this much walking," she said. "And these boots . . ."

"Brandi, why didn't you say something? We can't afford for you to get infected feet. And besides, you came close to getting killed today. How many more spiders? How many more things will I have to worry about?"

"So would you rather I had stayed at Pedro's Paradise or whatever that island was called?" She grumbled, blinking tears again. "I would be sitting there tonight all alone in the middle of the ocean wondering if you and Knoxi were even still alive." She leaned back against the wall and put her hands over her temples.

The sculpted soldier face Cody had worn all day softened, and the stress creases on his brow made a smooth retreat. He sat back, pulled off his hat, and surveyed every inch of her.

Brandi's hair was matted, and her ponytail reminded him of the frayed rope hanging from the flagpole at Pedro Island. Her Abby Torrance perfume had deserted her days ago. Exhaustion had wilted every centimeter of her face, and tear drops now gathered in the corners of her bloodshot eyes. She smelled like any other soldier after two hot days on the trail.

From the moment they had left Houston, he had treated her like a troublesome kid sister. Yet, defying death, she had rappelled from a helicopter into total blackness. When well-seasoned military professionals had no solution against impossible odds, Brandi had refused to back down in the face of ridicule, offering a prayer that had moved the hand of God.

She had won a staring contest with the most venomous spider on the planet. She had walked all afternoon on bleeding toes and a raw ankle without flinching. Could he have gone to battle with anyone more valiant than she?

He folded his blanket like a cushion and placed it behind her head. He delicately lifted her feet and slid his backpack underneath to elevate them. He poured water from his canteen over her feet and carefully draped them with a cool cloth.

"Oh, that feels better." She breathed a sigh. "Why the royal treatment? You're wasting water, you know."

A thin smile cracked his crusty face. "I just now remembered who you are," he told her. "You're that dangerous Wonder Woman that I can't live without."

Brandi shut her eyes. Suddenly, heaven and earth seemed perfectly in sync. Melodramatic words were mostly out of character for Cody, but she had learned to embrace those rare moments like a queen's treasure.

Knoxi came running and sat down. "What's wrong, Mama. Do your feet hurt?"

Brandi pulled her close. "That's not what made me cry, baby girl. Your daddy just said the most amazing things to me."

"Daddy, why do you always call her Wonder Woman?"

"Same reason I call you Fort Knox."

"And what reason is that?"

"Because, between the two of you, courage knows no gender, and courage knows no age. Simple as that."

Knoxi tilted her head.

Cody explained, "A couple of days ago, your mother asked me if I was sorry that I had met you both, because it had brought me a broken heart. But before we met, I didn't belong any place in this world. I didn't have anyone. But now, I know that everyone's heart needs someone to break for."

He rose to his feet, intending to signal Chavez to come, but Knoxi scooted forward, wrapped her arms around his knees, and refused to let go. He lifted her and let her squeeze him around the neck.

As the scene unfolded before her eyes, Brandi's spinning world suddenly made sense. This was perfect love—the kind that casts out fear—her daughter, sheltered and cherished in the safe arms of the man who had once belonged nowhere.

Cody had his own take. "Thank you, Fort Knox, for reminding me I was getting too big for my britches."

"What does that mean, Daddy?"

"It means I've been overestimating my own importance," he told her as he set her down.

Priscilla watched the exchange from a distance, then turned the other direction and walked alone toward the main structure of the site.

Cody called out to Chavez, pointing toward Brandi's feet.

Chavez trotted over. "What's the problem?" He knelt down. "Looks painful. Why didn't you tell me, ma'am? We could've stopped along the trail and treated this."

"I didn't wanna slow us down. And please call me Brandi."

Chavez cleaned and bandaged her injured ankle, treated the blisters with benzoin tincture from the field kit, applied an anesthetic for the pain, and then examined the torn boot.

"I can sew this boot up."

He dug a long needle and heavy thread out of the kit. This stuff is for repairing rafts and tents. It should work for a boot."

Knoxi saw Domingo arrive on the bike. "I'm gonna go debrief Domingo!" She scurried away like the littlest warrior on a mission.

Brandi's pride coaxed a weary smile from the corners of her lips as her daughter promenaded across the campsite with Cody's assertive stride.

Cody put his cap back on. "I gotta get Knoxi to bed, then debrief Mingo," he said as he departed and followed his daughter.

Chevy made an observation. "She's all him, isn't she?"

"One hundred percent, Mr. Chavez. One hundred percent."

"By the way, ma'am, Brandi, we've all been talking. You would've made a heckuva Marine."

"Thank you, Chevy. I just don't want to be too much trouble."

"Trouble, you say? I hate to think how much trouble we would have if you hadn't come along. And, you wouldn't be the first Marine to have blistered feet, either."

Brandi smiled. "By the way, what's Priscilla's story? She seems distant. Doesn't talk to anyone."

He was busy sewing the torn boot. "She doesn't have friends, just acquaintances. Her story isn't pretty. Her old man is a decorated Royal Navy Captain. Priscilla trained for British special forces, but ran afoul of her superiors."

"How so?"

"One night she was assaulted by five men. One was her CO. She had to resign. No one believed her. Her own father didn't believe her."

"Her own father?"

From a distance, Brandi watched Priscilla climb her way up the thirteen steps to the entrance of an ancient temple. She was now perched upon a banister near the entry door overlooking the camp. Low-hanging clouds obscured the top of the structure. She struck a match to light a smoke. In the darkness, the tiny flame illuminated her face and reflected into the overcast that hung a few feet above her head.

"She could be a beautiful woman if she wanted to be," Brandi observed.

Chevy finished sewing. "I don't think Prissy believes she's a woman anymore."

Suddenly, a commotion arose among the children. The evening quietness was pierced by loud screams from one of the kids. Chevy jumped up to investigate. The kids had bedded down on the blankets, but a small boy had leaped to his feet yelling and pointing to the ground. The little ones scattered every direction, running into each other—colliding, tripping, falling. Los Heridos began to bark.

Sabre and Chavez raced to the spot. Saber reached down with care and picked up a Goliath Bird Eater—from the largest tarantula species in the world. He placed the giant arachnid on his left shoulder and let it crawl down his arm. The Brazilian Wandering Spider they had seen earlier might have been the size of a breakfast plate, but this monster was bigger than a king's platter.

The child had not been bitten but was petrified by the scary-looking spider. Chavez explained to the children that this creature was not deadly, that its standard diet consisted of mice and birds.

Sabre took the tarantula into the jungle and let it go. When he returned, the children seemed certain the spider would come back searching for a child to devour. This was the second spider incident within a five-hour period. It was definitely time to panic.

Sabre had an idea. "Time for Tommy John," he said.

Cody's interest piqued. "Tommy John? What're you talkin' about?"

"Get all the kids together, Babe. I wanna introduce a couple of tricks I learned from Tommy John."

His real name was Alvin Maxwell. '*Sabre*' was his Navy call sign. He had graduated from MIT and had flown Naval aircraft for ten years. He was thirty-nine years old, five feet ten inches tall, and bore a strong resemblance to the actor Cuba Gooding Jr.

He had begun working on his electronic invention while still flying tanker missions. After resigning from the Navy, he had received a doctorate in quantum aerospace electrical engineering, courtesy of the US Government. After that, the Department of Defense employed him and financed the development of his call-tracking device.

After the children were persuaded to sit down, Sabre took over. He had earned points from the kids by letting the spider crawl on him, so their eyes were focused on his face. He asked Knoxi to translate.

"I apologize to all you kids, because I wasn't doing my job," he began.

Cody flashed an inquiring glance toward Chavez, who simply shrugged and stared back.

"Any idea what he's up to?" Brandi whispered to Cody.

"I have no clue," Cody answered as he leaned back against the wall.

Saber revealed that he worked for the United States Department of Defense. Part of his job, he said, was to make sure that all spiders stayed away from children.

Brandi grinned when she noticed Knoxi sitting on Domingo's shoulders wearing a skeptical face. The wild-eyed expressions of the spellbound kids made Brandi chuckle.

Sabre opened the leather case and pulled out five small lightbulbs, each a different color—red, blue, orange, white, and green. He explained that if a red, blue, orange or white bulb is burning, spiders are nearby. But if the *green* light is on, he told them, no spiders are detected within one mile.

He placed a bulb in each ear and one in each of his nostrils. They instantly lit up, *but none of them was green*. The kids screamed.

Next, he placed a green light in his mouth and clutched it securely with his teeth. The green bulb lit up bright as day, causing the others to go dark.

Everyone applauded. He pulled the bulbs from his ears and nose. The climax came next when he took the green light from his mouth, placed it in front of his face and released his grip. The shining green lightbulb began to orbit his head like an earth satellite.

Cody, Brandi and Chevy looked at each other in disbelief. The children's eyes were as large as silver dollars. No one made a sound.

Finally, Knoxi began clapping her hands frantically. *"Yaaaay!"* Once the silence was broken, it took several minutes to settle everyone down.

Priscilla came and sat next to Brandi and Cody. "Where do you suppose he came up with that bit of jiggery-pokery?" she asked.

"He's way ahead of me," Brandi conceded.

"He's worked on technology that folks like us can't even imagine," Cody added. "No tellin' what secrets hide inside that man's head."

The children had a new hero. They trusted his every word. He fastened the magic green light to a tree limb. It burned all night long, and the kids slept soundly until morning.

CHAPTER 18

FEED THE CHILDREN

O n the morning of Day 3, they decided to chance vehicle trails. This would allow them to make better time. Brandi welcomed these roads because she could wear tennis shoes which were easier on her feet than the combat boots. Her blisters had improved dramatically overnight. She ditched the helmet in favor of a camouflage ball cap.

Knoxi took Cody's hand. "Daddy, I've got it all figured out how Mr. Sabre pulled off those lightbulb tricks last night."

Cody and Brandi were amused. She sounded so grown up and showed no ill effects of her abduction. They looked behind and saw Priscilla, Sabre and Chavez on their heels. Priscilla wore her usual frown, but Sabre and Chevy grinned with anticipation.

"Well," Cody said. "Let's hear it, Fort Knox."

Knoxi's well-organized presentation began. "The bulbs had micro receivers that were tuned to wireless signals from Tommy John. The lights in his ears and nose were set to come on for five seconds and then go off. The green one was programmed to light up at the same time the others quit burning."

"How do you know it was all timed like that?" Cody asked her.

"Because, silly, I saw him counting off the seconds by tapping his belt."

Brandi pulled on Cody's arm. "Did you notice that?"

He shrugged.

"Of course he did, Mama. He is the person who taught me to

notice everything. Remember?"

Brandi asked again, "Cody. Did you notice that? Sabre tapping his belt?"

He ignored her. "So how do you explain the orbiting green bulb, baby girl?"

"That's easy! Tommy John controlled it like a drone with a signal that told it to fly around Mr. Saber's head by balancing the centripetal force of the orbit with the destiny altitude of his brain waves."

Brandi was unable to contain herself. Others ventured closer to get a front-row view.

But Cody, master of the granite face, continued his line of questioning. "Okay, so how do you account for the bulb defying gravity?"

Knoxi put her hand on her head. "Oh, yeah, I didn't think about that."

Cody chuckled again. "*Destiny altitude?* Where'd you get that term, Fort Knox?"

"Oh, I was reading one of your old flight-training manuals before we came on this trip."

"Trip?" Brandi reacted. "That's all this is to you?"

"The term is *density* altitude, not *destiny* altitude," Cody informed her. "And it doesn't have anything to do with brain waves. But if you're flying an aircraft, you'd better not load it to max gross if the *density altitude* is too high."

"Roger that, Daddy. I'll keep that in mind."

Saber spoke up, "I think my secret is safe for now, but Knoxi's getting close. Do you have her enrolled at MIT yet, Babe?"

Everyone loosened up. An orbiting lightbulb demonstration? A watchdog for the kids walking into camp just at the right moment? Food from Heaven? A child genius doubling as a comedienne? Maybe things were not so bad after all.

Morning went quickly, but the afternoon was a drag. With three hours of daylight remaining, everyone was hungry, thirsty, and exhausted. The marauders distributed food rations from their own backpacks to the children. They picked a few berries, but it was not enough. The drinking water had run out again, and they had not found the stream depicted in satellite photos.

The children, already depleted before the journey had begun, were running out of energy once more. Some had to be carried. Priscilla asked Brandi if she had any more miracles on tap for that night. After all, the trip to the coast would take at least three more days.

More prayer? Manna from Heaven? Would God multiply the berries like Jesus multiplied the loaves of bread and fish? If something dramatic and immediate did not happen, the mission and the children were doomed, and Priscilla made certain everyone knew it.

Soon, the exodus came to a grinding halt. Some of the younger children collapsed and refused to get up. Cody gathered the team.

Sabre pulled the sat photos from his backpack. "We're here," he said, pointing to one of the images. "We should've arrived at this stream by now."

Chavez agreed. "It crosses our path," he affirmed. "Edible wildlife should be found in the vicinity of that stream. Send a scouting team ahead to locate it. The rest of us will hang out here for a few hours."

"Children are resilient," Brandi said. "They just need something to get them going. Right now, things look bleak."

As the scouts departed, Brandi took Cody's arm and ushered him away into a clump of trees behind a large rock formation. She threw her arms around his neck and kissed him. "I've been missing you."

"Me too. How are your blisters?"

"Better, thanks to Chevy and some TLC from my husband," she answered.

Brandi then turned away from him and stood with her arms folded.

"Cody, I . . . I must ask you a question. The night we met, you unexpectedly swept me up in your arms and kissed me. I was so shocked," she chuckled. "Why did you do that?" She turned back, looked him in the eye, and waited for his answer.

"What?" He put his hands on his hips. "You brought me out here to ask me that?"

"Well, it was the most exhilarating surprise of my life, and I just wanna know what was running through that head of yours, okay?"

He rolled his eyes. "After *four* years?"

"It's important, Cody."

"Well." He rubbed his chin as if in deep thought. "Just wanted to see what I could get away with. I mean, you just looked like you needed a good kissin', that's all."

"Will you please be serious!" She grabbed his shoulders and shook him. "Now listen to me, Cody Musket. You kissed me because I was traumatized, and you knew the full impact of the attack at the theater had not yet sunk in. You feared I might wake up the next morning and become afraid to ever let a man touch me again. You were trying to save me from that. You wanted me to remember the kiss the next morning instead of focusing on the abuse."

"Where did you ever come up with that?" He sobered when he noticed she wasn't smiling. "Uh, kissing you while you were still kissable? You think I was *that* smart? I kissed you cuz I just couldn't help myself, that's why."

"Really, Cody?"

"Of course."

"So . . . were you . . . tempted to take it beyond a kiss?" She tilted her head, attempting to conceal her queen-size grin.

"What difference does it make? You want to know if I thought you were hot that night?" He looked through the trees toward the temporary camp as if preoccupied with more important matters.

"You didn't answer my question." She stepped in front to block his view. "Did you think about taking it to the next step?"

"Of course not. I mean . . . well, what I mean is—"

She placed her hands on his scruffy face. "Oh, you never did learn to tell the truth, and you're such a bad liar."

"I know."

She threw up her hands. "And you're so *arrogant* sometimes!" She turned away.

Cody stepped forward and held her by the shoulders. "I've never figured you out, Wonder Woman. Like right now, you stand there and smile but you look like you're gonna cry at the same time."

She turned back. "Can't you just admit that you wanted me that night, *Captain America?"*

Cody's knees gave way to laughter that collapsed him onto his back in the soft grass. Brandi fell on top of him.

"Okay, okay, I surrender," he said, straightening his face. "You have no idea how much I wanted you that night. Good thing your mom and dad showed up when they did."

"Cody, if you'll let me finish." She placed her head on his chest and listened for his heart. "I need to tell you something in case . . ." She ran out of words.

He finished Brandi's thought, "In case this difficult road doesn't lead to a beautiful place after all?" He pulled off her cap and finger-brushed her hair.

They became still and quiet enough to hear the children's soft chatter filtering through the trees.

Brandi finally broke the spell. "Yes, it was four years ago, but just remembering, I mean . . . that first week, it's one of my greatest treasures. I wanna tell you *so* many things I've never said." She raised her head, her misty eyes soft as the falling dew beneath the Kapok trees. "We may not have tomorrow."

Cody grinned and smothered her with a bear hug strong enough that she lost her breath. "Well then," he growled, "how 'bout one last kiss?"

Brandi giggled. "*Ohhh*, you are such a beast!" She wrestled, then suddenly raised her head. "What was that noise?"

They stood to their feet and hurriedly brushed themselves off.

"Sounded like a child laughing close by," Brandi said. "Didn't you hear it?" She put her cap back on.

He nodded. "I recognized the laugh."

They looked about, searching for a more secluded place, then stopped and laughed at themselves. Brandi looked deep into his eyes. "Cody, promise me you won't . . . I mean, if shooting starts, I don't need a hero. I already have one. Let the other people . . . they're trained for that sort of thing, right?"

Her eyes begged him for a promise, but he said nothing.

She turned sharply away from him. "Cody, I'm so scared. I dunno where my faith has gone."

He stepped toward her and wrapped her up. She leaned back into him and closed her eyes for a moment, then turned to face him. "Well, at least keep your backside out of the line of fire," she pleaded. "Lilly won't be here to patch you up this time."

"Lilly? You mean that skinny girl in Pittsburgh with the shaky hands?"

"I'll never forget," she reflected. "You were lying there with your butt stark naked, and you reached out and held her shaking hands and told her they felt like *healing hands*. You're such a barbarian sometimes, but then you say beautiful things that pop out of nowhere."

"Hey, I had to calm her down somehow if she was gonna dress my bullet wound. She prolly ended up marryin' some rich surgeon. She wudda never cut it as a doctor."

"Well, it was probably the most beautiful thing anyone ever did for her, telling her she had healing hands. Cody Musket, this world is way better off with you in it. I know I'm selfish, but—"

Just then, Domingo's bike sputtered into the camp. He was yelling his head off about something.

Cody took Brandi's hand. "Come on!" They rushed back to the group.

Domingo had talked to a couple of farmers. They had told him where to find water. They said to look for a large, pointed rock forty feet high. The rock had been pushed up from underground by a minor earthquake the previous month. Two hundred meters north of that landmark they would find a waterfall that ran off into a crystal-clear lagoon.

Joe Hampton knew his number had been called. He climbed a tall Barrigona palm to have a look. "I see it—the tall rock, secluded by trees about two hundred meters west."

Hampton decided to survey the entire area with his field glasses before coming down. From sixty feet up he looked north, hesitated, and stared.

"What is it, Hampy? What do you see?" Cody looked straight up, waiting for an answer.

"Might wanna have a look at this, sir. Could be nothing. Looks like a small school house or—"

"School?" Chavez jumped in. "You can't be serious. There isn't even a town within . . . what I mean is, get down here on the double."

Hampton descended to the ground. "It's in a low-lying area directly north. Small building. Frame construction. Orange school bus sitting outside. Most of the structure obscured by trees. That's why it doesn't show up on the sat photos. I almost didn't see it. Distance estimated two clicks."

It was decided that they would first find the lagoon. They needed water. The school and the bus could wait until the next day. Chevy had already sent scouts to search for water, so he called and gave them the coordinates to look for the rock and the lagoon. A half hour later, the scouts radioed back. They had found the water.

The news aroused the children. They arose and followed the marauders to a narrow road that led to the rock. They could hear the water—a spring that bubbled up and proceeded north.

They followed the stream northward until it spilled over a thirty-foot drop-off into a lagoon below, just as the farmer had said. From above, the lagoon was partially hidden by palms, ferns, and evergreens, and in the distance beyond, a narrow valley stretched eastward as far as the naked eye could see. They camped at the top of the falls and sent two men to test the water.

"The stream on the satellite photo probably rerouted itself underground due to that earthquake last month," Saber said. "That's why we missed it. The quake pushed the giant rock up from below, and that's where the water is surfacing."

"You think it's safe to drink?"

"I would bet on it, Babe. I sampled the water. It's warm with a slight mineral taste. It originates as an underground spring. There is no mining or manufacturing, nothing in the area to contaminate the water."

"And no dead animals around the water—a positive sign," Chevy added.

Cody nodded. "So, what about the school house Hampton found? What do you make of it?"

"Can't imagine a school way out here. I'm gonna send Hodges and Seaman up ahead to take a look tomorrow at daybreak."

Chavez pulled off his hat. "We need to chill here tonight."

Everyone was excited. Running water! They made camp and rationed what few berries and palm fruits they had collected. But it still was not enough to feed the children.

"That's it. No more food," Chavez said.

"The kids are knackered, can't go another day without eating," Priscilla insisted. "Any more bears around? I saw a couple of skinny monkeys earlier. Maybe I should've taken a shot at one. This time tomorrow, these rugrats won't move another inch."

The Spanish interpretation of Priscilla's words made its way through the child brigade. Some of the children were crying. Brandi wanted to scold Priscilla but held her tongue.

Just then, two ragged elderly men approached on the road, leading three sheep, two goats, and a heifer. Chavez and two others met them with guns raised. Chevy asked them to identify themselves. The two men were the only other humans they had seen all day.

The strangers were farmers. Several families had heard about the children, and had asked these men to deliver their animals to the *"niños que huyen"* (fleeing children) and to the *"valientes libertadores"* (valiant liberators) who had blown up Capistrano's compound. The animals were all they owned, and they sent apologies that they could not do more.

Brandi slowly fell to her knees. Priscilla laid down her gun and sat on the ground beside her.

The other marauders, painted faces and empty backpacks, marveled as Cody embraced the two dirt farmers. He placed his hands on their heads. "May God be with you and the other families who stand with us."

Thirty-eight dirty little faces smiled—Knoxi's Brigade would not starve tonight.

While the men organized a crew to prepare an early evening

meal, two young men and four older women suddenly approached on the road with blankets, worn out children's jeans, a large basket of potatoes, twenty melons, and one duffle bag filled with home-baked cachanga frybread.

These benevolent peasants had been walking since dawn, carrying food and clothing from friends and family. Along the way strangers had given them even more items to carry. Word had circulated through the countryside—feed the children.

Chevy weighed in. "Hard to believe these people knew exactly where to find us, and yet we've seen no sign of Capistrano or any spies."

"I guess you know these peasants risked their lives coming here," Sabre said. "If they encounter Capistrano's guys along the way . . ."

"Yeah, or if Capistrano learns that they helped us," Cody added.

Brandi stepped near. "Do you think Capistrano will ever figure out where we are?"

"He already knows," Chevy stated grimly. "You can count on it. These peasants told me something else. It's not what I wanted to hear. It's about that building, the school or whatever it is."

"The one Hampton saw?" Brandi asked privily. "What about it?"

Chavez lowered his voice. "The building Hampton spotted is definitely not a school. I've decided not to send the two scouts alone in the morning. Too risky."

Cody was edgy. "So, what is that place?" he asked straight up.

"These peasants said to avoid that facility at all costs. They go out of their way to stay clear—voices, crying, wailing, especially at night. They call it Den del Diablo, *The Devil's Den.*"

"Voices?" Cody frowned. "That's the direction we're headed tomorrow."

Chevy's next words sent chills shooting down Brandi's spine. "They said a benevolent American woman ran a clinic there until it was taken over by El Monstruo de Fuego Negro. That means *Monster of the Black Fire.*"

Brandi wavered. "Monster? Black fire? What's black fire?"

Cody put his arm around her and casually ushered her away from the children. "Come on," he said, "we don't want to scare the kids."

"Cody," she whispered, "tell me what *black fire* means."

"Hmm, not sure. I don't want to speculate. Need to find out more."

It took only minutes to slice the melons. They divided the loaves, passed out morsels, and started the fire at dusk. The air was warmer than previous nights on the trail. Clouds had finally dissipated. A giant yellow moon rose above the horizon beyond the distant valley.

Priscilla had not uttered a word since the brave locals had arrived with food and supplies. Now, she wandered off alone, descended a rocky embankment beside the falls, and wove her way through evergreens and ferns until she planted her boots firmly upon a smooth shelf at the edge of the lagoon.

On the north side of the pool, straight across from her, a cliff ascended straight up thirty feet. The falls, located on the west side, produced a soothing sound, cascading down over several shallow ledges and gracefully slipping into the shimmering pond. The moonlight, bright as day, reflected off bubbly ripples on the surface of the water. She was standing squarely in the center of a secluded tropical paradise. The scene would have made the perfect postcard.

She scouted for reptiles and other signs of danger, then tasted the water. It was warm, sweet, and metallic, probably containing traces of iron, lithium, and magnesium—all minerals with healing properties. She pulled off her boots and her thinning soldier socks and sat down on the rock shelf, dangling her aching, calloused feet into the surface foam. She warmed to the sensation of the gentle lapping at her ankles.

The moon hung like a gigantic beach ball. She felt the urge to reach out and touch it. Lunar glory. Even the rocks came to life like friendly faces, reflecting the soft light in every direction. The streaming water invited her to immerse her whole body with a promise to cleanse every pore and to purify her soul.

In the seclusion, she abandoned her hard-core dubiety, left her muscle shirt and the rest of her clothes on the shelf, and eased into the scintillating pool.

Suddenly her senses were alive. Something pure, ancient, and gentle held her, like soft hands massaging every muscle and joint. Submerged with just her face above the water, she breathed in the sweet air and reveled in the weightless floating—all burdens gone. Removed from the relentless, silent desperation that was her life, glorious and irresistible warmth and a delightful, almost playful Presence surrounded her.

She climbed back onto the bank and looked down at her reflection. The image in the water was someone she did not recognize. In the golden light, her wiry frame was at ease. Clothed only in a surreal glow, Priscilla's skin was smooth and innocent. She was a woman again, and only God was there to notice. For a few hypnotic moments, her pain was gone.

What was happening to her? She had no use for other women, and she hated men. She loved nobody, not even herself. *Why would anyone or anything love me? This can't be real.*

She gathered her clothes and yelled for Brandi, who promptly came running. "Have all the girls and the women come down here and jump in with me." *Did I really say that?*

Within minutes, twenty-four girls, all under age ten, stood at water's edge. Brandi addressed them. Knoxi translated. "The only clothes you have are the ones you are wearing. We don't recommend swimming in them because they will be wet all night, and the air may get cool later. Leave them on the rocks, but remember where you put them."

The girls shed their clothes as fast as they could and jumped in. Frolicking about, screaming and yelling, they lost themselves in the warm water and soft moonlight.

"Tell all the men to stay away!" Brandi shouted to Cody as she and the others skinny-dipped.

"Don't worry," Cody yelled back. "I told them if anyone went down there Prissy would break their neck!"

Brandi watched Priscilla engage with the girls. For the first time, Priscilla's hard face had softened.

Brandi paused to absorb it all—every inch, every ripple, every aroma. The new lagoon, created a month earlier when the stream had rerouted itself, had been incomplete until tonight. The sweet music of laughing children was all that had been missing, an immaculate symphony echoing upward over the steep walls and sailing home toward the heavens.

Someone had created and arranged this moment. Someone knew they were coming.

When it came time for the girls to leave the water, they protested, but the boys would have their chance to swim, and after that, dinner would be served.

CHAPTER 19

I GOT NO ONE

The women escorted the girls up the slope and back to the campsite above the falls. Everyone was chatty. The lagoon had brightened spirits, and the smell of roasting meat was in the air.

Brandi told the men. "If you guys don't take all these boys and get in that water with them, we're gonna grab you one by one and throw you in."

Priscilla added, "That includes you, Domingo."

Domingo tried to jump on the bike, but three men grabbed him. He filled the atmosphere with loud sacrilege as they separated him from his boots, dragged him down the slope, and threw him into the water fully clothed.

When he came back to the surface, he shouted. "*Wahooo!* Have I friggin' died and gone to heaven?" The rest of the male contingent followed him in.

Soon, Domingo was picking up boys and dropping them into the water. Laughter from his young playmates could be heard throughout the camp. Groups of them took turns jumping on Domingo en masse and sinking him to the bottom. Others decided to join them in a free-for-all.

Following the skinny-dipping and evening meal, the camp was littered with leftovers. The adults picked up enough meat for one more meal. They would save it overnight and munch early in the morning. The goat and heifer would be slaughtered at the next stop.

The frybread had been a big hit. One full duffle bag should have been barely enough bread to go around, but the kids had stuffed themselves and had not consumed it all. Priscilla volunteered to gather up the bread remnants. The leftover frybread was enough to fill *four duffle bags*. After rechecking to make certain, she was in disbelief. She would tell no one.

Finally, they told the kids to go to bed. The children complained, but as soon as they hit the blankets, they were sound asleep. No need for any green light tonight.

Brandi sat alone by the campfire while Cody helped bed down the little ones. After a few minutes, Priscilla somberly walked over and sat on the log beside her.

"I wanna know how in the merry trollies your little girl pulled off that stunt with the mud camouflage. How could a tot that young even think of such a thing?"

"My husband taught her."

"Come on. That's rubbish. You're just messin' with me, luv."

"No. Seriously," Brandi told her. "Cody used to play a camouflage game with her at Uvalde, Texas where our close friends have a ranch."

"Camouflage? What little girl plays camouflage games?"

"He taught her how to hide in plain sight."

"So then, he was preparing her in case she got herself snatched?"

"No," Brandi answered. "It was just a game. She once painted herself with yellow body paint and stood against a yellow wall in the barn."

"As you Americans say, '*Are you kidding me?*'"

"Not kidding," Brandi said with a chuckle. "Cody passed by several times and couldn't see her—more or less, that is."

Priscilla became quiet and leaned forward with her head down.

Brandi continued. "So, when Cody left the barn, we all watched while this tiny yellow girl came running into the open and sneaked up behind my 185-pound professional athlete husband and tackled him."

"How could she do that?"

"Oh, he fell six feet headlong and rolled over at least three times to make it look good." Brandi made a rolling motion for emphasis. "Afterward, he gave her a piggyback ride to the river and dunked her at least fifty times to wash the paint off. They screamed and laughed the whole way."

Priscilla's brooding eyes glistened with tears in the flickering light of the campfire. "How long did you know Cody before you had his child?" she asked.

"Knoxi was conceived before I knew Cody. I was in a relationship that ended violently. Afterward, I promised myself and God that I wouldn't sleep with another man until He sent me the man of His choice."

Priscilla frowned. "She's not Cody's daughter?"

"Cody is her father—the only father she has ever known."

Priscilla stood up and took a couple of steps toward the fire. "Your husband is popular in America." She nudged a fallen ember toward the flames with her boot. "Plenty of cheeky women throw themselves at famous men when they travel. Doesn't that set your knickers all-a-twist?"

"When I met Cody, I was an emotional wreck. I was vulnerable. He had opportunities, and I feared he would ask me to, um . . . you know, break my vow."

Priscilla turned around. "Would you if he had asked?"

"I loved him so much," Brandi said. "There were times I almost hoped he would push me just a little."

"Do you think he knew that?"

"Of course, he knew. He read my face like a comic book. But

he never took advantage. A man who would love me that much? Yeah. I trust him when he travels alone. I never worry."

Priscilla stared into the smoldering fire. "A man that damned honorable would find nothing in me. Besides, I can't stand for a bloke to even get close to me anymore. You're a blinding lucky woman, ma'am."

"I would call myself blessed."

"Well, I would've married him the first minute. So, when you finally did, was it like, as Americans say, 'Rockets red glare, bombs bursting in air?'" She flicked her fingers above her head to simulate fireworks.

Brandi shut her eyes and held her tongue.

"I'm . . . I'm sorry, ma'am. I just meant—"

"You know, Priscilla, you and I are alike. I believe in speaking my mind too, and right now, I can tell that something else is on yours."

Priscilla slowly sat back down. A solo teardrop rolled down over her weathered cheek. "I had a little boy," she whispered.

Brandi waited. The hypnotic sizzling and crackling of the logs in the fire became larger than life, as it were the only sound in the forest.

"When I was still in the army, I was gang-raped by five soldiers. One was my commanding officer. Never was sure which of those animals was the father. It was seven years ago. No one believed me about the assault."

She wiped her eyes with her fingertips, then re-galvanized her hard countenance.

"I resigned and became freelance. When I was seven-months pregnant, I desperately needed money. I finally found a low-life company willing to hire me for a week. A mission in Sudan. A five-day gig monitoring communications from a safe place." She stopped and reached for a smoke.

"What happened, Priscilla?"

"Two enemy soldiers broke into my vehicle. I tried to fight them off, but—" She shook her head. "I was rescued just as they started to carve up my face." She pointed to the scar above her eye. "Afterward, I wasn't pregnant anymore."

"What happened to him? What happened to your son?"

"I . . . lost him right there . . . beside the road. I held my little Jesse for an hour while they rushed me to the hospital. They had to pry him out of my hands. Anything that was still alive in me died with him."

"I'm so sorry, Priscilla. I'm so sorry."

Priscilla shrugged, then stood up and walked close to the fire again, still holding the unlighted cigarette. "So, was your God even watching when this happened? Maybe he was out to tea, or maybe taking a whiz." She lit her cigarette.

Brandi remained silent.

Priscilla sighed bitterly. "My father was British Navy. I disappointed him because I could never be the son he wanted." She paused and grimaced. "I never told him about losing a child who would have been his grandson."

"Your father never knew you were pregnant?"

She shook her head. "If only I had not gone on that gig. It was just about money. It's always been about money. But this mission here in this country . . . I mean, it's about things I've never seen before." She seated herself again, took a deep drag, and exhaled a cloud above her head.

The two women fell silent as the forest seemed to stir— crickets, birds, the occasional call of an animal wooing its mate. The moon-splashed leaves shimmered like crystalline angel wings, hovering, weeping, recording every word.

"Priscilla, I wanna tell you a story. Parts of it have never been made public. I must ask for your discretion."

Priscilla held the ciggy between her fingers motioning Brandi to continue. Tiny smoke loops swirled and rose slowly above her. "I'm listening, luv."

Brandi told her how Cody had discovered faith at Kandahar when he was not expected to live. She told about the miraculous recovery of his leg, the orthopedic surgeon who became a believer, the children, the RPG, the cage.

She revealed that Cody had later seen the Afghan children in Heaven, and she explained the meaning of '*amalga oshirish*,' a phrase in the Uzbek language which had launched Cody into his destiny.

"That's a pretty story, but sounds to me like he was on something," Priscilla muttered. "And he said something the first night about listening for God? How can you think you've heard from God?"

"Priscilla, I think—"

"It's too late for me," Priscilla interrupted. "But you? *Ha!* The bear and the deer showed up after you said that prayer. And . . . and the people bringing food and blankets, giving all they have. I gathered up the leftover bread, and . . ." She looked upward as the wind chimed through the treetops. "This can be a spooky place at night, like someone's up there."

"It's just the wind, Priscilla. It's only wind."

"I have been with so many men I've lost count," Priscilla said. "But love? I don't even know what that means. Love doesn't exist for me. You wanna know how I murdered out at rappelling school? Let's just say some officers expected me to perform like a man in the daytime, but like a woman at night. I did what I did to get ahead in a man's world."

Brandi waited. Priscilla wasn't finished.

"I mean, how can a rock-salt bitch like me find the peace you talk about? Bloody too late for me." She licked her left palm, then used it to smother her cigarette.

Brandi gathered herself. "You heard God, Priscilla, tonight in the water."

"*Ha!* That's worth a merry shilling," she snarked as she lit up another smoke. "And what exactly do you suppose He said?"

"He reminded you who you are. He created you to be a woman. To Him, you're *so* beautiful. You wanna know what love looks like? I saw His love all over your face when you were with those girls."

Priscilla raised one eyebrow. "How can you make that presumption? I mean, it's not true, none of it."

"You can see your son again, Priscilla. The peace you knew tonight is only a taste of what Heaven will be like. You see yourself as someone who has made too many mistakes, but when life brings you to a dead end, God just sees a brand-new place to start."

All was quiet again. The kids were asleep. Even the forest seemed mute.

Priscilla licked her chapped lips. "So, how do you pray to someone that's dead? You don't really believe Jesus came back after he was dead, do you?" She blew another cloud into the air. "I could never believe a thing like that. What proof do you have?"

Brandi cleared her thoughts. "So," she said. "To begin with, it is a historical fact that hundreds of Jesus followers were brutally martyred in the first century. Many of these claimed to have seen Jesus alive after he was resurrected. Would so many have been willing to suffer such unthinkable agonies in order to protect a lie? Think about that."

A hush settled upon them again.

Brandi continued quietly. "Priscilla, if Jesus isn't alive, Cody didn't rise off that operating table at Kandahar. And if Jesus didn't defeat death, He's a fraud, and all we can count on is the uncertainty of self-discipline and religion. He suffered to pay the penalty for our sin, then He arose to prove He is the Son of God. And only a *living* Jesus can heal a heart as broken as yours."

"I dunno, ma'am. I mean, you and Cody have a support system to help you. You're a family. I got no one."

"Well . . . you do now," Brandi offered.

"So, this is when we're supposed to hug? Like sisters? I'm not much for hugs, luv. Have you seen Domingo's left forearm?"

"You mean all those four-letter expressive metaphors?"

Priscilla chuckled. "Never heard it put like that, luv. But I refer to the one tat that makes sense: *'Only the strong survive.'* Domingo and I agree on that. People like him and me don't need nobody else."

Brandi turned toward her. "Domingo? T-Rex? The same guy who was splashing in the lagoon and laughing with the children because he had suddenly found little friends who loved him?"

Priscilla tossed her cigarette into the fire and stared at the glowing embers. She swiped tears from her face with her fingers again.

"Why have I never before seen things like I see on this mission?"

Brandi smiled. "Maybe because you've insisted on walking through this life alone, so He granted your wish and stayed away. But He wants you. That love? That peace? Run to Him, Priscilla. Fast as you can."

A strong gust swept through the forest, causing treetops to shed small berries and flakes of dead bark. Low clouds had returned. The moonlight had disappeared.

"I'm just not much for hugs, ma'am, that's all."

CHAPTER 20

A BEAUTIFUL PLACE

The horizon was endless. The galactic panorama was brilliant. A glorious light which seemed to have no source came from everywhere. The cosmic golf course was perfect—grass with thousands of individual blades humming melodies with limitless harmony as gentle breezes stirred them like fields of velvet.

Music, perfect music in every language, seemed to flow out of each and every object—rocks, brick pathways, and even from a clear shallow brook that made its way through the center of the course. Flowers, millions of them, released sweet aromas—fragrances that could be seen like ribbons of color ascending into a spacious blue sky.

As God and Moses prepared to tee off, it was decided that Moses would go first. He selected his favorite club, a driver that Jesus, an experienced carpenter, had customized just for him. Moses drew a round of applause from the great cloud of witnesses as he drove a perfect shot nearly 400 yards. The ball landed directly in the middle of the fairway, just off the edge of the green.

All were silent as the crowd anxiously awaited the opening drive by the Almighty. He swung the club with enough force to create a rushing mighty wind with tornado-like vortices that swirled outward and upward into the wildest blue cosmos. Everyone ducked for cover temporarily, but no one suffered any harm.

When the wind ceased and the dust cleared, the multitude was shocked. Despite a mighty swing, the club had barely grazed the ball, which had then dribbled out in front of the tee and had come to rest just a few feet away.

Moses glanced at Father God, who sported a sly grin. In the twinkling of an eye, a rabbit appeared. It pounced on the ball with a single bound, seized it with its teeth and headed straight toward the nearby wilderness at warp speed.

Just when it seemed the ball would be lost forever, a gigantic hawk swooped down from lofty regions and plucked up the rabbit. The big bird soared into the sky clutching the stubborn hare in its talons. When positioned directly over the green, the rabbit finally released the ball, dropping it directly into the hole.

Millions applauded.

Moses was frustrated, hands on hips. He turned to the Maker of all things and asked one simple question.

"Lord, did You come out here to play golf or just mess around?"

"Cody? Cody, stop messing around . . . Cody?"

He opened his eyelids. Two huge blue eyes stared him in the face. "Wake up, man of steel, we need to get moving. We can't mess around. Didn't you hear me?"

He sat up. Everyone stared. "I was just in the most beautiful place I've ever seen."

"Must've been a heck of a dream. We need to move on," Chevy said.

"What place were you in, Daddy?"

"Well," he said, hesitating and looking about. "I think it might've been Heaven."

Cody explained the dream—the living panorama, the light, music, golf course, and Moses' inquiry at the end.

"Really, Cody? You dreamed all that?" Brandi was mystified.

"Do you think the dream could have some meaning? It was so

real." He rubbed the sleep from his eyes.

Brandi scratched her head. "Well. Hmmm, let me think a minute."

"I know what it means, Daddy!" Knoxi's exuberant innocence turned every head. "God wanted to hit the ball in the hole, but the hawk needed to fly, the rabbit needed an adventure, and Moses was getting too big for his britches, overestimating his own importance just like you, Daddy!"

Those who had taken turns keeping watch through the night held their breath. Sabre broke the ice, doubling over trying to contain himself. The mirth then spread. Iron-hard faces began to crack and some laughed uncontrollably. Most of the children didn't understand, but they caught the thrill and joined in. Knoxi was the lone holdout.

She frowned, hands on hips like her mother oft displayed. "Well, Daddy, I was just sayin' maybe God had more important stuff to worry about than knockin' a silly ball into a stupid hole."

Cody pulled his daughter to his chest and collapsed backward onto the blanket. Most had never seen him laugh so hard.

Finally, he sat up. "We aren't laughing at you, Fort Knox. We're laughing because you nailed it. That was a very profound interpretation of my dream."

Brandi raised her eyebrows, but Knoxi wasn't finished.

"That's right, Daddy. Maybe God is telling you not to give up if things go all weird. We'll still get there . . . uh, to the beach I mean, but maybe it won't be a straight line."

He got up and folded his blanket. "I'll keep that in mind, Fort Knox."

As they broke camp, both hope and apprehension played with their minds. They all sensed it. The laughter had been good. Knoxi was a natural entertainer, but they weren't home yet.

Cody looked behind to make certain that Knoxi couldn't hear

him, then he asked Brandi, "What did *you* think about the dream?"

"You never know," she answered. "What did you and the others decide about that mystery building with the school bus?"

"We could use the bus," Cody answered. "We just don't know who's in that building. We're gonna find it, take a look from a distance, then maybe send a coupla' scouts in for a closer look."

Word had spread throughout northern Librador that Capristrano's compound had been set ablaze by liberators leading an exodus of little ones to freedom. But if the peasants knew, so did Capistrano.

CHAPTER 21

DEN DEL DIABLO

The group headed north, hoping to find the building with the orange school bus, but after trekking cautiously for an hour toward the estimated coordinates, the structure was not to be found—no building, no bus.

"We're moving on," Chevy said. "Somethin' doesn't smell right. A legend about a devil's den? A school bus way out here in the jungle, and now it's all disappeared? I don't like it. Smoke and mirrors. A trap. We gotta keep movin' if we're gonna outrun Capistrano."

"Understood," Sabre agreed, "but it might be worth a limited risk if that bus does exist. An extra ten minutes searching isn't gonna make much difference. Send Hampton up a tree. Let him take another look."

They sent Joe Hampton up a slender tree like before, but he could not get a visual on the building in any direction. They ordered him back to the ground. He slithered down, then sat on a log to put his boots back on. "It was there yesterday. That bus stood out like a big orange flag. Buildings and orange buses don't just disappear. I have a bad feeling 'bout this."

"We're movin' out!" Chavez barked. "Capistrano's either on our six, or he's waiting ahead. The longer we're distracted chasing ghosts, the easier target we make."

Suddenly, Los Heridos, Paco's wounded dog, startled everyone. *"Wooof! Wooof!"* He barked twice, trotted forward about thirty feet, stood perfectly still, ears alert, his neck bristling.

Chavez was ruffled. "Paco! Call your dog! He's gonna give us away. Maybe I should've just shot him when I had the chance!"

The dog, having been silent for two days, had now shown new life. He barked again, growled, ran into the forest, and disappeared.

"That dog knows something," Brandi said. "Something has caught his attention."

"Well," Cody warned, "if there *is* someone out there, we may not want to bump into them."

A moment later, Los Heridos reappeared, barked, then ran away again. This time, Paco ran after the dog at full speed and vanished among the trees. Cody bolted forward, caught Paco within seconds, and brought him back kicking and screaming. The dog was gone.

"This kid can run," Cody was panting.

"Paco, *cálmate,*" Knoxi said. *"Por favor,* be quiet, Paco. You need to be calm."

"That dog's gonna get that boy killed," Chavez said. "And if we follow, it could get us killed too."

"Let me go after him," Dakota suggested. "The dog has knowledge of something important. Maybe he'll find the bus. He will not lead us into danger."

"And you know this because?" Chavez wasn't convinced.

"Wha' chu think?" he snarked. "I'm an Indian, aren't I? Haven't you heard? All us natives can read the minds of animals."

"Come on, Tonto, you're an educated man. Harvard, right? You expect me to believe—"

"Actually, it was Yale," Dakota interrupted. "But I never let school stand in the way of my education."

Chavez took a look at Cody, glanced at the tearful Paco, then back at Dakota. "If you aren't back here in ten minutes, we're rollin' up and headin' for happier hunting grounds. You'll have to track us and catch up."

"Understood," Dakota agreed as he departed. In seven minutes, he returned with the dog. "You need to come see this." He breathed heavily. "We found a building that matches Hampton's description. The orange bus is there too."

The entire brigade followed Dakota to the edge of the same valley they had seen from above the lagoon the night before. They started down the hill and soon spotted the building, but the orange bus was no longer in sight.

"The bus was there a few minutes ago," Dakota said. "Maybe it just now pulled out." He trained his eyes deep to the right and left, and he listened for sounds of a bus.

"I don't like it," Chevy steamed. "Somethin' here's all wrong. How could a bus completely disappear that fast? I don't even see a road down there."

"It was a miracle that I even saw this building yesterday," Hampton informed them. "It's camouflaged with that natural unpainted wood. The bright orange bus caught my attention in the afternoon sun. That's the only reason I spotted the building."

The facility was nestled and well-hidden at the bottom of the lush, green valley. They continued with caution down the gentle slope and worked their way closer to their objective, taking advantage of thick foliage which provided cover. They finally positioned themselves behind an old stone wall about halfway down the grade, approximately 100 meters from the small wooden building. They would be required to cross a shallow clear-water stream which passed near the front of the structure.

Chavez surveyed in every direction with his field glasses. "I don't see the bus. It may be on the other side of the structure or may have pulled out like Dakota said. It's unknown if the building is occupied, but—Wait! I see movement." Chavez clutched the glasses tighter and strained to see. "People are coming out of the building. Looks like—*No way!*"

"What do you see?" Cody and Brandi were crouched next to him. "What is it?" Cody demanded.

"You aren't gonna believe this, Babe." He clenched his teeth. "That woman must be the benevolent American the peasants told us about. Here. Take a look."

Cody held the binoculars up and gasped. The back of his neck flushed like a rooster's crest.

"What is it, man of steel?" A cold wave rolled over Brandi. "Cody?" She shivered.

"This isn't happening. You hear me, Chavez? This isn't happening!" Cody handed the glasses back to him.

Brandi and Hodges were now crouched together. Chavez motioned to them. "Get these kids back up the hill. Keep 'em hidden."

"What is this place?" Brandi asked.

"Den del Diablo, ma'am. I always wanted to storm Hell. This is it."

Brandi caught her breath.

Chavez rattled off commands. "Babe, help guard the kids with the others. I'm taking the snipers." Chavez pushed his comm mic close to his mouth. "Perez, Hampton, Seaman, T-Rex, we're going down there. We gotta reposition for clear shots."

At that moment, the shaggy dog bolted toward the building, growling, running at full throttle on his three good legs.

Chavez jerked his head around. "Somebody grab Paco! Make sure that kid doesn't follow the dog!"

Dakota weighed in, "Los Heridos has unfinished business down there. He's only doing his duty like a good soldier."

"Come on!" Chavez called his snipers. "The dog is a perfect diversion. We gotta reposition now! By the time we get there, both victims may be dead." He tossed the binoculars back to Cody. "Here, Babe, keep these glasses so you can stay scoped in."

Chavez spoke into his mic again, "Priscilla, you come with us. We may need help with the women."

"Women?" Brandi glanced at Chavez and then Cody. "What women?"

Chavez, Priscilla, and the other four snipers began moving toward the building, trying to remain undetected. If they were discovered, it would be a major disaster.

Suddenly, the woeful voice of a woman—cries of agony— pierced through the dewy air. Brandi stared toward the building but could not get a clear view—too many trees, too many morning shadows.

"Cody! What's happening?" Brandi demanded to know.

"You don't wanna know. Believe me. Let's just get the kids back."

The screaming continued. Obviously, a woman was being tortured. Brandi yanked the field glasses away from Cody and stared toward the source.

"Ohh, Cody! No!" She dropped to her knees, her eyes glued to the gruesome scene. *"Oh, Lord Jesus, please! No!"*

Five armed men and one female were guarding eight scantily-clad women at gunpoint, forcing them to watch a stocky, robust man with a bottle in one hand, and a bullwhip in the other, brutally flog a young woman secured between two whipping posts.

A teenage girl, perhaps no older than thirteen, was tied to another post begging for mercy as she waited her turn.

"I told you not to look." Cody took the glasses back. "It's gonna take a few minutes for the snipers to get positioned. Chevy's doin' it by the book. They can't afford to miss. Their job is to shoot. Our job is to pray those prisoners will still be alive afterward. Come on, let's get these kids away from here." They started back up the hill.

The growling dog now began to bark frantically, announcing

an all-out assault. Brandi looked back over her shoulder. Even without the glasses she could see Los Heridos charging full speed, now splashing through the shallow creek near the action.

An explosion of gunfire rang out. Bullets splashed the water in front of the dog and ricocheted from partially submerged rocks. Cody counted five shots fired in rapid succession, and then three more blasts at random. Brandi jumped. Some of the children screamed. They crouched for cover as Cody pressed the field glasses tighter to his face. Though his view was partially blocked by trees, he determined that the charging dog had not been hit, but that the young girl and the woman tied between the posts had been shot.

More gunfire cracked the air as the enemy soldiers traded shots with the marauders, sending distant echoes into the upper valley. Afterward, all was quiet—no more crying, no more shooting, no more barking.

Chavez and the others sloshed through the creek and cautiously headed into the building. Cody strained to see, but the outcome was unclear. He counted all seven enemy combatants down, but both female prisoners tied to the posts appeared to be lifeless, slumping over.

"I'm going down there," Cody said. "The building hasn't been secured, so stay here with the kids and the soldiers. You understand me?"

Brandi looked up at him and shaded her eyes, trying to control both her anger and sorrow. "I will, Cody. I promise."

Justice Hodges held Paco and assured him that Los Heridos could take care of himself. When she saw Brandi crying, she moved close with Paco and placed her arm around Brandi's shoulders.

"They will secure the area, and it'll be safe in a few minutes, ma'am," Hodges assured. "I'll let you go down there then. I know you wanna be with your man."

Cody hurried down the gentle slope and crossed the creek. Chavez met him just as he arrived at the whipping posts.

"The building's clear, Babe. All enemy combatants down." He lowered his head as he looked at the two bloody female prisoners still secured to the posts. Miraculously, not one of the eight other female captives had been harmed.

The young girl was dead—nearly decapitated by a hollow-point bullet from behind. The blond woman, whom they assumed was American, had been shot in the back. The bullet had left a gaping exit wound on her right side. Chavez sent word to not let any of the children come down the hill, then he checked for vital signs on the American.

With arms still tied, slumping between the posts, she began to move and moan. Chavez and Cody cut the ropes and eased her onto a thin blanket obtained from inside the building. Her upper body was covered with blood, her green scrubs barely hanging on, having been ripped apart by the whip.

"Can you do anything for her?" It seemed like the right question to ask, but Cody already knew the answer.

"Gimme a hand," Chavez said. "Gotta see if I can slow the bleeding."

It wasn't hard for Chavez to access the wound. The worn-out medical scrubs were torn to pieces where the bullet fragments had exited. He tried to wrap her upper body to slow the bleeding as Cody supported her, but she screamed in agony.

"Lay her back down, Babe, we're only making it hurt worse. It won't help anyway. I mean, without a hospital . . ."

Chevy gave her morphine. She became still, her breathing labored.

Cody ground his teeth as he glanced over at the dead enemy gunmen on the ground. "These reek of alcohol, and they were prolly high on bobos. They musta' panicked. Didn't even know what they were shooting at. What a waste."

"We found plenty o' reefers and Oxy locked in a cabinet inside." Chavez ground his teeth. "I mean what t'ell kind of soldier does this?" he seethed. "First thing they did was shoot these two in the back."

"They weren't soldiers," Cody muttered. "No honor. Just butchers, high on something."

"This woman shouldn't be lying here, Babe. She couldn't be over twenty-five, twenty-six maybe." He laid a worn blanket over her to cover her wounds. "If only we cudda' been here a minute sooner." He shook his head. "The morphine will make it easier for her, but if you wanna talk to her, better make it quick."

Brandi had just come down the hill. As she waded through the creek, she slowed her steps, staggered by what she saw. The young girl tied to the post had no face. A large portion of her skull had been obliterated.

Cody knelt next to the fallen woman, her face and hair spattered with crimson, her wounds hidden by the worn-out gray blanket. The pinkish ground near the post where she had been constrained was littered with bloody smithereens of green clothing. The shaggy, panting dog whined, crouched next to Cody, and began licking the woman's face.

When Cody reached down to brush the bloody strands of hair away from her eyes, his mouth suddenly gaped open.

"Lilly?" He stared. "Lilly, is it you?" She opened her eyes.

Brandi was out of breath from the long run, and now a numbness took her as she recognized the familiar face. She stumbled forward but could no longer feel her knees. She dropped beside Lilly and tried not to imagine the grisly wounds hidden by the blanket.

"Is that you, Mr. Musket? I can't believe you're here. Did you free the women?" Lilly's weak voice was barely audible, but recognizable, even after four years.

Cody stroked her face. "Everything's okay, Lilly. The women are safe. I remember you from Pittsburgh . . . before Brandi and I were married."

"Yeah. *Ha!* I saved your butt once, didn't I?" She grimaced and coughed. "I see you brought Doctor Kildare."

"Doctor Kildare?" Brandi looked puzzled.

"My dog. Thank God he got away. They were gonna eat him. Please, he's no trouble. Can you find him a place?"

"Don't worry," Brandi assured her. "He's already found a boy who needs looking after. Doctor Kildare led us right to you, Lilly."

"Guess I sort of ended up in the wrong place at the wrong time today, huh?"

"No," Cody said quietly. "No, you didn't, Lilly. We just didn't get here soon enough, that's all. What are you doing so far from Pittsburgh?"

She swallowed hard. "Three years ago. Just a one-month church mission trip—an adventure. I saw how the people needed me, so when the others went home, I stayed." She coughed, then struggled to take a breath. "Lots of people lived in this valley back then. No doctor within forty miles."

Brandi stepped over to the creek to dampen a towel with cool water. She returned and bathed Lilly's face.

"A year later, Capistrano came to power and put Kola Mendoza in charge here—a total psycho. Turned my clinic into a whorehouse." Her respiration became rapid and shallow. "He used captured women to reward his soldiers."

"Don't talk about it, Lilly. Save your strength." Cody looked at Chavez for a sign of hope, but Chevy shut his eyes.

"Always high on something—Kola Mendoza." Lilly coughed again, her eyes open wide. "They call him *El Monstruo de Fuego*

Negro, Monster of the Black Fire. You just missed him. He drove away and left the guy with the whip in charge. Ordered him to punish me and Annabella."

Brandi held a cup of water to Lilly's lips. Lilly took one swallow. Domingo and Priscilla came near and listened in.

"I kept the women alive, treated their burns, cuts, bruises. Gave them shots for infection. They would lose hope so easily. I begged those animals to leave the sick ones alone. I nearly went crazy hearing them scream and beg. Once, I even offered to take the place of two women who were at the breaking point. Got myself drunk first—figured I could stand it that way."

"Oh, dear Jesus," Brandi whispered.

"They declined my offer. I guess I wasn't much to look at. They kept me around cuz someone had to keep the women . . . keep them working." She began to cry, then recovered. "I wasn't much of a drinker, either," she chuckled. "I threw up for two days afterwards."

Brandi's tears rolled down onto Lilly's cheek. "Oh, Lilly." She wiped Lilly's face again. "Why were they punishing you?"

"Last week, they brought four teenage girls—so young." She tried to clear the rattle from her throat. Brandi gave her another drink. "I couldn't take it anymore. I helped them escape. Told them to head east and try to find one of the villages. The soldiers caught one of the girls last night—Annabella. They made her talk."

"What about the other three? What happened to them?" Cody asked.

"They must've made it to the villages."

"Why didn't you escape with them?" Brandi asked her.

"And leave these women on their own? They wouldn't have survived a week."

Domingo hardened his fists and walked away.

"They drank . . . all night . . . to get worked up. I don't believe they wanted me dead. Just wanted to teach me a lesson. But sooner or later . . ." Her speech slowed. "Sooner or later, everything here dies. Don't feel bad for me."

She reached from under the blanket, tried to clutch Cody's sleeve, but lost her grip. "Mr. Musket, Cody, I prayed every day someone would come," her voice now a whisper. "Promise . . . promise me Mendoza will never come back to my valley. He destroys everything good."

"Don't try to talk, Lilly." Cody put his hand on her forehead. "Oh, God, this is . . . so wrong. But I know that You put Lilly in this wrong place because people needed her here." The marauders who had gathered around to listen removed their head gear.

"Mr. Musket? Are you still there? Cody? I can't see you."

Cody reached under the blanket and found her hands. "We're here, all of us. I'm holding your hands. Can you feel that?"

"Can't feel anything," she responded weakly. "Are my hands cold?"

Cody grimaced. "Healing hands, Lilly . . . They feel like healing hands."

Cody placed his ear next to her lips to hear her last words.

"God made them to heal, not harm. I always knew . . ."

"Always knew what, Lilly?" Cody waited. No more breath sounds. Cody moved his fingers over her eyelids to shut them.

"She's gone, Babe. I'm sorry." Chavez stared down at Lilly's face. "How does somebody get that brave? She was too good for this world. She wasn't like me."

"You heard what she said, Chavez." Cody stood up. "Everything here eventually dies. But not today. We rescued eight women that we're takin' with us. We did good here this morning."

"Not good enough." Chavez turned and walked back toward the building. "We need to see what we can salvage out of this place, then get back on the road."

Brandi excused herself and walked briskly toward the stream. "I'm gonna be sick," she said.

Priscilla approached the eight women. "Follow me. We can find you some better clothes inside the building. After that, you need to go with us." They understood enough English to comprehend, but they told Chavez they wouldn't leave until Lilly had been buried.

Chavez emerged from the clinic. "They want to bury her, Babe. I've already assigned two guys to dig the grave. The ground is soft in this valley—didn't take 'em long. Gotta leave it unmarked cuz somebody'll desecrate it. We'll bury them together. Gotta expedite."

"Roger that. By the way, what's Seaman carving on that piece of wood over there."

Chavez turned to look. "He's a wood craftsman. Supports himself that way. He said someone should place a marker on this place so nobody forgets what happened here."

After they had buried the two bodies, they did their best to disguise the unmarked grave, then lingered for a moment. Brandi had returned from the creek, her face and shirt wet from splashing in the cool water. She held Cody's hand and leaned close. "You should say something, Cody." The marauders removed their hats again.

Cody cleared his throat. "I'm not good at this," his gutty voice faltering, "not good at all. I regret that we did not know Lilly's little friend, Annabella, whose body lies here with her. I can tell you that Lilly . . . she was the bravest warrior on this field of battle today. She was a tiny woman who loved large. Some reach the end of life wondering if their lives ever mattered, but Lilly, she—" He tightened his lip and bitterly shook his head.

Brandi squeezed his hand. "That was perfect, sweetie."

"Amen," Chavez said as he donned his cap and his battle face again. "Ladies and gentlemen, we still have the living to care for. Capistrano isn't gonna slow down."

He radioed ahead and told the marauders on the hillside to have the children ready to move out. They started walking back toward the stream, but someone was missing. Looking back, Brandi beheld Doctor Kildare lying on top of the grave, his tail motionless, his eyes shut.

Brandi walked slowly back to the gravesite. She knelt beside the heroic animal and gently lifted up his chin. His brown eyes were resolute, understanding, all-knowing.

"Doctor Kildare, come with us. Let's go see Paco. He needs you now. The other children need you. Chevy can rewrap your paw."

The grieving dog whined, then wobbled to his feet and followed her, limping badly.

As they crossed the stream before starting their climb up the hill, Brandi moved between Cody and Chevy and caught their arms. "You guys need to wash before we get back to the kids. Look at yourselves."

Cody and Chavez stopped. They squatted down in the water to wash their hands and clothing. Brandi knelt behind them and placed her hands on their shoulders. She was lost in a sea of emotion, remembering that Cody had once tried to explain the feeling you get when so much sorrow and anger flood your mind at the same time. Now she understood.

When the two men rinsed, the water became bright red and ran away from them, carrying Lilly's blood downstream. As it dispersed in the pure, cool water, they heard a tapping sound behind them. They looked back to observe Seaman nailing something over the front door of the building. It was a hastily-carved wooden marker with these words:

"Lilly of the Valley — Healing Hands"

CHAPTER 22
CAN I STILL BE HUMAN?

The detail returned sadly from the gun battle at the clinic, moving up the hill to join the exodus once again. They numbered eight more souls than when they had departed two hours earlier. The rescued women cried softly.

The long walk was agonizing for Brandi as she leaned into Cody and clutched him with both arms. "I can still hear the air escaping from her lung through the bullet hole," Brandi said. "That wheezing sound—I'll never get it out of my head."

"You shouldn't have gone down there," Cody told her. "Some things can't be unseen after you've seen them. You'll get past it, but I wish you had kept your promise to stay here with the kids."

"I could not have stayed here," she confessed. "And I don't know how I'll ever get past it."

"Yes, you do. You'll keep doin' what you've always done— layin' it down for somebody else. It's what defines you."

Priscilla offered a cigarette to anybody who wanted one. It was the first time she had offered to share anything.

Justice Hodges offered stogies to any takers. "I ain't usin' these no more," she stated plainly. "I didn't bring enough to finish the trip anyway. Figgerd I'd be dead by now."

Six of the rescued women and three of the snipers, including Chevy, divided up what few she had remaining.

The mournful appearance of the detail alarmed the children. "Mama!" Knoxi cried. "What was all that popping? Guns? Did someone get shot? Why are your clothes so wet? Who are all these women? Why are you crying?"

Chavez reminded everyone they must keep moving. Explanations could come soon enough.

As they started north, the eight rescued women began to interact with the kids. Some of the eight had lost children of their own, and the little faces gave them hope. Domingo headed in the opposite direction, scouting behind for Capistrano.

Once they hit the trail, Cody moved forward to converse with Chavez. Justice Hodges walked beside Brandi but kept her distance. She knew the look on Brandi's face.

Brandi acknowledged Hodges with a simple nod. She wanted to cry again, but was determined to remain strong for the children.

Cody and Chavez had a heart-to-heart. The two men had been in battle together in Afghanistan, but scarcely knew each other. Cody had moved on to a lucrative baseball career. Chavez had known only one thing—armed conflict.

Chavez spoke without emotion. "One of the women we rescued showed me the marks Mendoza put on her. Not pretty. He's a giant—about seven feet tall, jet-black hair, with orange locks and a long beard."

"How did he earn his name *Monster of Black Fire?*"

Chavez never looked up. "You really want me to tell you that right now?"

Cody cleared his mind with a deep breath. "So, did you find anything in the building that we can use?"

"Not much," Chevy answered. "Found some clothing for the women, some pain killers, some penicillin. No radio, no sat phone. Can't get satellite reception here anyway—somethin' still jamming." He tossed away the partially-smoked stogie. "Is your wife okay?"

"She's seen violence before," Cody told him. "She's always bounced back. But . . . this one hit us hard. We knew this woman once upon a time. At least, we thought we did."

"You never get used to it, Babe. If you ever do, you'll be just like Capistrano. We're all just barely holdin' it together—even Prissy. Humans aren't built for this. Nobody should see what we saw."

Cody's eyes clouded.

"When you first join up," Chavez said, "you want to fight at least one war in your military career—the chance to prove yourself. You're itchin' for that first battle. You think it's gonna be like the homecoming game. You think you'll feel a sense of accomplishment if you win, but . . ." His voice trailed off.

The two men walked silently for a few paces. No wildlife sounds, just the low murmuring of the children and the soft shuffling of so many little feet. Chavez wearily looped his assault weapon over his shoulder before continuing his thoughts.

"In the beginning, I would tell myself the gunfire in the distance would never come any closer. I thought I was the only one, but I soon figured out everyone else was just as scared. Your IQ goes to zero when the bullets start to fly, and you can't remember a single reason why you joined up in the first place."

"You've proved your worth time after time, Chevy. That counts."

"Worth? How do you figure? I was naïve enough to believe that the purpose of war was to gain something like freedom or taking back stolen terrain, something worth fighting for. Sniper training seemed so punk-ass sweet, so impersonal. But when I deployed, the reality hit me that my primary duty was to eliminate unsuspecting individuals, *real people.* It's hard to see the purpose when nothing is gained and there's always someone else you have to kill next time."

Cody was quiet while Chavez pulled his sunshades from his pocket.

"Sometimes you're sent to the most beautiful regions," Chavez continued. Seems almost like a vacation. You can even pretend there's no war going on, until you see what happens to the innocent."

Cody couldn't think of anything to say. It was awkward. He had never heard Chevy put so many words together at one time.

Chavez swatted a fly away from his weathered, sunburned cheek. "In the end," he said, "you just try to hold on to something beautiful. You try to remember how it feels to hold the hand of a child or wake up and watch the sunrise over Subic Bay. Anything . . . anything to feel human. Otherwise, all you have is your training and your knowledge—the kind of knowledge you wish you didn't have."

"Maybe it would be easier if we didn't have a heart," Cody said. "But *heart* is what separates us from animals."

"I might've had a heart once," Chevy sighed deeply. "I lost it when I lost the purpose."

"People need us, Chevy. That's what gives us purpose."

"Lilly needed us," Chavez pointed out. "Problem is, we had the opportunity to eliminate Mendoza, but we were five minutes late. All we did is get Lilly killed and miss the one chance to take somebody out and make the world a better place."

Cody searched for words. "You asked me earlier how somebody gets as brave as Lilly," he reminded Chavez. "Lilly's heart broke for the people of her valley. It's why Mendoza was afraid of her. Love made her *fearless, dangerous*, and I didn't even know her last name."

"Lilly of the Valley," Chavez declared. "That was her *real* name. That's how this country will remember her. For all it's worth, I hope we meet up with that Mendoza. Can I still be human and wish that?"

Cody cleared his throat. "For all it's worth, amigo, you're one of the best humans I know. I lost the purpose once. I regained my self-worth when I realized that Jesus thought I was worth dying for."

Just then, something tugged on Chavez's right hand. He looked down. It was Knoxi. "You do have a heart, Mr. Chavez. It's just broken right now."

Chevy found himself folding his hardened fingers around the tiny hand of the seven-year-old girl. Knoxi looked up to smile.

Cody drifted back a few paces and wrapped his right arm around his wife's shoulders. Together, they watched their daughter adopt a new uncle.

CHAPTER 23
T-REX

At noon, they came to the end of the forest. Ahead lay a narrow canyon a half mile long, and beyond that, a lengthy stretch across rocky, sandy flatlands. They decided to rest while still beneath the shade trees. Chavez deployed scouts to make sure they would not be ambushed in the canyon ahead.

The trees masked the intensity of the high noon rays, but one look toward the distant north, their intended path, was more than enough to discourage. It would be grueling—sandy, rocky, sunny.

Cody and Brandi sat together next to the trunk of a thirty-foot silk tree. The horizontal leaves were prickly, so Cody and some of the men cleared spots on the ground where leaves had fallen. Cody looked to his left. RJ Seaman, one of Chevy's snipers, had moved in to help clear spots for others to sit.

"Hello, Seaman," Cody said. "Nice job back at the clinic. Chavez says you scored two of the kills. You saved lives this morning."

Seaman acknowledged with a brief nod. "Thank you, sir. This mission might be . . . I mean all these kids . . ." He looked toward the children who had collapsed on the ground in a large group. "You gotta wonder if some of these will even be able to get up. It's only noon, but seems like a whole day has already gone by."

Brandi spoke up, "That was a very nice thing you did, carving that beautiful marker for Lilly. Very thoughtful. She won't be forgotten."

"Yes, ma'am." He paused, and then looked at Cody. "Uh, Cody . . ." He sat down. "Did you know I had a brief career in the big leagues once? That's how I got the nickname, '*Lefty*.'"

"I heard that," Cody responded. "Saint Louis Cardinals?"

"Nope. It was Cincinnati. I got into one major league game and that was the end of my career. The next day, I joined the Army. We played Seattle. It was the eighth inning, and since I was the only lefty in the pen, the skipper brought me in to face a rookie— Ken Griffey Junior. I figured on throwin' my breakin' ball on the first pitch so he wouldn't hit it out of the park. It was the best slider I ever snapped off."

"So, what happened?"

"He hit it out of the park. Last time I checked, they were still searching for the ball on the other side of the river."

"*Haha!* Well . . . rest assured, Lefty. I know a lotta guys who can hit it outta the park, but they can't shoot under fire like you."

"And not many can make something meaningful out of a rough ol' piece of wood, either," Brandi added.

"It's good you were here today, Mr. Seaman." Cody shook his hand.

Before getting underway again, Chavez called the leaders together for a briefing. "We need to keep a diligent watch for that bus," he began. "Dakota and Hampton are the only two who've seen it. It's a mini bus—maybe fifteen passengers if you cram it full. It won't carry everybody, but it would be an important asset if we could capture it. Some of these kids are weakening. We don't wanna have to carry 'em. We're already fatigued."

Priscilla brought up a related matter. "What about *Pyro-Jack* who likes to carry black fire in his hood? Are we gunna capture him? Or do we kill him?"

"Pyro-Jack, or *Monster of the Black Fire* as the locals call them, is the most dangerous part of encountering that orange bus.

Reliable intel, courtesy of Lilly of the Valley, tells us Kola Mendoza was last observed with his big butt sittin' in the driver's seat. So, if you encounter the bus, assume the worst."

"So, sir," Priscilla pressed her point, "if we encounter him, do we capture, or do we kill?"

Chavez's sharp brown eyes looked right through her, his teeth clenched. "Just don't destroy the friggin' bus in the process. Next question."

"I hear he's a legend with the locals," Dakota volunteered. "They believe he can't be touched by a bullet. He was once reported in two different places at the same time a hundred miles apart, and the two individuals who reported it were found later that night gut-burned from the inside out, or so the legend goes."

"Gut-burned?" Brandi whispered. "Cody, what does that mean?"

"Means somebody has to stop him," he muttered.

Hodges decided to join the public discussion for the first time. "Well, I don't b'lieve in none of them monster legends!" she announced. "Yep, they said the same thang 'bout Goliath, but David struck him down wid jus a shepherd sling, then cut off his head and showed it to evabody! If I spot Mista Black Fire, I'm gonna take him down and decapitate him right then and there and do what David done. Yessuh! He ain't steal no more precious kids!"

"I agree, Hodges," Chavez said. "Even in modern warfare, that kind of thinking will get you ahead."

For a moment, confusion sat upon them—*ahead?* or *a head?* Had Chavez intentionally invoked a humorous double entendre? His face revealed the obvious—He had no clue why everyone was staring. He was all business. Brandi couldn't hold back a giggle, and soon, resistance to laughter became futile. The children had no idea what had just happened, but it must have been good and must have been funny. Everyone joined in, Cody and Chevy the lone holdouts.

When they finally picked up and started moving again, they were juiced. Chavez's accidental wordplay had loosened up everyone. Several came by and congratulated him on finally doing something human.

"So, what did you think of Chevy's verbal stumper about getting ahead? Or did he mean a head?" Brandi asked Cody.

"Getting a head? *Ohhhh,* now I get it."

She swatted his shoulder with her free hand. "Don't play dumb with me. Do you think he did it on purpose?"

"Considering the mood Chevy was in? I doubt it. Besides, I've never seen him crack a joke except . . . except when things look . . . hopeless."

"Daddy, what was everybody laughing about?" Knoxi had left her 'post' with the brigade and joined her parents. "And why were you and Mama rolling in the grass yesterday? Are you trying to get a baby?"

Cody had held his laughter after Chevy's word snafu, but this time he could not. Brandi, however, saw things differently. "Why were you spying on us?" she scolded. "I knew I heard somebody. And where did you hear about rolling in the grass and babies?"

"I'm sorry, Mommy," she declared with abject tone. "Sometimes Mia and José forget I understand Spanish. I heard Aunt Mia tell him she was surprised they didn't have a baby after all that rolling around in the grass the last time they were at the ranch."

Brandi was suddenly speechless, but Cody had regained his composure. With a soft chuckle, he lifted his daughter. "What a wonder you are, baby girl. Your mother and I were *only talking* in the grass yesterday. Meanwhile, don't repeat any of that, okay?"

"Woo-hoo!" Knoxi brightened. "It didn't look to me like you

were *just* talking."

Brandi's mouth fell wide open. "What did you say?" She grappled for words, trying desperately to wipe the smile from her own lips.

Cody's long sigh assured his wife he would have the last word. He addressed his daughter softly enough that his comments could be heard by only the three of them.

"After everything that happened at the clinic this morning . . . I mean only God knows how much I needed to hear what you have to say. Your mother and I are glad to know that nothin' around here escapes your notice—not even someone rollin' in the grass."

"I want to go home, Daddy. I'm tired," she pouted. "When can we leave here?" She laid her head on his shoulder, then sprang back to life. "Wait, Daddy! Put me down!" She began kicking her feet.

Brandi's alarm bell sounded. "What's wrong?"

"See that little girl over there with the black hair? Her name is Angel. She's from Nicaragua. All her family is dead. She's crying again. I told her last night that my mama and daddy want to have more children and maybe we could be sisters."

Cody and Brandi watched as their only daughter went to embrace a new sister. In the moment, how could they possibly object?

Within an hour, temperatures rose and the company began to drag. Scrubby bushes afforded little shade. Clouds had long since dissipated.

By late afternoon, all were exhausted. This time, there was no rain shower and no lagoon. Leaders were concerned about Domingo who was overdue for his daily report on Capistrano.

Dunes were scattered throughout the immediate area, and the sun-soaked rocks were like hundreds of mini radiators. In the distance they saw what looked like an oasis of evergreens. With tortuous determination, they struggled on until they reached the clump of trees which had flourished around a dry gulch. It was an hour before sunset. They had to stop. They would roast the remainder of the meat for those who were hungry, and drink the rest of the water. The coast was still two days away.

The open road was exposed—no cover, no jungle in which to hide. Domingo called in and screamed over the comm that he was just minutes away. When he arrived, he dropped the bike and hit the ground running. Panting, out of breath, he barked out loud metaphorical maledictions which added up to only one thing—*trouble.* Capistrano was only a half day behind with approximately 150 troops and heavy artillery. The marauders and children would be overtaken and outgunned on the sandy plains the next day. The kids were terrified.

Leaders gathered to discuss options, but no one had any answers. Even if they were to travel all night, they would still be overrun long before they could reach the coast.

That's when Domingo shocked everyone into disbelief. He placed himself squarely in the midst of the thirty-eight frightened children, and in strongest terms, demanded that Brandi pray again.

Priscilla raised her eyebrows and threw her ciggy into the gulch. "Now, I've heard everything."

Cody offered an alternative. "God will hear each of you if you wanna pray. Just talk to Him. Be yourself. Tell Him how you feel. Be honest with Him."

Cody's suggestion gave rise to an unexpected event. Domingo immediately jumped aboard. He did exactly as Cody suggested.

He cupped his hands around his mouth and yelled loudly toward the heavens, *being himself* and pleading desperately for the lives of the children.

Knoxi stood with eyes wide open. "Mama, do you hear that?"

"*Shhhh.*" Brandi motioned. "Domingo doesn't know any other

way to talk. Maybe later you can teach him some better words."

Domingo stormed Heaven the only way he knew—straight on, straight up, and loud. His irreverent petition, employing full use of his colorful phraseology, might have made the angels want to cover their ears and shut the windows of Paradise, but his impassioned plea brought battle-tested warriors to their knees.

The unlikeliest of candidates, the man reputed by some to be part reptile, had pled with utmost urgency for his little playmates. Beneath his cold-blooded crust, T-Rex had a beating heart.

Priscilla had her own take. "Do you call that a prayer? If there is a real God, I hope he wasn't listening, or we're buggered."

Domingo wiped his dirty face with a tattered sleeve. The gritty marauders, spellbound with hats in hands, remained perfectly still, waiting for Cody's response to the most amazing event they had ever witnessed.

Cody approached the fifty-nine-year-old former Army Ranger. "Mingo, I've never heard any man knock on God's door with more love or compassion." He put his hand on Domingo's shoulder, then looked at the others. "Are y'all thinking the same thing I'm thinking?"

"*Mount up!*"

The two words reported loud and clear, but from where? From whom? Heads turned, looking for the source.

Despite exhaustion, they changed their minds about making camp. An hour of daylight remained. No one could give a sound reason to move on. What benefit would an extra hour bring? Nevertheless, everyone was compelled to keep marching. The exodus had a new pulse.

The marauders, in harm's imminent path, could have fled to save themselves, but none did. Instead, they took to the road again, determined to march until sunset.

CHAPTER 24

THE HAWK

As darkness approached, their path took them through another temporary stretch of jungle, and finally brought them face to face with an old rusty bridge spanning a deep chasm. The bridge was wide enough for a truck to pass, but they had not encountered a single vehicle on this road so far. The rusty structure appeared to be at least a hundred years old.

Enough daylight remained for the marauders to visually inspect the bridge before sending everyone across. They cautiously searched for signs of explosive devices—booby traps or heavier charges placed underneath the trusses which might be rigged to sabotage the entire structure. Ten minutes later, they declared all clear.

Cody stood in the middle of the bridge looking straight down at a fast-moving stream which ran at least a hundred feet below. The water was crystal clear like the lagoon the night before. He turned and gazed toward the sunset. The radiant blue, orange, and golden cirrus sky was all that remained of the day. The sun had now dropped below the horizon. Would tomorrow's sunrise be their last?

They would cross the bridge and make camp tonight. Tomorrow's task meant more flatlands with no cover—the final leg to the north coast—two more days of walking. Time was running out. Capistrano was closing in.

As Cody stood alone, his mind struggled to find an answer. Brandi had always been able to receive some sign, a simple word, or instruction from God. Why could he not?

A Sea Stallion or Chinook helicopter could easily land on the flats ahead and rescue them, but even if they had the means to call for outside help, would anyone beyond the borders of Librador even know they were still alive?

Brandi joined Cody. They crossed the bridge together. The marauders and children followed. The kids were quieter than they had been all day.

Cody glanced at the fading sunset once more, then shut his eyes. A brief vision of Lilly's fair eyes and flowing golden hair filled his head—the way she had looked in Pittsburgh four years earlier.

Priscilla caught up with Chavez. "So, looks like this might be it, luv."

"Maybe," he responded. "But this isn't the first impossible situation for Cody and me."

Chevy told her about the ridge in Afghanistan—his SEAL team backed up against the escarpment with no path to escape.

"So, how did you make your getaway?" she wanted to know.

"Cody gave himself up as a decoy and led the hostiles away from us. He was captured. The rest isn't pretty. I mean, they don't exactly treat captured pilots with love and respect. It bought us time to escape."

"Now, I am puzzled," she brooded.

"Oh, you thought I came on this mission for the money?"

"Well, I just assumed . . ."

"Why are *you* here, Prissy?"

"Money. Simple as that," she told him.

"You sure?" He didn't wait for her answer. "Cody's a generous man when it comes to his family. I knew him when he had nobody. You and I both know what that's like."

Priscilla stared at the rushing stream far below.

"I've seen combat," Chavez told her, "but I've never seen a clearly-defined purpose like we have here. These kids, they need us. This country needs us."

"But this blood-awful country isn't yours or mine," Priscilla insisted.

"Does that matter? Besides, if somebody doesn't stop this bunch, they'll eventually get so strong they'll be snatching kids off the streets of London and New York. This may be a small corner of the world, but we have a chance to make a difference this time."

"I've never met a woman so bloody lucky as Brandi Musket," Priscilla ranted. "What is it with her?"

"I'm not sure it's luck, Priscilla."

"Go hang it up! You mean the God thing? If you ask me, it's rubbish. Like today, like what happened to that Lilly girl."

"I can't stop thinking about her, either," he said. "Innocent face—the same kind we all had once."

"So, why would a smart God let that happen to someone like her, luv? I wouldn't argue if it happened to me. But she didn't deserve it. She was the one good thing in that hellhole. It's always the ones who try to make a difference that die. If there's a God, he's definitely lost the plot."

At that moment, they were surprised to hear an aircraft approaching from behind. Everyone turned to look. Sabre and Cody recognized the type. It was a Cessna 208 Caravan, a single-engine turboprop with a seating capacity of sixteen. The wing flaps were deployed and the power was near idle—landing configuration, descending northbound as it passed just above them.

Cody, Sabre, and Chavez had an immediate powwow. The plane was on an approach to an airport, but where? None showed up on the satellite photos.

"There's a landing strip ahead," Cody said. "Let's find it."

The three men followed the path of the aircraft, and soon they stumbled upon a primitive landing strip positioned in a sandy field. The dirt runway was marked by streamers. As they warily approached, a frame building came into view at the edge of the landing area. A dust cloud, which had been created by the arrival of the turboprop aircraft, still hung in the air.

The plane was parked next to the building entrance. Its propeller had stopped turning, but no one had yet deplaned.

They took a secure position behind an enormous pile of rocks next to a bulldozer about fifty meters from the front door. Chavez surveyed with the field glasses. In the last fading moments of daylight, he noticed that the structure was similar to Lilly's clinic. He could barely make out the sign above the door: *"Edificio de Oficinas."*

A dim light inside the building shone through the only window. Then, something partially hidden behind the structure caught Chevy's eye.

"That must be our missing bus," he said as he handed the glasses to Cody. "Here, take a look."

Cody confirmed. "Yep. Orange, just like the bus we're looking for. And here comes our unfinished business—Mendoza, the black fire guy. He just walked out of the front door."

Cody shivered as a cold dread took him temporarily—a feeling he had hoped would never haunt him again. He couldn't take his eyes off the giant figure who now walked slowly toward the parked aircraft. Chavez yanked the glasses away and pressed them against his face, then handed them to Sabre.

The light shining from the open door was just enough to see every ghastly detail. The "unfinished business" was indeed a mountain of a man with snake-like orange dreadlocks and a bushy black beard. His grisly appearance gave new meaning to the term *nightmare*. With a snarly face and biceps like footballs, he was at least seven feet tall, and wearing boots somewhere around size 25.

Mendoza popped a handful of pills and chased them with the last swallow from an Aquila longneck. He tossed the bottle away. Sabre was enraged to observe two armed hostiles exiting the aircraft leading a string of twelve frightened children tied together with a cattle rope. "You don't wanna see this."

"We can see it without the glasses," Chavez seethed.

"Looks like we arrived on time," Cody added. "So now what?"

Just then, a young woman with dark hair stumbled from the building whimpering and wailing, chasing after Mendoza. Chavez grabbed the field glasses, straining to see her in the dim light. Her arms were pocked and marked with brutal scars. The right side of her face was a thing of beauty, but the other side told a gruesome story. She wore a black halter top with matching shorts.

Mendoza pushed her down, but she came crawling back to him, reaching, pleading, crying. This time he kicked her, sending her sprawling and rendering her motionless on the ground.

The imposing figure approached the two men holding the fettered children. He slapped one of the gunmen so hard it knocked him down. The unfortunate subordinate staggered back to his feet with wobbly knees. Lilly had warned that Mendoza was usually high on something.

Mendoza loosened the rope so he could examine each child. One by one, he picked them up, looked them over and set them back down. He placed the seven girls on his right side and five boys on his left. The children cried and sobbed.

"I've seen enough of this." Cody scooted forward and stood up.

"Wait!" Chevy grabbed him by the arm and pulled him back. "You're not dying on my watch! And neither are those kids. The moon's ready to move behind that cloud," Chevy said, pointing to the distant sky. "Let's wait 'til we lose the moonlight."

"If we're gonna save these kids," Sabre said to Cody, "we gotta do exactly as Chevy says."

The two gunmen took the seven girls to the bus and padlocked them inside as the moon ducked behind the cloud. Chavez, Cody, and Sabre seized the moment and moved to position themselves closer. They hid behind a sizable bush.

A minute later, the two subordinates returned from the bus and followed Mendoza and the young boys into the building and closed the door.

"Okay," Chavez motioned. "Let's move."

From inside the building, the little boys began to scream. Chavez hastened his steps. "Weapons, gentlemen. We're going in."

Chavez was first to push through the door. The petrified boys were locked in a large animal cage while Mendoza threatened and taunted them with a blowtorch unlike anything Chevy and the others had seen. The flame hissed like a snake, a pink glow at the center with an outer plume that alternated between black and invisible. This torch had no hose and no cord—a simple hand-held portable device with no visible delivery system to supply it with fuel or power.

When the gargantuan Mendoza spotted the intruder standing in his doorway, his lightning-quick reflexes propelled him into motion. Howling like the midnight wolf, his intimidating eyes wild and raging, he thrust the ghastly torch toward Chevy with his long arm.

But Chevy's nerve held. His gun was quicker, his aim deadly.

When Mendoza crashed to the floor, the entire building rattled. He had fallen squarely on top of the lighted torch, trapping the flame underneath his huge chest. Like Goliath, the Philistine champion with whom David had tangled in the valley of Elah three-thousand years before, a single shot to the head sent him to his eternal destination.

Chavez now stood over the destroyer of Lilly's valley. "You played with fire for the last time."

Mendoza's accomplices threw their hands into the air, begging the rescuers not to shoot.

They made the two gunmen open the cage and liberate the seven boys. One of the kids was screaming and wouldn't stop. Cody started toward the child, but Chavez stepped in front of him and gently placed his sweaty arms around the terrified youngster. He spoke softly to the young victim in his own language until he calmed down.

The smell of burning flesh now filled the room. Mendoza's body was smoking. The unthinkable became obvious—the torch beneath Mendoza's dead body still burned.

Chavez turned around still holding the boy and rattled off instructions in rapid succession, "Cut off that torch and tie these men hand and foot. I need to interrogate them to find out what they know. Get those little girls out of that bus! Secure these weapons. Search the building for anything we can use—communications, fuel, ordnance, in that order. And here, take my comm and let Priscilla know to prepare for twelve more kids and possibly a very disturbed woman. And speaking of the woman, somebody check on her."

Sabre was edgy. "Help me move this monster, Cody. We need to proceed carefully with the black fire. We gotta cut off that torch and destroy it."

"Do you know what that black fire is?" Cody asked, as they began to move the huge body inch by inch. "I never saw a flame like that."

"Next-level stuff. Experimental," Saber answered. "I didn't know anyone had developed it to this extent. A blowtorch that burns like a microwave and never leaves an external scar. Or, you can change the field terminals and make someone's face look like scrambled eggs. It's like holding hellfire in your hand."

He and Cody dragged Mendoza's huge body off the torch.

"Horrible smell," Cody said. "Burnt flesh. Can you cut off the flame?"

Sabre cautiously lifted the burning torch and carried it to the other side of the room. "This device is just a primitive prototype of what could be a horrible weapon of the future," he said. "Here's the receptor adjustment, and this button must be . . ." He pressed the button. "Got it!"

The pink and black flame disappeared.

"No tellin' how this guy got the technology," Sabre said while examining the pistol-like mechanism. "Top-secret. Operates off antimatter principles combined with a seven-dimensional metric, similar to Heim's theory, worse than a science-fiction horror flick." He set the torch down and knelt beside Mendoza's body again. "Help me turn this guy over."

They rolled Mendoza over and made a hideous discovery. His chest was now a large vacant cavity. Even the heart was missing.

"Where did the flesh go?" Cody swallowed hard. "There's no trace of tissue. Part of him is . . . just gone, like something took a big bite out. No blood, no fried body parts, no nothing."

"Researchers believe this gizmo can send human flesh to one of seven other dimensions if the vortices are synched," Sabre answered. "When this guy fell on the torch, it could have changed the setting. His flesh may have been transmitted to another dimension. That part's just theory of course, a quantum possibility, a bad dream."

"Maybe it's not theory anymore," Cody said. "How do you destroy that thing?"

"It draws gamma rays from electromagnetic radiation in the atmosphere and channels it through a component no more powerful than an atomic watch," Saber told him. "I just need to smash this conversion oscillator on the handle and—"

Chavez interrupted, sounding ragged, "What about using it against Capistrano before you destroy it?"

"Unfortunately, this contraption is just an instrument of torture, only effective at arm's length," Sabre said. "My dream is to someday utilize the same quantum technology for deep tissue repair, or to make inoperable bullets and shrapnel disappear from someone's body. Maybe my research will pay off, but this weaponized version . . . I mean, in the wrong hands it could be developed into a weapon capable of destroying an entire army from a hundred miles away."

"Or send a whole city to some other place in the universe," Cody grumbled. "Destroy it!"

"My pleasure," Sabre agreed. "The world doesn't need another WMD."

At that instant, a single gunshot sounded off. Everyone hit the deck. Chavez crawled toward the entry door and nudged it open. A whiff of gun smoke rushed into his nostrils. The woman with the disfigured face lay on the porch in a pool of blood with a small caliber pistol in her lifeless hand.

"Where did she get the gun?" Chavez knew the question was meaningless, but he could think of nothing else. He dropped his head and coughed up the gunpowder breath he had just inhaled. "You know," he said plaintively, "God must've had such high hopes for the human race once."

Sabre unlocked the bus. The girls scrambled out and scattered across the field as fast as they could, headed for the trees. The darkness may have scared them because they slowed down as they approached the ominous jungle.

"Chavez! Come tell these kids we can feed them and take them with us."

Chavez ran out and called to them in Spanish. They all stopped. Cody and Sabre searched the facility. It had only four rooms. One of them was padlocked.

"Maybe we can load up the plane with people and make several trips to the coast tonight and get everyone out of here," Cody suggested.

"Good idea," Sabre said, "except the plane has maybe fifteen minutes of fuel on board. I already checked. There are no refueling facilities here."

Chavez came in with the seven little girls he had rounded up. He interrogated the two prisoners, and they told him they were forced to land because of low fuel. Their destination had been farther south, but headwinds had slowed them down and their fuel was running low. Their commander had planned to be elsewhere, and was angry because they had failed to manage the fuel more carefully.

"There goes the plan to escape by air," Cody said. "Wonder what's behind this padlocked door?"

"Let's find out." Chavez walked outside and returned with a crowbar from the bus. He broke the lock. "Hey, guys! Check this out. This stuff is enough to blow that bridge! Capistrano won't be able to cross the gorge."

The three men had a round of high fives as they beheld a room full of explosives and demolition accessories.

"How long will it take to rig it?"

"Six hours, Babe, give or take. But that's if everything we need is here, including remote detonation equipment. Also depends on if it works."

"Okay, let's find what we need and get the stuff loaded on the school bus. How much fuel is in the bus?"

"It's on empty, too, Babe. But maybe it'll get us to the bridge. I have no idea how Mendoza planned to get fuel for the bus or the airplane."

"I'm beginning to see . . . I mean just think about it," Cody said. "Mendoza's plans were disrupted. He didn't plan on being here at all, but because of the headwinds, the plane full of kids shows up here just in time for us to meet up with 'em."

"So . . . you think it was some sort of divine arrangement," Chavez muttered. "It was just headwinds if you ask me."

Cody changed the subject. "You load everything, Chevy, since you're the demolitions expert. Sabre and I will walk the kids to the camp. I don't wanna give 'em a ride on this bus with explosives on board."

"You got it."

~   ~   ~

As Brandi waited anxiously for Cody and the others to return from the small airfield, she paced back and forth near the bridge, praying that Capistrano and his minions would not appear on the other side. Priscilla approached her and sat down on a flat rock.

"I guess this is the time for—how do you say it in America— put up or shut up?" She pulled off her hat and scratched her head.

"What do you mean?"

"If there is no God," Priscilla explained, "we're dead by this time tomorrow. There's no escape unless Capistrano gets struck by lightning. This is when your God has to show up, or we're history."

Cody and Sabre suddenly came into view, approaching the camp with the twelve children they had rescued at the airport. Knoxi ran ahead to welcome the traumatized youngsters and offer them food. She spoke to them in Spanish and explained the situation from her point of view. "There is plenty of food for everyone," she said. "If we need more food, some very old people will come walking on the road and bring it to us."

Cody revealed their plan to blow the bridge. "If we hadn't walked another hour," he told them, "we wudda' never seen the plane or found the explosives. We also rescued these twelve kids and ran into Mendoza."

Brandi glanced toward Priscilla. Their eyes met briefly.

"What happened to Mendoza?" Priscilla asked Cody.

"Mendoza's dead. He thought he could beat Chevy to the draw. Bad move."

Everyone clapped. Some cheered.

The marauders wanted details, and the question on everyone's mind seemed obvious. Would Hodges be the one to ask Chavez if he had cut off the head of the giant? But Hodges was reluctant to hand Chevy's misspeak back to him, even if just in fun. Perhaps it was because she recognized the clouded, distant stare on Chevy's face, or maybe because Chevy had just slain the most dangerous man in the country as if it were all in a day's work.

Chevy was oblivious, all business. He wanted only to start rigging the bridge. The task would be long, dangerous, and draining. He hesitated when he noticed everyone staring, but was not in a mood to gloat or spout details about the kill. He wiped perspiration from his face and exhaled a long, clearing breath. He obviously hated awkward moments.

Priscilla quickly stepped to his side. "We're good," she assured him. A paper-thin smile slipped through her usual scowl. She locked eyes with Hodges momentarily. Hodges returned an amiable nod.

They feasted on the rest of the meat and refreshed themselves with clean drinking water collected from the stream at the bottom of the ravine. Knoxi's Brigade, which now numbered fifty, bedded down under a starry sky. Eight marauders were busy most of the night preparing for the demolition of the bridge. Domingo departed again to keep watch on Capistrano's troops.

At sunrise, they moved the entire group four hundred meters farther north to make sure everyone would be clear of the blast and falling debris.

"Daddy, maybe Domingo was the rabbit and the plane was the hawk?"

Cody gave her a glance but was focused elsewhere.

"Daddy? You know the dream you had? Remember?"

"Alright, let's do a head-count." Cody wanted to make certain no one had lagged behind.

"You can ask Daddy later," Brandi told her daughter. "We're pretty busy now."

All was set, everyone on pins and needles. The sun had risen, but was obscured by a solid low overcast. They waited only for Domingo to return. Finally, they heard the bike, then saw him speeding across the bridge from the other side. When he arrived, he was frantic. Capistrano had broken camp at midnight and was but an hour away.

"No problem. We're ready." Chavez looked at Cody and received the signal—thumbs up.

Chevy pulled the switch. Nothing happened. He reset everything, double-checked all connections, and tried again— nothing.

He tore open the switching device. It was completely functional. Chavez, Sabre, and Cody jumped into the bus and sped to the bridge 400 meters away. They checked the relay box. It was an antique, but it had passed Chevy's inspection earlier. Now, it was smoking, unusable.

"It's toast, Babe. This was the only relay I found last night at the hangar. I didn't see this coming."

Fifteen minutes had passed since Domingo's announcement that Capistrano was closing in. The early morning overcast was beginning to show patches of blue sky. Now the other marauders came running toward the bridge.

"We could put a few kids on the bus and in the plane and try to outrun Capistrano," Chevy said, "but there isn't enough fuel."

Cody began to see flashes of Afghanistan again. He raised his volume. "We haven't come this far to let these kids die!"

"Stay cool, Babe. Don't lose your head, especially now." Chevy knew the reason for Cody's panic. It was his family—all of them, including Knoxi's entire brigade.

Chevy was calm, resolute. "There is one other way, Babe. One way to finish it."

Cody stared through dazed eyes. "Copy that," he said quietly.

Priscilla nodded. "I understand," she agreed. "The six charges underneath this bridge must be detonated manually. Count me in, luv."

Chevy's eyes narrowed. "I'm with you, Prissy. We just need four more volunteers."

Cody's gut burned within him as he contemplated the options. He knew every man and woman would likely volunteer, and that the final decision would be his. Who would live? Who would die? How could he choose?

Hodges had overheard. She exchanged a glance with Cody. She knew his struggle—having to make a choice he would live with forever.

Cody scanned toward the north and spotted Brandi and Knoxi coming toward the bridge, still a distant fifty meters away. How could he possibly face them now? How could he say goodbye? How could he tell his little girl?

Chavez read Cody's thoughts. There was no way he could let Cody be one of the six. He walked up behind his friend and prepared to render him unconscious with a chokehold.

Just then, the bus engine started. They turned to observe Sabre driving away from the gathering crowd, aggressively blasting the horn to clear the way. In a few seconds, he was bouncing toward the airport, a swirling cloud of dirt in his wake.

"Where's he going, Babe?"

Cody made no response. He walked forward slowly, his head bowed. Tommy John, neatly tucked into the black leather travel case, was sitting on the ground where the bus had been parked. Cody dragged his feet ten paces and picked up Sabre's greatest contribution to humanity, the device that had saved his little princess. He tucked it under his arm, then turned and stared at Chevy.

Chavez took charge. "All right, the rest of you, let's get away from this bridge. It's gonna blow!"

At first, everyone looked confused.

"Come on, Cody. We have to go." Chavez waved his arms. "Double time Prissy, let's get everyone moving!"

Brandi met Cody on the road. "Did they get it rigged to explode? What's happened?"

"We gotta move away." He hustled her along. "Where's Knoxi?"

"I just now sent her back to the group. Cody, what's wrong?"

"Let's catch up with the others. I think . . . I think things are under control. But—"

"But what? Cody? Under control?" She glanced back toward the ravine. The solid overcast was breaking up, allowing scattered patches of sunlight to shine upon the dated, rusty bridge.

By the time they approached the others, everyone was short of breath. Priscilla met them before they caught up with the group. At that moment, everyone heard an aircraft and looked skyward. The Caravan passed overhead staying just beneath the low, patchy gray clouds. It was southbound, headed toward the canyon. As it flew over the brigade, the wings rocked sharply side to side. Cody then stopped on the road, stepped away, and saluted.

Brandi tried to read his face but could not. She gazed back into the low sky to watch the Caravan bank left and descend into the ravine on a collision course with the bridge. Her mouth gaped open when the reality of the moment overtook her.

She recognized the sound of the turbine engine advancing to full throttle. Brandi squeezed her eyes closed and buried her face against Cody's left shoulder. "I can't watch."

Three seconds later, seven loud concussions rocked the ground, sending flames, smoke, and debris skyward. Brandi jumped with each blast. She shuddered and clutched Cody's shirt.

"No! No! No!" She pounded Cody's chest, and then reined in her anguish. The children were watching.

Knoxi came running full speed, crying, screaming. *"Daddy! Daddy! What's happening? Daddy?"*

Cody reached down, caught her with one arm and lifted her.

"Daddy, was it Sabre?" She yanked on his collar with all her might. *"Daddy!"*

He pulled her close. "The hawk, Fort Knox. It was the hawk. He finished his mission, then flew away to his home in the sky, just like in my dream."

Priscilla stood alone five feet away. Her face was ashen, streaked with tears that cut little pathways through the sandy dust on her cheeks. Cody reached toward her. At first, she was stoic, but then, she opened her arms and walked into a tight embrace with the three Muskets.

Everyone stared like frozen figurines, mesmerized as gray and black billows rose up and intermingled with scattered cotton clouds that stubbornly hung overhead. Booming echoes traveling down the canyon now faded into silence. The old bridge groaned and creaked as it finally gave up the ghost and collapsed piece by piece into the deep chasm.

CHAPTER 25

NOWHERE TO HIDE

The faces of Cody's Marauders were drawn, hollow, and shadowed. Their camouflage face paint, now several days old, was hidden by layers of dirt, sand, and sweat. The men wore a week's bearded grunge and the women dealt with tangled hair matted and dirty from the gritty breeze.

The adrenaline which had driven them to push the limits for five days was spent. Exhaustion was now their greatest threat. Second-guessing and grief was their brutal adversary. Rest stops became more frequent. The tired group nursed their blistered feet at every stop.

Lilly's death had profoundly impacted Chavez. He could understand Sabre's conscious decision. His life had not been *stolen*. He had given it. But Lilly's death made no sense. His own decision to lead a rescue attempt had backfired. If they had arrived just minutes earlier, or if they had simply moved on, Lilly and her friend would still be alive.

Cody was trapped in his head as well. He glanced back a dozen times until he could no longer see the hovering smoke. He remembered a famous quote, though he could not recall who had authored it:

> *"To snatch victory from the jaws of certain defeat is the greatest thrill a commander can experience."*

But this morning, the thrill was missing. They were delivered from the jaws of the reaper only because a brother had paid a heavy

ransom. The big explosions of the early morning still hung on—
the vibrations yet tingling in his breast. Escape from Librador was
within reach, but no one was talking. Every warrior has limits. Had
they reached theirs? Chavez was right—humans were never meant
for this.

"Can we retrieve his body and have him buried in Arlington?"
Brandi interrupted Cody's thoughts.

"No one can know how or where he died," Cody responded.
"He has a son at MIT named Ryan. He's even smarter than Sabre,
but we cannot tell him or anyone else what happened here. This is
an unauthorized mission, and I don't want to create an international
incident or jeopardize Ryan's safety and reputation. Burial at the
bottom of that canyon is as honorable a resting place as a man can
have. Besides, Sabre isn't there, *just his body.*"

"And Lilly, too," she reminded. "She's not in that hole."

Cody wore a thin smile, remembering the beautiful place he
had visited in his dream. "Knoxi was right," he said. "It hasn't been
a straight line to the beach, like my dream when God didn't hit the
ball directly to the hole."

"Hmmm. You know, Cody, the timing of everything was
perfect. If we hadn't been delayed at Lilly's, we would have been
ahead by three hours, and we would have passed way beyond that
bridge yesterday. We would never have seen the plane last night.
Mendoza would still be at large, and Capistrano would have caught
us on these plains today."

"I guess you're right about the timing." He wrapped his arm
around her waist as they walked and pondered. "We also rescued
twelve more kids and captured a hideous futuristic weapon that
could eventually destroy—" He tightened his lip and decided not
to finish.

"Weapon?" she inquired. "Was it something about the black
fire?"

He pulled his cap low on his brow. "Don't go there right now."

"I didn't want to know anyway," she conceded.

Cody's bloodshot right eye gave up a tear. "Chavez was ready to just move on 'til they brought Lilly and Annabella out and tied them up. That's why these brave men and women . . . they just couldn't walk away." Cody breathed deeply. "I need to clear my head."

Brandi responded, "Sweetie, when I first laid eyes on these 'brave men and women,' as you call them, I was horrified. These gallant individuals have issues, mostly because of their occupation. But the world needs them, and none of them will ever be the same after this mission."

Knoxi joined them. "Mama, did you make Daddy cry?"

"Men sometimes cry," Brandi told her. "They can hurt too."

"I'm glad your mother's brain isn't wired like mine," Cody grunted. "She can figure stuff out way before I do."

Cody looked ahead and noticed that Priscilla had joined Chavez at the front. "See that?" He pointed.

"Chevy and Prissy?" Brandi smiled. "Life does go on. I saw them together for a few minutes, yesterday. Wonder what they're talking about?"

"They're lovers!" Knoxi blurted. "I saw 'em kissin' on the bridge last night!"

"Knoxi! Shhhh!" Brandi glanced around to see if anyone else had heard. "You aren't supposed to talk about people like that," she scolded. "And just why were you nosing around last night?"

Knoxi's face was easy to read—she was in trouble.

Brandi leaned close, took another look around, then whispered, *"Really?* You saw them kissing?"

Knoxi, exhilarated to learn that she wasn't facing discipline, decided to really spill the frijoles. "Yes ma'am! And the other day, Mia told Uncle José she was never gonna wear any pants again!"

"What?"

"That's right! I heard it myself. She told José in English that she was tired of wearing the pants in the family!"

"Ha!" Cody couldn't hold back, but Brandi kept a straight face—more or less.

Knoxi then revealed that she had been teaching Domingo how to say some good words. "I taught him how to say *'amen'* yesterday," she told them.

"Amen? Well," Brandi said, "that's certainly a good start."

~   ~   ~

The explosions had terrified the kids, but most were unaware that the "lightbulb man" was dead. The news slowly circulated. By evening, everyone knew. When they stopped to make camp. Cody gathered the people. He asked his daughter to interpret for the children.

"We are only one more day from our destination," he told them. "By tomorrow evening, we should be on a big ship headed home."

Knoxi's interpretation made the kids cheer. They smiled for the first time since the bridge had collapsed that morning.

"You should know that we're alive and free because this morning, your friend and mine, the man with the green bulb, sacrificed himself for us." Cody awkwardly pushed his hands into his front pockets.

"Greater love has no man than this, that he lay down his life for his friends." He cleared his throat. Knoxi moved next to him and reached for his hand. He pulled his right hand from his pocket and clasped hers.

Cody continued, "Someday, you will hear the story about an

ordinary woman—a *doctor*—one who chose sides and changed her world. Her enemies spent the whole night getting high, working up courage to carry out an order against this small woman who carried such a bright torch for God."

Priscilla turned her head away. Chevy placed his arm around her.

Cody removed his cap. "Last night, I did not know if we would see another sunset like this one." He pointed to the western sky. "I know where Sabre and Lilly are tonight, because I visited that beautiful place yesterday before I awoke."

Domingo and the others removed their hats. Several stared at the sandy ground, while a few turned and gazed toward the sunset. The children showed little reaction. For them, it was simple—freedom was near. One more day. Just one more day.

The next morning, morale improved. They could taste liberty. The children jostled for position at the front of the brigade, each wanting to be first to spot the ocean.

It was the sixth day of their exodus. The adults were running on adrenaline again and a sense of relief. The constant vulnerability and the task of babysitting so many children had left them depleted. But now, with the gentle breeze in their faces and the smell of saltwater in the air, everyone was jovial—jesting, trash talking, laughing. It was the last leg of their journey.

At noon they spotted the coastal waters two miles in the distance. Their ship awaited offshore. It was but a speck. Everyone cheered. Some of the kids were ill with fever. Most had insect bites, cuts, and scratches, but even they brightened up.

Clouds that had blocked the sun during the early morning burned off at midday. With no trees for cover, they would be forced to travel the final distance in bright sunlight again with temperatures in the high 80s. A warm headwind faced them.

Deep, sandy soil made walking tedious and exhausting. The

ground was hot, but nothing, not even gritty eyes or burning feet, could dim their hopes. The ocean was in sight. Within a few hours, they would dine aboard ship.

Suddenly, they heard Domingo's bike at the rear—maximum speed and spinning wheels cutting through heavy sand, kicking up clouds of dirt and debris. He had gone back earlier to scout once more for possible trouble. Now, he brought his final report. The news was bad.

Capistrano had taken a long way around the canyon and was in hot pursuit within ten miles. His motorized troops were heavily-armed with automatic weapons, RPGs, and the addition of a Vietnam era 155 mm artillery weapon. Within an hour, Capistrano's hellions would wield an arsenal against the exodus from which escape would be impossible.

The coast was still two hours away, their footing slow and exhausting. Even if they somehow reached the shore, they would require small boats for the final distance to the ship, which was anchored just beyond Librador's territorial waters. In that event, their small vessels would be vulnerable to artillery.

Cody frantically scanned the landscape—no buildings, no rocks, no hills—nowhere to run, no place to hide. They were outnumbered ten to one. This wasn't Afghanistan. This time, Super Cobra gunships would not show up to save the day.

He fell on his face and covered his ears. Panic filled the air—children screaming and crying, commanders calling out orders that no one could hear. Chaos—it haunted Cody like a ghostly echo. He had heard it before.

Brandi spotted him on the ground. She ran to him and attempted to lift him to his feet. Priscilla and Hodges arrived and helped her get him up.

"Cody, you have to lead these people!" Brandi yelled.

"There's no way to make it on time," he screamed back. "All

these kids! It's happening again!"

"Babe! Get outta your head! *Number seven, remember?*"

Priscilla reacted sharply, *"Number seven? What's that?"* She watched while Brandi and Cody stared at each other, then screamed again. *"Well? What in hades is a number seven?"*

Brandi answered, "In the heat of battle—"

Hodges interrupted, "It's from her father's list of leadership principles. Numba' seven: 'In the heat of battle when you's losin ground, be still and know that He is God, and He will speak to you!"

"Yeah! I know, I know. But this situation is—"

Brandi cut him off. "This situation is what, Cody? Too big for God?" She was animated. "Do we need the waters parted?"

"I'm no Moses!" he shouted.

She shook him. "Cody! Step up! You hear me?"

Hodges spoke out. "That's right, Cody. You ain't no Moses. But God is still God, and He trust you sure enough to put you in charge o' these kids."

"Is that all you people can think of at a time like this?" Priscilla raised her gun above her head and stormed away. "Number seven? Hell's bells! I'm going for one last smoke!"

For Cody, it was happening again. What if the kids were recaptured? What would become of Planned Childhood if he and Brandi died? He took one last look at the ship offshore and thought about Moses and the Hebrew nation trapped against the Red Sea, facing an all-out assault from horses and ironclad chariots. Cody wasn't the first freedom fighter in history to be faced with impossible odds in a game of sudden death.

He recalled his thoughts at Moca Punache—*Maybe today I die, but go with God, and never let them see you sweat.* He chuckled. *Yeah, I wonder if Moses ever thought of that?*

He put his feet in gear and outran everyone to the front of the stampede. He raised his arms and commanded the group to halt where they stood. Incredibly, everyone stopped moving. Most fell to their knees, out of breath, depleted, resignation on their faces.

He cupped his hands around his mouth, a la Domingo, looked to the sky, and bellowed out a raspy prayer loud enough to raise the dead. "God, I'm no Moses, but I'm asking You to part the sea or . . . or whatever you can think of! You're good at this kinda stuff, and I know You didn't bring us this far just to leave us!"

Then, for better or worse, T-Rex weighed in. *"Amen! Amen, dammit!* I—I mean, God . . . Sir." He removed his cap. "I'm a lost case. I never learnt no proper ways. But, now hear me out. Even a old fool like me knows that Musket's right! If You don't get here double-time . . .

The rest of Domingo's *prayer* would forever remain a mystery. The balance of his petition was drowned out by a sudden explosion of fiery passion among the adults and kids alike—raised hands, shouting, jumping, clapping, calling on the Maker of all things to make it right.

Priscilla had never seen a moment like this—a mission commander crying out to God in front of his troops with one of the Devil's own running interference.

Suddenly, a clamor not unlike galloping horses drew the attention of all. The sound of beating hooves became louder and louder. The ground shook. A hot wind began to blow. The sand they stood upon became airborne, swirling around them, lowering the visibility, darkening the high-noon sky.

Chevy's experience told him to look upward. "Wait!" he shouted. "What's that?"

Everyone gazed skyward. The sun overhead was partially blocked by the blowing particles, but an object appeared like a dark shadow descending through the gritty cloud.

Chavez raised his field glasses to his eyes and employed the filter mode. "I don't believe this!"

Prissy pulled the glasses out of his hand and had a long look. "I thought I'd seen it all 'til I saw this!" She refocused the lenses. *"It's a merry UFO!"*

Chavez snatched his binoculars back and took another look. "That UFO is a Chinook! I've seen a million of 'em." He handed the glasses to Cody.

"Confirmed!" Cody shouted. "But who sent it?" He wiped the sand from his eyes and looked again. "I don't recognize those markings."

The giant helicopter hovered above them.

Chavez shouted, "Everybody back up! It's gonna set down on the sand. Back up! Back up!"

It hovered overhead for a few seconds, then moved sideways a safe distance away and sat down.

It was 100 feet in length, olive drab, with bright red stripes and two gigantic sets of rotors. The children coughed because of the dust cloud. The ragtag brigade, completely out of options, gathered beside the big bird as its spinning rotors finally stopped turning.

When the door slid open, a giant appeared in the doorway. He wore a dark helmet too small for his head and dungarees that reached only to his knees.

"Slap ding, yo! Yawl git in here!" the creature bellowed. "Ladies first!" His smile appeared twice the width of his face as he removed his undersized helmet.

"Dawg?" Cody wiped the sweaty grit from his unbelieving eyes. "What are you doin' here?"

"Oh, jes pickin' up my brotha and his new family. A big 'splosion showed up on satellite yestaday morning. Decided to pull some strings and git down here. I tol' em you was alive! I jes knew it was true!"

He stepped onto the ground and lifted the helmet high above his head. "Man, I'm feelin' it today like thunda-n-lightning!"

Behind him, Silverbelle appeared in the doorway. "He was determined," she told everyone. "Somehow, he knew you were in trouble three days ago, and when the explosion happened yesterday morning, he knew that was it. The Pistons won't miss him. They're not gonna make the playoffs this year anyway."

"Yep, and I managed to git a sprained wrist so I couldn't play, jes in time to make dis trip."

Cody had a question. "So how'd you get access to satellite intel?"

"Don't ask," he shouted as he entertained everyone with a gritty tap dance in the sand. "And don't tell nobody!"

Silverbelle folded her arms. "My husband is such a clown."

"Lemme give yawl a ride to my boat. Shouldn't be hard to git evabody on board this here choppa. Might have to double up the kids in the seats. In fifteen minutes, we's on da' boat!"

Cody saluted Dawg. Brandi jumped up into his mammoth arms and squeezed him as hard as she could.

Cody hugged Silver. "Get him a helmet that fits next time. And those pants?" He shook his head.

Brandi smothered Silver with an embrace. "I must look a fright," she said.

"Well, my husband made sure we leased a boat with a salon and spa," Silver countered. "He was sure the girls would appreciate it. The boat's gonna be home to these kids until we can get them back to their parents or into one of our facilities. We tried to think of everything."

Some of the children were frightened because they had never seen such a giant of a man. Some were hiding behind older kids, afraid to board the huge transport.

But Dawg's hopeful smile put them all at ease. *"¿A cuántos de ustedes les gusta las galletas?"* ("How many of you like cookies?")

Little hands reached up. *"¡A mí, a mí, queremos galletas!"* Needless to say, visions of cookies now danced in their heads.

Dawg was exuberant. *"¡Esperen hasta que vean lo que hay en mi barco para todos ustedes!"* ("Well, just wait 'til you see what's waiting for you on my boat!")

Priscilla approached Cody as the children boarded the big bird. "So," she asked, "if you hadn't stopped and prayed to God, would the Chinook still have shown up?"

"All I can say is, it was right for me to pray, and it was right for Dawg to be here. The rest is a mystery."

"God can hear us before we ask," Brandi told her. "He answered Cody's prayer yesterday when Dawg saw the bridge explode, even though Cody didn't voice his prayer until today."

Chavez put his arm around Priscilla's shoulders. "We're comin' back, Babe. We talked about it—unfinished business." He looked into Prissy's eyes. "We want to find the purpose. I mean this kind of life is hell, but it's the only one we know, and we're good at it. Several others feel the same."

"We're reopening the clinic," Priscilla announced. "If anybody else tries to turn it into a merry knocking-shop, they gotta come through us."

"I don't recognize you, Priscilla," Brandi said. "Is this country really your problem to fix?"

"Both of you have earned a quiet life," Cody said. "You've done a good job here. The money you've earned from this mission would give you a good start together. Come to Houston with us. You're gonna be outnumbered here with no government behind you. Sit this one out."

"Sooner or later . . . you gotta pick a side if you wanna remain human," Chavez said. "What you said about Lilly carrying that big torch for God; she reminded me why I became a SEAL. A quiet life you say?" He looked at Priscilla again.

She shook her head. "We don't do *quiet* very well, Cody."

Knoxi tugged on Cody's arm. "Daddy, Domingo won't get on the helicopter."

"Why not?"

"He says it brings bad memories. It makes him hate everybody and hate himself. How can he hate himself when Jesus and so many people love him?"

Brandi had a suggestion. "Why don't you go ask *him* that question?"

Knoxi was gone in a flash. Cody and Brandi observed from a distance while their daughter approached terrible T-Rex, sitting alone with a blank expression on his face. They watched Knoxi place her hand on his knee and plead her case.

The aging warrior laid his weapon down, stood to his feet, and placed Knoxi on his shoulders. He carried her straight to the Chinook and set her on the ground by the entry door. Knoxi reached up and took hold of his huge right hand. Together, they stepped on board.

CHAPTER 26

TALL TALES, LITTLE HERO

Four days later, Central Panama

The Muskets lounged on the second-level veranda at the sprawling Aviles Cattle Ranch in Central Panama. A fiery sunset gave way to the same rising moon that had kept watch over Knoxi's Brigade during the previous nights.

Their ship had arrived in Panamanian waters 18 hours earlier in the wee hours of morning, and had anchored offshore in the Gulf. The couple doubling as Brandi and Cody had flown by helicopter to meet the vessel for a "glorious reunion" with their daughter, who had reportedly been ransomed.

The real Cody and Brandi had then departed the ship with Knoxi and had flown back to the ranch before dawn. The Musket impersonators had secretly stayed aboard the ship, and would sail with the children and the eight rescued women to Managua. The boat was to meet the Red Cross there. A cover story had already been constructed by an unlikely source.

The colorful open-air veranda was vintage Old-World design with classic arches exhibiting the finest in Spanish craftsmanship. With the brilliant moonlight and authentic flame lanterns, one could even imagine the famous masked avenger of folklore emerging from the shadows, his flaming blade drawn, ready to challenge any malefactors.

But their warfare was over for a season. The children had been set free. The mask, cloak, and sword would remain in the closet until needed again. Superheroes would now become healers, and this was cause for celebration.

The Muskets were treated to a banquet of beef ribs and all the trimmings, courtesy of their hosts, the Aviles family. The veranda was the perfect place to dine at sunset. A special dinner guest, a prominent media personality, departed after dinner and made her way down to ground level with her crew for a live report on the front lawn of the hacienda. The Muskets turned their attention to the built-in 89" flat screen to watch the broadcast.

"Good evening, ladies and gentlemen. Tonight, I am here in Central Panama at the magnificent Aviles Ranch, where I am now privileged to share an exclusive interview with the person we have been waiting to hear from. It is my pleasure to introduce Miss Knoxi Musket.

"So, Knoxi, can you please tell our television audience how you managed to become free, and why you arrived here by ship last night with the other children? Tell it exactly the way you told me earlier."

"Well, Ms. Cassidy, like I said, I was abducted by some very bad men at Wrong Way, Texas when I was with Uncle José and Aunt Mia."

"Uh, that would be José and Mia Bustamante, right?"

"Exactly. After that, I was taken to an undisclosed location."

"Undisclosed? Do you know what that means?"

"Sure, but I don't know the definition."

"Okay, so go on and tell us what happened."

"At first, I was really scared, so I asked Jesus what to do. He told me to cover myself with mud and spend the night in a tavern. The next morning I saw T-Rex for the first time. He's part reptile. He smelled, and he used bad words, but he was sweet. I kissed him, and later on he let me sit on his shoulders and ride him across the desert."

"Well, tell us about the other children."

"All these kids just showed up in the street, and one of them ran up a tree wearin' nothing but his underpants."

"Well, exactly how did you get him down?"

"Oh, it was easy. Hampy slithered up the tree like a snake and got him down, smooth as cake."

"Hampy? Well, did anyone else help you?"

"Sure. A man with an undisclosed name had this green lightbulb flying around his head to scare off spiders. Another unnamed contributor shot the monster in order to get ahead."

"Uh, monster? What kind of monster?"

"Really scary! He had these orange snakes coming out of his hair, and he drove an orange school bus to work every day. We walked a long way until a flying object with red stripes and bucket seats came right out of the sky and picked us up! So, here I am!"

"There you have it, folks. Who can doubt the word

of this little hero? No one else in the family is talking, and many questions remain unanswered. Speculation is that the Muskets, who stayed right here at this ranch until the ship arrived at one o'clock this morning, somehow obtained the release of their daughter and some fifty other children from an 'undisclosed' location by some 'undisclosed' means.

"Anita Crown Cassidy, reporting from the Aviles Ranch, Central Panama."

CHAPTER 27

THE CALM AFTER AND BEFORE THE STORM

In Librador, things fell apart for Capistrano and the Rizal regime. The exodus sparked hope in a demoralized people. Within weeks, a national revolt gained traction, aided by a group of seven mysterious hooded commandos wearing oversized Detroit Pistons jerseys. Their exploits resulted in the liberation of women and missing children by the hundreds.

The raiders also succeeded in confiscating five million dollars in medicine, health-care equipment, and weapons—all within a six-month period. No one knew who the masked raiders were, but their deeds of valor became legendary. Grassroots Libradorans called them *"Los Vengadores Enmascarados de Detroit, or "The Masked Avengers from Detroit."*

Lilly of the Valley Clinic flourished. The one million dollars Chavez and Pricilla had earned from the Muskets' rescue mission went a long way toward equipping the clinic. It was rumored that the regime had twice sent forces to take back the facility, but that both attempts had failed, and the attackers had never been seen again. This gave wings to a widely-spread story that Lilly of the Valley Clinic, once known as Den del Diablo, was now guarded by angels.

Within eighteen months, Capistrano disappeared. The successful escape of Knoxi's Brigade and the subsequent raids on his compounds had ignited a storm of protest and a thirst for liberty. The losses were too imposing for Capistrano and his dwindling underwriters to overcome. Without Capistrano, the Rizal regime collapsed, creating a leadership vacuum which fractured the people into multiple groups seeking power.

But the people of Librador were soon reunited by a dynamic forty-five-year-old former tavern owner named Benito Santiago, whose vision and charisma offered hope and the promise of democracy. Benito had disappeared during the morning raid on Capistrano's compound, and the marauders had wrongly assumed him dead. He had escaped with his wife. He was duly elected and became the country's first president.

Santiago would later claim that his courage to oppose tyranny had been born in him one night when God sent one tiny girl and sixteen warrior angels to the doorstep of his tavern.

~   ~   ~

Eight years later

October in Librador—A yellow school bus full of energetic elementary school children pulled off the road and parked in the shadow of a tall monument sitting next to the new bridge. The students were on a field trip.

The rebuilding of the bridge across the deep canyon was symbolic of the reconstruction of the entire country, engineered by President Benito Santiago. Children were safe. Librador had climbed out of its dark past.

A visit to this site was mandatory for all elementary school children in this small country. Each time, the story was retold of the daring rescue and exodus. It was part of Librador's history, as famous as the midnight ride of Paul Revere in America. It was also fraught with mystery.

A bronze statue of a nameless avenger, fifteen feet in height, stood overlooking the ravine. Underneath the figure lay a stone marker with words etched into the surface in Spanish and English:

> *"Dedicada al libertador desconocido. A otros salvó, pero no pudo salvarse a sí mismo"*

> "Dedicated to the unknown liberator. He saved others, but himself he could not save."

~ ~ ~

Later that night in Houston, Cody played his last baseball game. It was the seventh game of the World Series against the LA Dodgers. Cody was now age 39. Injuries had slowed him down, and he had decided to retire at the end of the season. But tonight, with his team trailing by one run in the ninth inning, Manager Jason Stearns called on Cody to pinch hit.

Despite a bruised Achilles, Cody limped to the plate with runners on base and two outs. He slugged a hanging slider to deep right field which looked like a game-winner until Dodgers right fielder Jay Toro leaped high against the fence and snagged the ball. Series over.

After his retirement, life became quiet. Too quiet. Boring. Planned Childhood was solidly in the hands of younger, stronger operatives, and Cody spent most of his time guest-speaking on talk shows and benefits, raising awareness about homeless children and the ages-old menace of trafficking.

Little did he know that a sudden, unexpected event would soon upend his life, and that the Muskets would face their greatest test ever.

Chapter 28

Muzzle Flash

January, four years later

Friday night—The Muskets' Houston estate rejoiced. Brandi and Knoxi had returned home that morning from a lengthy trip to Europe, where Knoxi, now eighteen years old, had addressed an international trafficking summit in Rome. The Muskets had finally given the green light for Knoxi to reveal the truth about her escape from Librador.

Rumors about the child exodus had circulated for nearly a decade. The family had remained silent, and the rumors had become distorted and speculative, nearing mythological proportions. Cody and Brandi decided to let their daughter set the record straight in her own words.

Her presentation had been riveting. Correspondents crowded the airport, causing traffic jams and flight delays as they attempted to get pictures and comments from Knoxi before her flight departed Rome.

Having completed their two-week trip, Knoxi and Brandi had returned to Houston worn thin and seriously jet-lagged.

Cody and Brandi enjoyed an intimate reunion in their bedroom, then slept the afternoon away. Meanwhile, their two sons, eleven-year-old Raymond and nine-year-old Cody Jr., rode their bicycles to the home of a friend.

Cody was committed to hosting a child-trafficking awareness benefit in downtown Houston that night. He would be forced to leave his depleted wife at home, but he promised to return early. He kissed her passionately and then departed, feeling as though he were leaving his heart behind.

A strange blend of sadness and gratitude filled Brandi's soul as her lover departed from their bedroom. Their lives had always been like a whirlwind. Often separated, they had worked hard to grow and guard their intimacy like a priceless treasure. In public, they were clothed with enormous charisma, but the mystique fell off when they were alone, and Brandi's heart always quickened to Cody's touch.

Cody had always preferred to drive his truck to downtown events, yet this evening, he had decided to drive her antique blue Mustang instead. Why his sudden desire to take her Mustang? Why did it feel so wrong? Should she be concerned?

~   ~   ~

Cody hastened his steps from the back door of their stately southwestern villa and onto the lighted pathway to the barn. He opened the large wooden doors, turned on the lights, and removed the cover from Brandi's antique blue Mustang. He opened the driver's side door and slipped into the worn leather bucket seat, then closed his eyes.

He and Brandi had once taken refuge in this classic vehicle, splashing through the wet Pittsburgh streets to evade the hit squad only hours after they had met. Sixteen years had passed, and the sweet memories yet lived in this vintage muscle car.

But much like this once-upon-a-time queen of the road, Cody had lately wondered if he too were a relic. At the age of 43, did anyone believe he was dangerous anymore?

Minutes later, he was on his way. The bright January sky was reminiscent of those euphoric Pensacola nights during his flight training when he would gaze upward through the canopy and become lost among a billion stars.

Abruptly, his mind was forced back to earth as approaching red and blue alternating strobes glared in his rearview.

Within seconds, the unrelenting police vehicle pulled directly behind his rear bumper. Cody steered onto the shoulder lane, rolled down the window, and waited. A large police officer emerged. *What could this guy want?*

The officer slowly stepped toward the Mustang, holding a blinding flashlight in his left hand and resting his right palm on the grip of his holstered sidearm.

"Keep your hands where I can see them." He shone the light at the Mustang's rear license plate as he approached. "License and registration please, sir."

The tall, robust officer examined Cody's driver's license, then glanced at the former ballplayer's face.

"Liquor store holdup. Blue Mustang. You aren't doubling as a thug these days are you, Cody?" He grinned.

"Don't gimme any ideas, officer. Retirement can be boring."

"*Haha!* I didn't recognize the car. I had no time to run the plates. I know where you're headed—that dinner downtown. My brother Mike Cannon is receiving an award there tonight."

"You're Mike's brother? He used to be my teammate. I'm gonna present him a citizenship award tonight."

The hefty lawman glanced toward another vehicle approaching from the opposite side of the boulevard. The coming headlights illuminated the big officer's nameplate on the breast pocket of his dark blue uniform—*Morris Cannon*.

Officer Cannon turned back again and pulled a notepad from his pocket. "Cody, I have a grandson who'd appreciate your autograph. Any chance you could—" The officer never finished.

Without warning, the deafening boom of a rifle shot at close range shocked Cody's senses. A muzzle flash had originated from the open rear window of the approaching sedan. Despite his suddenly-ringing ears, Cody detected that other grisly sound he had hoped to never hear again—the sordid thud of a bullet striking a human body.

The stunned policeman dropped his pad, fell against the door, then clutched his chest, spitting blood as he slid down to the pavement.

The red sedan pulled directly alongside the blue Mustang with the smoking gun barrel trained on the downed officer for another shot.

Cody instinctively reached between the bucket seats and gripped Brandi's .380 Ruger pocket handgun. He aimed and fired, emptying the magazine into the back window of the other automobile. The surprised driver burned rubber and screeched away, but not before the rifle had fired its second shot.

Cody attempted to exit the car, but the bulky officer slumped against the door, so he was forced to climb over the console and exit on the passenger side. He glanced at the fleeing sedan as he scooted around the front of the car and then knelt next to Cannon.

An ocean of blood expanded rapidly underneath the vehicle. As Cody endeavored to assess Cannon's condition, his peripheral vision signaled red alert. The sedan was now in reverse, barreling backward at an angry speed, tires smoking, returning to the scene.

Cody was out of bullets, the squealing sedan becoming danger close. He fumbled for Cannon's sidearm, still holstered underneath the officer's body. He frantically ripped the gun from its holster, pointed the weapon at the approaching vehicle and opened fire. The car slid to a halt, then reversed course again. It raced away at high speed, charged through a flashing red light, swerved out of control, and slammed into a gigantic oak tree a quarter mile away.

Cody resumed trying to save Officer Morris Cannon. He shed his blood-spattered evening jacket, then yanked off his shirt, rolled it like a snowball, and crammed it against the wound. He glanced away momentarily. Flashing lights—*help is on the way.*

"Hang in there, Morris. Hang on. Help's coming."

Morris clutched at Cody's wrist. "Cody, I was at your last game, the World Series." He coughed. "It was my brother's last game too."

"I remember," Cody said. "I wasn't in the lineup. I had an Achilles injury."

"Help him, Cody—my brother Mike. He's in a lot of trouble."

The officer's words were now barely audible. "I . . . wasn't ready, Cody. I dunno how to do this."

"How to do what?"

"Die."

"Come on, Morris! Don't give up!"

"They've killed me. Got what I deserved." He struggled to gain his breath. "We were gonna get rich—me and Mike. Bad . . . choice. Mike's in over his head. I can't be forgiven. Help him, Cody."

Cody fumbled for words. "Extreme sin requires an extreme sacrifice to cover it," he said. "Jesus made that sacrifice. Trust Him. Ask Him. He'll forgive you." He spoke with urgency. The officer was fast slipping away.

Morris Cannon gripped Cody's arm, then exhaled his last.

Immediately, the street was alive with responders—more flashing lights, police and fire vehicles, scratchy radio transmissions.

"Lemme see your hands!" The first officer on the scene was a rookie. Four others arrived a moment later.

Cody glanced up. Five weapons aimed at him. Both handguns that he had fired lay on the ground next to the deceased. Steam rose into the chilly night air from the hot muzzle of the blood-smeared Glock.

In the darkness, with his bloody face and hair, he was not recognized by any of the traumatized police. All they saw was a shirtless, bloody, unidentified man kneeling over a fallen officer. First responders did not recognize the Mustang, and no witnesses were present. The nervous officers had no idea what had just occurred.

"I live just a mile from here. My name is—"

"Move away from him! Step away now and get on the ground!"

Cody rose from his kneeling position with his bloody hands in the air, intending to step over Cannon's body and lie face down as instructed.

But his weak left Achilles, remnants of an old World Series injury, betrayed him, and he toppled back to the ground. He reached out with his left arm to break his fall, but his hand landed only inches from the two weapons lying on the pavement.

Five police officers fired their weapons. Cody fell across the dead officer's chest.

~   ~   ~

Meanwhile, back at the Muskets' villa . . .

Something about a hot shower had forever been a mood-lifter for Brandi, but Friday nights had become extra-special. It was shower night for Brandi and her man. It had become a tradition. They would plan all week for their precious Friday night encounters.

On this particular Friday night, the encounter was off since Cody had been called away by duty.

But even without him, she was invigorated just to be back in her own bathroom—their bathroom—where Cody's presence lingered even when he was absent. The warm, pulsating water flushed away her road-weariness, rekindled her sense of touch, and heightened her anticipation for his late-night return. She had promised to have his bed warm when he came home, and she would be certain that everything was perfect.

She punched an overhead button, enabling the built-in FM receiver to bring the outside world into her waterworks. She had interfaced her smartphone before entering the shower so that it would interrupt the radio signal if she received a call. The *Sam Black Hawk Freedom Ain't Cheap Show* was in progress:

> "... and I'm tellin' you folks, this is not some wild conspiracy theory fantasy, and it's gonna bring this country down if someone doesn't wake up! Am I still the only one talking about 'ideological cleansing', as I have termed it? I've been preaching this for three years now. I've been shot at. I've received death threats ... I mean someone doesn't want me talking about this, and it will destroy our way of life if we don't wake up!
>
> "Uh, folks ... I've just been handed a bulletin ... A shooting has taken place in Houston ... We're trying to confirm—"

Just then, Brandi's phone beeped, interrupting the program. She turned off the water, stepped out of the shower, and donned Cody's robe, which hung next to the door. She reached for her smartphone and tucked it underneath her wet hair next to her ear.

It was the Houston Police.

She dropped her phone into the floor of the steamy room and ran toward her clothes closet. *"Knoxi! Knoxi!"*

She could hear her daughter racing barefoot up the stairs. The bedroom door flew open, and Knoxi burst into the room.

Brandi was frozen, standing near her closet door. "Help me find my clothes! I can't think straight!"

Knoxi helped her mother get dressed as Brandi filled her in. "That's all I know," Brandi cried. "They didn't give me any details. Contact your brothers!"

Eleven-year-old Raymond and nine-year-old Cody Jr. were not home. They had sent text messages, explaining that they had gone to the home of a school friend on the other side of the subdivision. In the confusion, Knoxi and Brandi had failed to notice the text.

Their Mini-Coupe they had driven home from the airport earlier was nearly out of gas, so they frantically jumped into Cody's truck. The rear tires screamed as Brandi backed out of the garage, turned, and then accelerated down the circular driveway toward the street.

She turned on Cody's AM receiver, where a special news bulletin was in progress:

". . . where a tragic event has just occurred. The former Houston Astros star third baseman and designated hitter Cody Musket, who played twelve seasons, has been shot. He was rushed in critical condition to Methodist Hospital with multiple gunshot wounds. Tina Anderson of station KPRC in Houston is standing by at the scene."

"Thank you, Kareem. One question asked is why Musket was not driving his F-570 truck with the CODY-12 license plates tonight. Officers say they would have recognized his truck had he been driving it. But tonight, for some reason, he was in

his wife's Mustang. The story gets even more bizarre. There is a dead police officer at the scene. Another vehicle has been found a half mile away with two armed gunmen dead inside. The motive for the shooting is unclear. Was Musket the target, or was it the officer? More to come. Back to you, Kareem."

Knoxi located the text from Raymond, then called him. "Raymond! Where are you guys? The Riveras' home? Listen, Ray. Daddy's been shot! Turn on the news. They took him to Methodist. We're coming to pick you both up."

Brandi raced through the subdivision, screeching past intersections and swerving around corners. She turned into the Riveras' driveway honking frantically.

The boys said hurried goodbyes to their friends and rushed to the truck. Cody Jr. jumped into the back seat, but Raymond hesitated, ready to take matters into his own hands.

"Want me to drive, Mama?"

"No, Raymond. Just get in."

"But sometimes Dad lets me when—"

"Are you kidding? You're only eleven! He lets you drive?"

"Well, sure. At José and Mia's ranch sometimes."

"Too many crowded roads and you don't even have a license. I'm gonna have to fight traffic all the way. Three conventions in town and the Rockets are playing the Spurs tonight."

"But you're crying. How you gonna drive like that?"

"Raymond! Just get in!" She sniffled and wiped her tears.

Knoxi spoke up. "Mama you should let me drive."

"You?" Raymond sneered. "Just because you can fly a plane doesn't mean you're a good driver."

"Kids! Please! I'm driving! That's final! Get in, Ray!"

CHAPTER 30

A note from the author: This section contains graphic descriptions of Heaven, where Cody enters into a dramatic, intimate conversation with Jesus. Heaven is infinitely more glorious than we mortals can conceive, but we do have glimpses from scripture. Apostle Paul was caught up to Heaven and then returned. The book of Revelation also adds clarity. Years ago, I spoke face to face with Don Piper whose death in a plane crash was confirmed by medical records, and whose book entitled Ninety Minutes in Heaven offers stunning descriptions.

In writing this chapter, I relied upon these and similar sources. Beyond that, I could only yield my imagination to God. I hope you will excuse my inadequate depictions of things far beyond the reaches of my own mind, and that you will simply look for the heavenly truth behind this story.

—James Miller

~   ~   ~

Sunday, two nights later

Cody's eyes were loosely bandaged. He could hear people talking nearby, but did not recognize the voices. One man and two women discussed his medical condition.

"I don't know how he has survived this long," the male voice said. "Life support was discontinued an hour ago."

"Oh, how my heart goes out to Mrs. Musket," one of the women said. "I have admired her so many years."

A third voice, shrill, female, "Vitals are dropping, doctor. He's going fast. We need to get the family back in here."

Cody opened his eyelids. He blinked, but saw no one. Where was he? The voices were fading, now distant. He was floating, but how? Had he ingested something? The peace and euphoria were overwhelming.

Suddenly, new surroundings came into focus. He was seated in a Chinook helicopter which was fully occupied but not cramped. The other passengers were smiling, their faces focused on his as though he were their guest of honor. They all knew him, but he couldn't place any of them.

He stared out through the window and recognized the Houston skyline silhouetted against an orange setting sun. Just then, the city fell away. His instincts told him the Chinook was fast gaining altitude, yet he felt no sensation of movement.

He took a second look around, studying carefully the faces of his fellow riders. This time, he recognized them all, save one. The familiar faces belonged to the children who had died violently in Afghanistan. Once marred beyond recognition, they were now perfect, strong young adults clothed like royalty.

One of them reached her hand toward him with a beaming smile. He could lucidly hear her thoughts: *"It's all good, Cody. You're coming home."*

Cody remembered her, the teen-aged captive whom the Afghan terrorists had tried to force upon him as he lay in the street, beaten, depleted, humiliated. She had been merely an object, a plaything in the hands of evil doers with no one to save her.

On that day, Cody's excruciating thirst, unbearable pain and delirium had robbed him of all but a tiny glimmer of life, but he had offered her his last ounce of hope with an outstretched hand and a look of kindness—a reminder that she was, in fact, human, *not an animal*, and that someone understood her pain. It was all he could think to do. It had been enough. She had never forgotten his selfless gesture which had brought her a moment of sweet serenity just seconds before the RPG exploded. Curiosity drove him from his seat straight toward the cockpit. All eyes followed him. The pilot looked to be a young version of Sabre Maxwell, and the copilot chair was occupied by Elias Chavez.

Cody gazed through the front windshield. Where were they headed? It certainly wasn't Dallas or San Antonio. Darkness suddenly gave way to a brilliant landscape which came perfectly into view. What had happened to the Houston sunset? Where had the night gone? This was not a dream. It was more real than anything he had ever experienced.

Chavez turned to him. "Go back and have a seat, Babe. Someone back there wants to meet you. We're almost home."

When he seated himself again, a tiny girl—a beautiful, perfect child, the one whose face he did not recognize—approached and stood beside him.

"My name's Goldenbelle," she said. "You know my parents. Please tell them I can't wait to meet them. My mommy lost me when I was still in her tummy. My daddy plays basketball and drives a big motorcycle. I may be all grown up by the time they get here. Tell them not to be sad anymore. Soon, we can all explore the Father's kingdom together!"

Cody stared at her tiny face. Her eyes—he had seen them before.

The Chinook hovered just above the surface of a land that seemed familiar. Then, somehow, he found himself standing on solid ground. His feet sank inches deep into grass that resembled green velvet waving gently in the soft breezes, each blade individually illuminated. The horizon was endless.

Cody's wonder was unbridled more than he could take in. It was the same place he had visited in his dream while in Librador, but now more brilliant, more vivid, deeper, sweeter, brighter than day. Light which came from everywhere pervaded his body and was the essence of the most powerful love he had ever felt.

He remembered the singing rocks, brick pathways, and the shallow brook that shimmered through the rolling field. As he stepped into the creek, the cooling water flowed over his bare feet. He stood strong again, like in his rookie season, but without the pain in his heart and soul. He stared down at his body, naked but fully clothed, beautiful, without scars. He lay down in the stream and closed his eyes. The soft currents carried away the last remnants of painful memory.

Then, someone chuckled. "Hello, Cody. I seldom bring people here by helicopter, but I have more creative ways of transporting people to this city than you can count, even more than the number of humans ever created on earth. A few of your friends were anxious to ride along and escort you home. Before you go, I want you to see something."

Cody opened his eyes and gazed upward at the most magnificent individual he had ever seen—His face like the sun, His eyes like deep waters. His voice was both warm and chilling, young and ancient, profound yet simple, and more engaging than Cody had ever imagined.

"I AM the only one who wears scars here, Babe." He extended His hand to Cody. "Follow me."

Cody was amazed that even in this Place, he was addressed by his aviator call sign. When he rose up from the stream, he was wearing an Astros game uniform with the number 12 on the back.

They began walking. "Cody, I know about the times when you called and it seemed I did not answer . . ." He paused, his voice breaking.

Cody wanted to fall before Him, but he followed and listened.

"I was there when you lost your parents. They are waiting for you here. I felt your pain when I brought Hanna home before you could marry her. I always had your back, even when you couldn't hear my voice. I created in you the spirit of a warrior because one was needed where you were destined to set your feet. I allowed you to stumble that you might lift the fallen. I caused you to feel the sting of tyranny, so that you might overcome injustice.

"I let you mourn for the children so that you would be strong to lift up my arms to the helpless. I led you where you did not wish to go, because I had heard the prayers of so many who needed to be liberated.

"There is no child's cry that I do not hear, no agony of soul that I do not feel, no hurdle so high that I cannot breach, no road so steep that I cannot climb, no distance so far that I cannot touch instantly, no grave so permanent that I cannot open, and no pit so deep that I AM not deeper still."

They continued, and soon paused at a fork in the road. A giant stone highway marker stood beside the intersection with an arrow pointing to the right. The sign had been engraved in a language that Cody was unfamiliar with, and he wondered why they had stopped. The meaning of the words was immediately revealed to him—*The Dark Angel of Moca Punache Resides Here.*

"Construction is just beginning for this dwelling. Some of my angels like to joke around. They thought it was funny when someone mistook you for an angel, and they decided to rub it in."

Cody was confused, but still had not spoken a word.

"What? You didn't think angels could be funny? Hey, in My Place humor is an art form! You think I'm into creating puppets? Sad, sappy, one-dimensional beings? There are as many personalities among the angels as among humans. My Father and I are not into making cookie-cutter robots. Nothing around here is boring."

This wasn't what Cody had always pictured.

"And speaking of Moca Punache, all Heaven stood at attention when your prayer from that tiny hut ascended up before us like a sweet fragrance. You were exactly where I had placed you, doing precisely what I had prepared you to do. My glory descended upon you the moment you stepped into the street. That's why Salvador ran. It's why he was afraid."

"I—I had no idea, Sir."

"Of course, you didn't. You knew only that you could not bear the thought of losing My children. When you told Salvador you were not alone, ten thousand angels stood before Me wanting to go in your defense. I chose to go Myself, hoping that Salvador would repent when he saw My glory round about you. But Salvador . . . Salvador chose his own place." He turned His face away from Cody briefly, then his smile returned.

"But this is not a moment to be mournful. I have wonders to show you, and someone else you need to see."

They walked again. Cody sensed no passage of time. He could see a magnificent city in the distance with a wall that extended high into the air. It appeared to be at least ten miles away, but he could see it clearly. A radiance at the center of the city extended outward and upward far into the cosmos—brilliance that could be felt like particles of hope penetrating everything, giving purpose to all creation. No shadows. Love so overpowering it temporarily brought Cody to his knees. Mountain ranges rose in the distance behind the walled city perhaps a hundred miles away, yet visible in the smallest detail.

They came to a forest which produced aromas more exhilarating than any he had ever encountered. Once upon a time, he had known the stench of war and death. Now, his senses were energized by fragrances so sweet that even eternity would not be enough time to become accustomed. He wanted to stop and simply inhale, but they kept moving.

Through the trees he caught glimpses of enormous chateaus

made of stone, gold, and jewels of unimaginable colors. Many appeared to hover, while others seemed multi-dimensional, with some components distant and others at arms' length.

Finally, they turned onto a winding stone pathway which took them deeper into the forest and led to a massive edifice more magnificent than any he had ever encountered. It was the size of a small city but was constructed like a grandiose mansion. Gigantic stones which comprised the walls were finely cut and perfectly fitted with no mortar—walls which rose at least one hundred feet straight up. Decks, pools, and built-in staircases in the inner portions were clearly visible through open windows larger than the replay screen in right field at Minute Maid Park.

The building itself reverberated with delight. He heard laughter and saw children playing. Once, the sounds of hell and the cries of suffering children did haunt him in his night seasons. If only he could tell Brandi that those horrors were now completely swallowed up by the sweet, sweet sounds of Heaven.

What was this building? A city? The most elaborate resort in the universe? *Is this God's personal mansion?*

"*Ha-ha!* I hear what you are thinking, Cody. Do you want to see who lives here?" He pointed toward the door at the top of a crystal stairway. "I will leave you now to get reacquainted. *Ha-ha! Yes!* I'm loving this so much!"

He left Cody standing near the massive entryway. The steps before him were of transparent gold. A giant pair of diamond-blue praying hands hovered and floated unattached above the doorway. The exterior front wall was of salmon-tinted glass with inlays of ebony and gold phasing in, phasing out, the two colors switching places every few seconds. When the door finally swung open, a familiar figure emerged—young, energetic, smiling, with golden hair and dancing feet which never touched a single step as she came down the stairs toward him.

"Welcome, Mr. Musket." She giggled. "I have plenty of room in my house for all the people we lost. They have their own dwellings, but they come here to help me mentor children into adulthood if their parents are not here. Your home is just as magnificent, but it isn't quite ready yet."

Cody looked above the praying hands where a modest inscription was etched for all to see:

— LILLY OF THE VALLEY FOREVER —

"Dad!" Someone was calling him—a familiar voice, youthful, authoritative. *"Dad! Nobody dies tonight! You hear me?"*

CHAPTER 30
IT AIN'T OVER 'TIL IT'S OVER

The shooting of Cody Musket had become the biggest news story in America. It had been two days since police officers had shot him, having failed to recognize him on the street just a mile from home.

The five officers involved had been placed on administrative leave, and were viewed as public enemies by the media and by the majority of the American people.

Cody had retired from baseball, and was due to be inducted into the Baseball Hall of Fame the next year. He had been headed to a benefit in downtown Houston when the shooting had occurred. A police officer, Morris Cannon, had been gunned down on the street by a hit team. No one knew why.

Cody had tried to save Cannon's life, but was mistaken for a perpetrator by first responders.

Reporters from all over the world were camped in and around the hospital. It was Sunday night. Surgeons had revealed that one of the bullets had penetrated his skull and damaged his brain. Another was lodged in his spine. He had never regained consciousness. He would never recover. Life support had now been discontinued. The death of Cody Musket was imminent.

In the lobby of the hospital, at least a hundred people had gathered for a prayer vigil. Someone brought a radio to the front of the room and turned the volume up. Everyone in the lobby stopped to listen.

"Good evening, ladies and gentlemen. This is a special Sunday night broadcast of the Sam Black Hawk, Freedom Ain't Cheap Show. I am your host, Sam Black Hawk. Since Friday night, this nation has been in a state of shock over a senseless shooting. Tonight, Cody Musket fights for his life.

"I cannot imagine what is going on in the minds of his family, but I can tell you what goes on in mine. As I sit here in our Nashville studio, speaking live to fifteen million people in this country, as well as a large Armed Forces Radio Network audience, my heart is on the sixth floor of Methodist Hospital in Houston. The time has come to tell you about the first time I met Cody Musket."

Nurses' stations now tuned in to the broadcast which normally was heard only Monday through Friday.

"As most of our audience knows, I lost my legs in Operation Desert Storm. The things I saw, and what I experienced all but destroyed me. My great-great-grandfather was a Comanche war chief. I had wanted to be like him, but living in a veterans' shelter in Galveston, my life seemed over.

"A few days before Christmas, ten short years ago, I sat in my wheelchair at my usual spot near the Galveston seawall, and this guy wearing an Astros cap comes along with his eight-year-old daughter. He asked me about my legs. I was angry at first. 'None of your freakin' business,' I told him. Then he showed me his scars—nasty, ladies and gentlemen, simply nasty."

By now, the entire hospital was tuned in. Brandi and her three children listened while sitting next to their comatose husband and father.

Knoxi now recalled the meeting beside the seawall. She had accompanied Cody to Galveston for a speaking engagement. She had worn a pink holiday jump suit with the words 'Santa is Wonderful' written on the front in scarlet letters, and 'But Jesus is Even Better' written on the back.

She had never forgotten how lonely Sam looked, sitting motionless on the concrete sidewalk staring at foamy whitecaps that were inbound atop each wave that rolled in over the beach.

In another reality, he would have made the perfect Santa Claus—early fifties, wide nose and face, long, thick, wavy hair, mustache, and a heavy beard. But his cheeks were leathery, not rosy, his eyes were hollow, not jolly, and his hair shadowy gray, not snowy white. He drove no sleigh powered by eight tiny reindeer, but rather a wheelchair propelled by his own two arms

After two decades staring into sunlit ocean surf in the face of salty winds, no one even noticed Sam anymore. He was a fixture—just part of the scenery waiting to blow away.

"I didn't even know who this guy was. I wasn't much of a baseball fan in those days. After a minute, he wanted to say a prayer for me. I mean, right there on the pavement. I told him I didn't believe in Jesus, God, or any of it. He told me that was okay, cuz he and his daughter did.

"I told him to go ahead. After his prayer, the little girl decided it was her turn to pray. She actually took my hand. Are you kidding me? Can you imagine how I looked? How I smelled? I was nobody. After they left, I wondered why anyone

would do that for me. A bystander told me the stranger played third base for the Astros. Wait a minute! With no cameras? No press on hand? Nothing to build his marketability, his brand? What was his motive?

"When I got back to my room, I did something I had never done before. I actually prayed to God and asked that if He was real, would he reveal Himself to me. Well, I can tell you that nothing happened. Absolutely nothing.

"But a week later, I was getting ready for bed, and for some reason, I could hear that little girl's prayer bouncing around in my head after all that time. I mean, the way she talked to God, you'd think she knew the Almighty personally. Now you know me. I never blubber on the air. I'm not a very emotional guy. But that night, I cried.

"Something seemed to lift me. A love surrounded me that I never knew existed. I felt forgiveness I never knew I needed. You can say what you want, but I believe I was in the presence of God, and I have to say, it was life-changing!"

Brandi reached across the table and held her daughter's hands. Raymond and Cody Jr. were silent, but each managed a smile as Black Hawk concluded.

"The next week, I spent my entire savings on a Christmas dinner for all the guys at the shelter. The story was picked up by Fox News and I was interviewed. The next week, I was asked by the local

*Fox station to be a news contributor for veterans'
affairs. After that, one thing led to another, and
here we are.*

*"I wanted to be a warrior like my great-great
grandfather. But, who would've ever bet a nickel
that ten years after Galveston, I would be sitting
here addressing millions, fighting for what is right
in this nation and lifting up wounded warriors over
the most powerful media in the world?"*

Knoxi smiled broadly, even as she wiped tears from her face.
She turned off the sound. Cody Jr. left the room.

Jungle Dawg and Silverbelle quietly entered. They embraced
Brandi and Knoxi. Dawg shook hands with Raymond.

Everyone was silent when Cody stopped breathing seconds
later. Brandi, Knoxi and Raymond moved to the bedside and stood
with heads bowed. Two physicians entered the room, each
pronouncing Cody Musket dead at 7:03 p.m.

Brandi gathered her two children into her arms. "Where's
Junior? Did he leave?" Cody Jr. had not returned. Ray and Whitney
joined the Muskets for an embrace with Dawg and Silverbelle.
Time seemed to stand still in the sudden quietness.

Then, a small voice pierced the silence. *"Dad! Dad! Nobody
dies tonight!"*

Everyone looked up. It was nine-year-old Cody. He had
quietly walked back into the room with Pastor Phil Tutor of Church
on the Meadow, and was now standing over his father's deathbed.

"Dad! I said nobody dies tonight! In the name of—"

"I think I hear a Musketeer," Cody responded with a weak
voice.

Brandi's knees buckled. "Awake!" Cody's arms were moving.
His mouth was open, trying to speak. "That's . . . my boy. I would

know that voice anywhere in the universe."

The head nurse ran into the room. "Mrs. Musket, I need everyone to step out."

Silverbelle helped Brandi through the door. In the hallway they huddled. "He always calls us the Musketeers," Knoxi said, unable to contain her elation.

"Paging Dr. Bonner. Paging Dr. Bonner."

Ten minutes seemed like forever. A medical team gathered around Cody. Finally, the family heard the news they waited for.

"Mrs. Musket, your husband is awake—for now. We're not sure why."

Brandi entered the room trying to control her heartbeat. "Cody? It's me, sweetie. The children are waiting in the hall. They told me I could talk to you for a minute."

"Hi, Wonder Woman."

"Oh, Cody, they told us you weren't coming back."

Cody's voice strengthened. "You remember what I told you on our wedding night?"

Brandi grinned. "Well, as I recall, you didn't say much after my parents took Knoxi with them and went across the hall."

"I said you were the hottest 'Brand' going."

"I do remember that!" She leaned over and kissed him.

"I thought you were hot then, and it still goes," he said.

"I hope they can take these bandages off your eyes soon, and I'll show you just how hot." Brandi was alive after two days in shock.

Cody spoke again. "I need to tell you something. Be strong. I'm gonna ask you to reach out to some people."

"What are you talking about?" Brandi asked.

"First, I need to see each of the officers who shot me."

"You want to do what? They have lawyers. Do you think their attorneys will let them talk to you? I mean, your own sons will not even let them get close to you."

"So, I need to talk to my children first," he told her. "They need to hear what I have to say. Trust me."

"OK. Done. Anything else?"

"I need to talk to Mike Cannon."

"Mike Cannon? You mean the retired catcher? The brother of the slain police officer?"

"His brother asked me to reach out to him just before he died on the street. Said he was mixed up in something bad."

"Okay. Who else?"

"When are Dawg and Silver getting here?"

"They're already here," Brandi answered.

"I have something to tell them," he said. "Something very important."

"Cody, I need to tell you that Chevy died yesterday. Priscilla messaged me. His heart gave out. He was so young."

Cody chuckled. "I know. He is."

"Cody, what do you mean by 'he is?' He is what?"

"Young."

~   ~   ~

At 8:00 a.m. the next morning, Cody had a visit from his children.

"Well, if it isn't the Three Musketeers. Aren't you kids supposed to be in school? What day is it?"

Knoxi took the lead. "Daddy, it's Monday morning, and we had something more important than school. And don't you think the Musketeers joke is getting old?"

"You always did have your mother's flair for words." He reached for her. She took his arm with both hands.

Raymond asked, "When are they gonna remove the bandages from your eyes?"

"That's not important right now, Ray. I don't need to see you, but I want to say some important things to the three of you."

They gathered closer.

"I don't want any of you to join the fans or media in demonizing the police officers who shot me. Bitterness will rob you of your destiny."

"What do you mean? You want us to forgive them? Forget it!" Raymond crossed his arms. "I wanna sue every last one of 'em! *They* should be in this bed, *not you*."

"Cody, do you feel the same way?" he asked his younger son.

"Well, Dad, you don't know what you're asking."

Raymond broke in. "Dad, you weren't even armed!"

"Fort Knox, what do you think?"

She was in tears by now. "Daddy, are we gonna lose you again? Why couldn't you wait until later to ask us this?"

"I need to tell the three of you some things that only your mother knows. I want to be the one to tell you. It happened in Afghanistan before I ever met your mom."

He told them about the children in the cage, the RPG, and about the people who died because he had disobeyed the order to withdraw.

"I was awarded the Medal of Honor for saving lives, but the body count was greater than the number of people I saved. I have lived with that." His speech was strong and commanding.

"There is a young man in Springfield, Indiana who grew up fatherless because his dad shielded me with his own body to save me. And there were thirty-two children who burned to death taking an RPG that was meant for me. When it was over, I picked up my Beretta and shot the enemy commander after he was already captured and unarmed. Fortunately, he lived, but, you see, I know something about forgiveness because I have needed to be forgiven." His heart rate and blood pressure now fluctuated on the monitor.

"Why didn't you tell us this before, Daddy?" Knoxi was crying.

"You didn't need to know this before," he said. "But now you do. Retribution may satisfy in the short term, but it won't heal your pain. Hatred and peace cannot occupy the same ground in the human heart. A man who can forgive becomes stronger than a general who takes a city."

His voice trailed off. He slept again. The three quietly slipped out.

Later, in the afternoon, Cody had brief meetings with two of the officers who had responded to the 911 call. The other three declined his invitation.

~ ~ ~

At 4 p.m. Dawg and Silverbelle walked in. "*Ha-ha!* Slap ding, little bro! How you doin? Ain't no bullets gonna *eva'* keep you down! By now, evabody know dat!"

Cody reached up with his hand. "That sounds like my numero uno B-ball practitioner. You come here for a little one-on-one? I know I could beat chu today for sure! You got that beautiful lady with you?"

"I'm right here, Cody." Silverbelle took his other hand. "We rushed as fast as we could. Got here late yesterday. Been waitin' patiently to see you today. What an answer to prayer! We didn't expect . . . I mean we—"

"I been dyin' to tell you something," Cody interrupted with a chuckle. "I mean literally! Yeah, that's right. I been dying to tell you both." He paused and weakly squeezed their hands.

"Wasso important?" Dawg asked. "We listnin' now. C'mon,

spill it."

Just then, Brandi tiptoed into the room and stood in the back. Whatever Cody needed to tell Dawg and Silver must somehow involve Planned Childhood, since the couple were major donors. Shouldn't she be there too?

"I have these bandages on my eyes," Cody told them, "but I see things more clearly than ever."

In the years she had known Silver and Dawg, Brandi had never seen either of them cry. Life had made them as hard as the iron that sharpens iron, but while holding Cody's hand, Silverbelle's eyes became moist and cloudy. Something was up, something personal, something painful. Brandi decided to slip out, but she stopped where she stood when Cody's next words stunned everyone.

"I met Goldenbelle," he said as he tightened his grip on Silver's hand. "She has your eyes. It's no mistake. I don't know the history, but she asked me to tell you both that she—"

"Goldenbelle? Who's that?" Silver glanced at her husband. They traded blank expressions. Then suddenly, Silver raised both hands to her face and gasped.

Cody turned to Dawg, "And the child has your thirst for adventure, excitement. Have you taught Silver to ride yet? I mean Goldie wants all three of you to explore—Uh, yeah, wait, I'm gettin' a little ahead of myself."

"Oh, Cody!" Silverbelle finally breathed again. "Are you saying what I think you're saying?" She looked up into Dawg's eyes and threw her arms around him.

Watching their tearful embrace was a first for Brandi, and was a thing of beauty and grace. Brandi did not know the story, but one thing was obvious—grief had ended, years of hidden anguish gone in a flash. Dawg lifted his wife off the floor and waltzed her around the room, swaying, gliding as though floating on air.

He finally set her down. "We lost our child ten years ago," he told them. "First trimester. We wasn't expectin' no trouble. I was on the road. The team was playin' in Denver. If I'd been home, I mighta' been able to get her to the hospital. I mean, we didn't even tell our friends afterward. We just wanted to move on."

Silver stroked his face. "Baby, it wasn't your fault. I have told you that a million times." She turned to Brandi. "We didn't even know 'til now if the child was a boy or girl."

Brandi's knees weakened again. Dawg noticed and reached across with his long arm to steady her.

"I should go and leave you for a few minutes," Brandi said. "I feel like an intruder. This is your moment."

"We're glad you're here, Brandi." Silver showed her a soft smile. "You're family, and it's only right that you share this minute with us."

~   ~   ~

After dinner, Brandi, Knoxi, and the two boys went up to see Cody again. Mike Cannon, the brother of the slain officer, had just left. Cody was resting comfortably.

"How are you feeling, Daddy?" Knoxi asked.

"This has been a great day," Cody answered. "I feel like I just won both ends of a doubleheader."

Then he reached for Brandi. "And speaking of doubleheaders, remember that hot day in Chicago when we played the White Sox in the afternoon, and then played the Cubs that same night in a make-up game? We were all furious when the commissioner ruled that we had to play two games that day against different teams in different stadiums."

"How could I forget?" Brandi snickered. "Your feet were itching so bad that you were going crazy before the second game."

"Yeah, and you came storming into the clubhouse at Wrigley

to doctor my feet, and all the guys headed for cover."

Knoxi giggled. "Well," she said, "I never heard this story."

"Wait," Raymond interrupted. "Is this the story about the naked shortstop?"

"Rookie shortstop from Panama," Brandi affirmed. "What was his name? Marco something?"

"Yeah, Marco Rojas. He was stark naked, so he jumped into his locker and closed the door and stayed there until your mom left." The kids laughed.

"He went 0 for 5 that day and blamed your mom."

"Dad, that's hilarious." Cody Jr. was hyped. "Can I tell the kids in my class that story?"

"Um, I'm not sure that's a good idea," Brandi advised.

"By the way, son," Cody said to Junior, "you should know that I heard you all the way from Heaven last night. God let you call me back, but not before I had flown to that place so high that all-a-sudden everything in life made perfect sense."

It was quiet for a few moments.

Knoxi broke the silence. "Daddy, when are they gonna take these bandages off your eyes so you can see us?"

"Don't worry, Fort Knox, I see everything I need to see. This was a wonderful day. I think my job is done. By the way, tell Sly and Julia to come on into the room and bring Jeremy."

Brandi glanced toward the door then back at Cody. "What are you saying? Jeremy was competing at the Winter Olympics in—I mean they aren't supposed to be here until . . ."

All was quiet.

"I'll see you all in the morning . . ." Cody drifted off.

No one wanted to leave. Ray and Whitney slipped into the room. The head nurse escorted Tanner, Julia, and their nineteen-year-old son Jeremy inside the door. They had been waiting in the hallway for twenty minutes.

The nurse offered an empathetic smile to Brandi, and then left. Julia stood behind the chair and placed her hands on Brandi's shoulders. Dawg and Silver embraced each other by the door. The only sound was Knoxi softly crying while Jeremy held her in his arms.

Cody whispered once more, "Sabre, you never looked better." Afterward, he took his last breath.

Brandi saw the monitor. She knew it was over, this time for good.

Then came a startling knock at the door. Everyone turned to look. A young man pushed the door partially open. When Brandi caught a glimpse, the blood rushed from her face.

CHAPTER 31

HEAVEN CAN WAIT

The face looking through the opening was stunning—beautiful bronze skin, captivating brown eyes—a ruffian tempered by suave academia.

Knoxi swallowed hard and was the first to utter a sound, *"Sabre!?"*

Brandi jumped up and stared. She rubbed her eyes then looked again. The face in the doorway was real.

"I'm sorry to intrude, but I must see Mr. Musket."

Brandi's knees were like jelly. She sat back down. "Sabre? No, of course not." With shaky voice she tried to convince herself. "How could this be?" She stared again.

The young man pushed the door fully open and stepped into the room. "Sorry to make this kind of entrance, Mrs. Musket. I've been told a thousand times that I look like my father. I'm Ryan Maxwell. Sabre was my dad."

Another familiar face appeared in the doorway behind Ryan. It was Secretary of Defense Amy Foster.

"Madame Secretary?"

"Hello, Brandi. Good to see you again. I am so sorry it is under these circumstances. We would have come sooner, but we needed approval from the president, and it took a couple of days. The president insisted that I come personally, but we've taken steps to keep my presence here a secret."

The president? The Muskets stared at each other in disbelief. They could see into the hallway, where several armed US Marines stood guard. Why on earth would the Secretary of Defense show up with an armed Marine escort?

Brandi glanced once more at the flat lines on the monitor above Cody's bed. "I'm . . . I'm afraid you're too late, Madame Secretary. Uh, approval from the president? Approval for what?"

"I will let Ryan explain." She handed Ryan a leather pouch. He pulled out a small device.

"Please trust us, Mrs. Musket," Ryan assured.

"Mama, that device looks like Tommy John," Knoxi was quick to point out.

"Tommy John? Who's that?" Ryan asked while he scanned Cody's body with the device. "No respiration, but still some brain activity. So here goes. I need more room."

Knoxi motioned everyone to back off. "Okay, Mr. Star Trek, this is your show for now, but I'm only letting you stand next to my dad because I knew your father. What the heck are you doing?"

"Wait, I need to concentrate," Ryan insisted.

The device reminded Knoxi of a tricorder, a fictional device seen in the old television series *Star Trek*—a little screen on the front and that squiggly little sound. It was similar to Tommy John, the device Sabre had used in Librador, but with a few upgrades.

Ryan made several adjustments, tuned the instrument to different frequencies, and then waited again. The device finally became silent, after which he scanned Cody's entire body once more.

"Okay, it's done," he said. "Ma'am, we need to resuscitate your husband immediately. We have a team standing by."

"Resuscitate?" Brandi stood to her feet. "What have you been doing all this time? We have a 'Do Not Resuscitate' order in plain sight. Can't you read these big red letters on this chart?"

"Mrs. Musket, please trust me. We need to clear the room. You can stay, but I and everyone else needs to leave."

Brandi glanced at the Secretary. She nodded her assurance.

"Julia and Silverbelle are staying with me," Brandi declared. "We're gonna sit here in the corner of the room and pray. My daughter will show everyone else out."

Knoxi watched as a team from the National Naval Medical Center in Bethesda, Maryland rushed into the room and surrounded Cody. *Bethesda? What's going on?*

Knoxi ushered her brothers and everyone else out into the hallway. She shut the door behind her, then noticed that men with earpieces and dark suits were stationed up and down the corridor— obviously a Secret Service detail in addition to the Marines.

As they waited anxiously, Knoxi decided it was time to dig for answers.

"So, what's your story, Ryan?" She nervously kept one eye on the closed door to the room where they were attempting to revive her father. "What did you do to my dad?"

"Well," he replied. "We'll know in a couple of minutes. The bullets in his brain and spine could not be surgically removed without killing him, so I . . ." He stopped and crossed his arms. "Sorry, it's top secret."

Tanner bristled up. "You wanna smooth that out for us, son?" The retired Pirates right fielder frowned as he stood with his right arm around Knoxi. His son Jeremy stood next to her on the other side. Tanner's "Cap'n Sly" scowl had only grown more intense with age.

"So," Ryan said to Knoxi with a nervous chuckle, "I could tell you everything, but I would have to kill you afterward."

Ryan's smug grin faded from his face when the younger McNair bore down on him with a *shoot-to-kill* facial expression.

Dawg moved forward, towering over Ryan. *"None of us thought that remark was cute."*

"Okay, okay. I give up," Ryan said. "I relocated the bullets to another dimension."

Knoxi snickered and glanced around at the others. No one was buying it. Dawg rolled his eyes at the ceiling.

Knoxi looked Ryan in the eye. "Another dimension?" She put her hands on her hips. "I've seen clowns that can lie better than you."

Ryan glanced toward the secretary, then proceeded with caution. "I can tell you only that I graduated from MIT soon after my father mysteriously disappeared somewhere in South America twelve years ago. I found his research and continued where he had left off, hoping I could discover what he was working on. I thought I could figure out who or what might've led to his disappearance. Then, the DOD brought me on board and wanted me to . . ." He looked toward Secretary Foster again.

"Gentlemen," Madame Secretary said to her Marine guardians, "follow me down the hall. I need to get a tall cup of something with a lot of caffeine in it. They'll notify me when there is news. These kids need some privacy."

The secretary, her Marine detail and Secret Service agents moved out of sight, then Ryan scanned the hallway to make certain that his only audience was Cody's inner circle—no press, no patients, no personnel.

"Do you trust all these people with you, Knoxi? Because what I'm about to say . . ."

She crossed her arms. Her catch-fire blue eyes made Ryan blink.

"Okay," he began. "You see, everything in existence has its own frequency, and consists of two basic energies—light and sound."

He took a deep breath, then started again. "The interaction of two separate physical systems is attributed to a field that extends from one to the other, and is manifested as an exchange between the two systems, but it's the combination of mathematics and quantum algorithms which allows us to isolate and quantumate an object trans-dimensionally, and if we utilize the correct—" He stopped when Knoxi grabbed his shoulders.

"Uh, what's wrong, Knoxi?"

"Do you ever come up for air? *Quantumate?* There is no such word. I mean like, whatever . . . Look, I get it already. You can't tell us, cuz it's top secret."

As she stared quietly into his face for a moment, Knoxi's eyes mellowed. "Seriously, Ryan, do you not know what happened to your father?"

"You know something about it," he asserted. "I can see it on your face."

Knoxi sighed. "Ryan, if it hadn't been for your father, none of us—"

Suddenly, she was interrupted by commotion in the hallway. They turned to see the secretary and her escort running toward them full speed. The door to Cody's room flew open.

"Kids! Your father is back! He's awake!"

~ ~ ~

Cody left Methodist Hospital in a wheelchair a few weeks after his so-called "surgery," but it wasn't easy to get him out of the medical center. His Houston doctors had expected him to have permanent paralysis in his legs, but he began to have feelings in his lower extremities immediately after the Bethesda medical team departed.

Despite exhaustive tests over the following weeks, neurosurgeons and therapists could find no indications of brain damage or diminished motor capacity. Noted medical researchers from around the world flocked to Methodist Hospital. They were baffled most by the complete disappearance of the bullets from Cody's body. It did not take long for the media to ascertain that the Bethesda specialists had performed some sort of futuristic surgery which had left no scars and had taken only a few minutes.

The media pressure and continual medical exams were oppressive and exhausting. Within three weeks, Brandi and Knoxi were desperate to sneak Cody out of the hospital and get him into a secret and secure place. They would no longer allow him to be used as a guinea pig. It was obvious that he needed time to heal and digest all that had happened.

A call to Anita Crown Cassidy got things started. The cagey veteran reporter, always up for a spin game, devised a story to divert the press. Next, a little help from Rosa's Cantina and some smooth-as-cake motor-mouthing from Captain Sly yielded results. Suddenly, Cody was gone.

Rumors circulated that he had died, but none of his friends or family would offer a word. Hundreds of Cody Musket "sightings" began to surface. He was reportedly seen by eyewitnesses at medical centers from Toronto to Rio and a dozen points between. *"Cody has left the building"* became a popular theme for nighttime comics.

After two months, Cody got antsy. He made a snap decision to reappear and return to a normal life after reading a Tulsa, Oklahoma newspaper announcement that a Cody Musket look-alike contest would soon be held on the campus of Oral Roberts University.

He figured it was a brilliant idea to return to society by entering the contest.

Cody arrived on campus with no fanfare. He entered the competition using the name *Willie Nelson*. There were nineteen contestants in addition to Cody. At the end of the day, he placed 5th. So much for his plan to reappear. He decided to return to his refuge—his hiding place where everyone accepted and loved him as a flesh-and-blood person, and *not* as a celebrity or an experiment.

No one, save his inner circle, knew his whereabouts, and even they did not know how his life would be affected by having been shot, dying twice, and coming back from the dead. No timetable was set for his return, and no one could speculate as to what his role would be in the future.

~ ~ ~

Mike Cannon, former Astros' catcher, disappeared after his meeting with Cody at Methodist Hospital. Shortly after that, 1500 arrests were made by the FBI because an unknown witness had exposed an organized *ideological cleansing network*, made up of political figures, celebrities, law enforcement officials, and known crime bosses.

The well-organized sinister conspiracy involved character assassination and murder of politicians and prominent activists whose views were in opposition to those of the network. Word was that Mike Cannon had been the whistle-blower, and that he had been relocated with a new identity. Most believed that the death of Police Officer Morris Cannon was the work of the same secret coalition.

Sam Black Hawk's conspiracy theory turned out to be dead on. He was credited for initially calling out the instigators. They even used the name *Ideological Cleansing Network*, the term coined by Sam in his broadcasts.

~ ~ ~

In the months following Cody's failed look-alike contest, Brandi and Knoxi routinely enjoyed life in the evenings, relaxing in the garden behind the Muskets' Houston villa. They reminisced about Librador and subsequent events, having finally come to a place of quietness and acceptance. They speculated on the future of the Muskets, and they often intervened in brotherly squabbles between Raymond and his younger brother Cody Jr.

Knoxi became more and more in demand as a speaker after details about her Librador escape became public. Despite her busy schedule, she was a brilliant student, and was quite a phenom on the basketball court. She constantly texted back and forth with Jeremy McNair, whose baseball career was just beginning in the Dodgers' minor league system.

In late August, as she sat in the garden with Brandi and her grandparents Ray and Whitney Barnes, she pulled up her phone and sent a text. But the message was not to Jeremy:

"Hello, Coach. I'm all in!"

REAL EVENTS THAT INSPIRED PARTS OF THIS STORY

The conversion of Sam Black Hawk — Inspired by the true story of Michael Morton of Round Rock, Texas, who had spent more than 20 years in prison for a murder he did not commit. When finally losing hope after two decades, sitting on his bunk, having prayed a desperate prayer a week beforehand (like Mr. Black Hawk in our story), his life was changed forever. Shortly after that, a chain of bizarre events led to his release. Chapter Nineteen of Morton's personal story entitled *Getting Life* (pub. 2014 by Simon & Schuster) was the inspiration for Sam Black Hawk's life-changing encounter with God.

~ ~ ~

Children in Heaven — Cody tells his friends, Dawg and Silverbelle, that he has met their unborn (miscarried) child in Heaven. This event was inspired by several real events. I will share one of them.

On March 5, 2003 Colton Burpo, age 3, had emergency surgery. During that time, he had a near-death experience, after which he returned with information about people that seemed impossible for him to have known. He met his great grandfather "Pop" who had died 24 years before Colton had been born. He said he talked to Pop, but that he didn't look the same as the picture of him (at age 70) on the mantle in the living room. His mother then retrieved another picture showing Pop at age 25, to which the three-year-old boy replied, "Yep, that's him."

He told his parents he had met his older sister in Heaven, but his parents informed him he had never had an older sister. When he told his mother he knew she had "lost a baby in her tummy" years before, she was speechless, because Colton had never been told of this. His unborn sister had been miscarried by his mother in 1998.

This verified his experience as genuine, after which he revealed much more, including the discovery that Angels loved to laugh. In fact, the youngster's suggestion that they sing "We Will Rock You" was one request the Angels found particularly delightful.

Colton's story is told in the motion picture *Heaven is for Real.*

~   ~   ~

Descriptions of Heaven — The depictions of Heaven were inspired by several individuals. One of those is Dale Black, the sole survivor of an aircraft crash at age 19. Immediately after the accident, his life hanging in the balance, Mr. Black visited Heaven, so he claims. His colorful, detailed descriptions were incorporated into Cody's story. But there is more.

Mr. Black was treated by renowned orthopedic surgeon Dr. Homer Graham, who, after multiple surgeries, declared that Black would never again walk normally or regain use of his left shoulder. Dr. Graham was prepared to amputate Dale Black's left foot and ankle.

But, like Cody in the story, Mr. Black submitted his life to Christ, trading his own ambitions for the great adventure of finding friendship with God and a new life, even if that meant losing his mobility. Mr. Black's unexpected, miraculous recovery was so complete that within two years he was back in college and competing successfully on the baseball team. He later became an airline pilot and was eventually recognized as an expert on air safety, testifying before Congress. His recovery had such an impact that Dr. Graham, known as "doctor to the (Hollywood) stars" became a believer and spent much of his later years performing volunteer medical missions with Dale Black on several continents.

Dale Black's story is told in his autobiography entitled *Flight to Heaven* (published by Bethany House Publishers, May 2010).

Another individual, whom I had the privilege to interview personally, is Don Piper, who was instantly killed in an automobile accident on a bridge at Lake Livingston, near Huntsville, Texas. He was pronounced dead by two paramedics at the scene, but ninety minutes later, while a fellow Pastor prayed over him, he returned.

With lacerations over most of his body, and nearly every bone broken, the trauma center in Conroe, Texas had never seen anyone injured that badly who was actually alive. They transferred him elsewhere since they didn't know where to start. Had his heart continued to beat after the crash, he would have bled out, but because he had been killed instantly, his body retained most of its blood count. This proved he had actually been dead.

Some of his descriptions of Heaven are also found in Cody's story. Don Piper's autobiography is entitled *Ninety Minutes in Heaven* (published by Revell, Dec. 1, 2006). His and Dale Black's medical history is a matter of public record.

~   ~   ~

Miraculous provision and multiplication of the food — I could list many sources for this subject. Again, I will share one. You need to look no further than to the country of modern Mozambique to discover a recent history of miracles, many of which are found woven into the novel No Pit So Deep. Roland and Heidi Baker, who have established faith-based orphanages, schools and feeding centers in Mozambique for more than three decades, have seen it all.

An article published May 18, 2012 by Tim Stafford in *Christianity Today* was my first introduction to this couple which has lived among the poor and ministered in the back-country mud huts, where almost daily they see verified miracles — healing, multiplying of food, and even several individuals raised from the dead. Feeding over 10,0000 orphans per week and praying for the afflicted has changed the spiritual landscape of this impoverished country.

Heidi has become known affectionately in recent years as "Mama Heidi" to a nation of people starved for someone to love them. Stafford proclaims, "One thing is for sure: She loves the poor like no other in this forgotten corner of the planet."

Check this couple out. I do not know how their ministry is supported financially, because their YouTube presentations which I have watched do *not* appeal for money.

~   ~   ~

Trans-dimensional quantumation — Yep, that part was pure fantasy. But as Cody says, "You never know."

Knoxi's World (Book 3)

"I'd rather be a fool for Jesus, than a wiseguy for somebody else."

Knoxi, a scholarship athlete and American heartthrob, lays aside her basketball career to take down a web of corporate corruption involving child slavery.

Knoxi's World will grip your soul, as she must "slip the surly bonds of earth" to rescue one 3-year-old child who holds the key to the freedom of thousands. In the midst of all, she finds love.

"Like watching a thrilling movie through the pages of a book!" — Official Review, *ILoveUniqueBooks.com*

"Electrifying! Superbly written, with a flawless ending."– *Readers Favorite*

Land Without Shame (Book 4)

Cody Musket Jr. assumes leadership of his parents' continuing battle against trafficking. After training with Navy SEALs, he struggles with his identity: Is he an avenger, or is he an evangelist?

Diamond Casper is an Oscar-winning film star whose career has blossomed after appearing in compromising roles. But her beauty hasn't brought her what she desires most.

Diamond and Cody, strangers, must work together after their commuter flight is hijacked. It crashes near an uncharted Caribbean Island, which they soon discover is a gold mine sitting under a volcano. The mine uses homeless underaged laborers.

A true thriller, a moving love story, a tale of honor and redemption.

Black Pearl (Book 5)
A Cody Musket Political Thriller

What matters most is how you meet the moment when the fate of the world hangs in the balance. The Musket family must pull together, circle the wagons, then come out fighting, as a powerful leftist force attempts to enslave the world.

"Black Pearl is a sensational, unforgettable Christian thriller. A secret file belonging to the president of the United States threatens an undercover agent and his family. Set twenty years in the future, the book contains technology that not only enhances the storyline, but is realistically credible! Breathtaking, electrifying, fast-paced, with a Christian overtone." – Susan Sewell, *Readers Favorite*

Award-Winning Author James N. Miller has been described as a realist, comic, writer, and entrepreneur. With 8000 hours as a pilot, he has carried the message of hope across the land as a gifted speaker and entertainer. He has also founded two aviation companies which have financed outreaches to displaced children and disaster victims in various regions.

Today, he's making a difference in another way through an exciting new 5-book novel series which presents the spellbinding 30-year journey of a faith-bound family fighting child trafficking. No Pit So Deep, The Cody Musket Story, fiction containing real events, has received accolades from both Christian and mainstream reviewers.

He lives in Waco, Texas with his wife Carla, whom he still refers to as "my first wife." They have been married 52 years and have been blessed with two sons and four grandchildren.

Email James Miller:
codymusket@gmail.com